WHERE LOVE
DWELLS

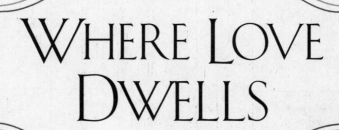

WHERE LOVE DWELLS

A NOVEL

Delia Parr

BETHANY HOUSE PUBLISHERS
Minneapolis, Minnesota

Published by Bethany House Publishers
11400 Hampshire Avenue South
Bloomington, Minnesota 55438

Bethany House Publishers is a division of
Baker Publishing Group, Grand Rapids, Michigan.

Printed in the United States of America

Library of Congress Cataloging-in-Publication Data

Parr, Delia.
   Where love dwells / Delia Parr.
     p   cm. — (Candlewood trilogy ; 3)
   ISBN 978-0-7642-0088-5 (pbk.)
   1. Boardinghouses—New York (State)—Fiction. I. Title.
   PS3566.A7527W48   2008
   813'.54—dc22

                                                 2008014236

Dedicated to
Joseph and Gerard
with humble gratitude
for the gift of your loving presence
in our lives

1

Candlewood, New York

Early April, 1842

Y OU'RE AN ODD WOMAN, Widow Garrett."
Emma shifted in her saddle and wondered why Zachary
Breckenwith was so determined to court her if he thought her
odd. "How gallant of you to say so," she quipped before shaking
off the water clinging to her rain cape. They had ridden through
a shower of hail, but the driving rain now forced them to seek
shelter under a heavy copse of pine trees, and Emma found she
had no interest in discovering the surprise he had planned for her
today during their outing.

Not now, when he obviously had such a low opinion of her.

"Forgive my choice of words. I don't find you odd, exactly . . .
I meant to say you are unusual. Even remarkable," he offered. His
gaze met hers and held it. "Most women I've known have neither
the interest nor the character to focus so entirely on other people
that they make little time for themselves."

Although his words soothed her doubts about his opinion of
her, Emma was uncomfortable with his compliment and deflected
it easily—as she had often rejected some of the advice he had given
her as her lawyer over the past five years. "Perhaps it's more a mark

of my professions, rather than my character. After serving patrons at the General Store for most of my life and now accommodating guests at Hill House, I've always had to focus on what other people need. I've never had the luxury of worrying overmuch about what I wanted to do for myself," she argued.

He smiled and cocked his head. "But you can choose to have the time to think more about yourself now if you'd agree to marry me. Build a new life . . . with me," he whispered. "Say yes. Say you'll marry me."

Her heart skipped a beat and she held his gaze. The true affection simmering in the depths of his dove gray eyes nearly scattered every reservation she had about the issues that needed to be resolved if they did marry. With his dark looks and tall stature, he was a handsome man by any woman's standards, but it was his wit and his acceptance of her as his equal on many levels that endeared him to her more than anything else.

Emma added persistence to his other good qualities and smiled. "I thought you agreed that I would give you my answer after all of my sons had come home to Candlewood with their families to celebrate my birthday. That's only a few weeks away."

The twinkle in his eyes sparkled just a bit brighter. "True, but you could say yes today simply because you have a bit of time to yourself right now to think about it, thanks to the rain," he said with a smile. "You did just argue that you've never had the luxury of having time for yourself, did you not?"

She laughed out loud. "I did. And you are an incorrigible master of words who has an uncanny ability to direct the topic of conversation in exactly the direction you choose. Would you say that's a mark of your character or your profession?" she asked, deliberately turning her earlier words back at him.

This time, *he* laughed out loud. "I suspect it's a bit of both."

He paused for a moment. "You've proven yourself to be quite a challenge during this courtship of ours, just as I suspect you'd be if we were adversaries in a court of law."

"Your adversary in court?" Emma snorted. "Assuming I overlook the fact that practicing law is the one domain I would have chosen to claim for myself had it not been refused to me because of my gentler sex, I would be curious. Would you find me to be an odd adversary in court or a remarkable one?" she teased, although truth be told, her inability to pursue her interest in practicing law because she was a woman still created an undercurrent of disappointment. She had come to accept, however, that it was a path God had not chosen for her.

Zachary smiled. "I'd find you quite remarkable, of course."

Emma was fashioning a suitable reply in her mind when droplets of rain began to filter through the canopy overhead. Torn between wanting to leave their shelter to continue their outing—before he pressed her again for an answer to his proposal—and the exasperating reality that the weather was becoming far too foul to entertain that notion, she let out a deep sigh. "I don't think we can stay here any longer. The rain is getting much heavier. I'm afraid your surprise for me will have to wait," she added, deliberately avoiding any mention of his marriage proposal.

"You're right, of course. We really should turn back and save our outing for another day. Perhaps I could salvage a bit of our time together by simply telling you exactly what my surprise for you is."

Her eyes widened. "You'd actually tell me?"

"Yes, I would."

More than satisfied with his offer, she smiled at him. "Please don't tell me your surprise. I do believe I can wait another day to learn what it is that you've planned for me."

"You can wait," he repeated, then shook his head as they urged their horses out from beneath the protection of the canopy toward Hill House. "You're sure?"

"Absolutely. Surprised?" she prompted, enjoying the banter that had always been a hallmark of their relationship, although their conversations had become decidedly more personal once they had begun courting.

"Completely," he admitted. "Maybe it's better if I do tell you," he insisted, with his head bent low against the driving rain.

"What irks you more, that I am content to wait or that *you* have to wait to surprise *me*?" she teased.

"Neither," he said. "At the moment, I'm more concerned with how I'm going to explain to your mother-in-law that I let you talk me into venturing out today in the first place. If you take a chill from riding in this rain, I'll never forgive myself. And forgiveness is not something I'll be likely to receive from your mother-in-law, either."

"That's not true," she countered as their horses plodded slowly toward home. "Mother Garrett will forgive you rather quickly because she'll be too busy telling me, 'I told you so.' " Emma smiled. "After living with her for over thirty years, I've grown accustomed to the fact she's almost always right. With our outing canceled today, though, I'm not certain how much longer I can bear her teasing about this surprise of yours," she admitted and shook her head. "How a woman who hasn't been able to keep a secret for the better part of her seventy-odd years has been able to keep yours so well is a wonder I can't begin to fathom."

"Your mother-in-law knows how important my surprise is," he insisted.

"Indeed," she said, more perplexed by how quickly her mother-in-law had allied herself with this man against Emma than by the nature of the surprise he had planned for her.

They skirted the town boundaries of Candlewood, avoiding Main Street, where they would no doubt attract attention, along with more gossip than either one of them cared to invite. By the time they crossed the canal at the north end of town, the rain had blessedly slowed to a drizzle again.

Emma's rain cape had kept her body dry, for the most part, but the brim of her bonnet was sagging down to her brow, and her saturated leather riding gloves numbed her hands. When she caught sight of Hill House, perched just ahead, she smiled. "Almost home and almost none the worse for the experience," she announced. "At least Mother Garrett won't be able to find fault with me for not dressing properly for this abominable weather. How are you faring?"

Zachary shook the water from his rain slicker and chuckled. "Well enough, I suppose," he admitted as he led them through the woods at the base of the hill. Once he had tied both horses securely to trees at the edge of the woods, he helped her dismount and offered his arm. "I'll see you to your door before I take the horses back to the livery. I don't suppose you'd be inclined to give me an answer along the way," he said, locking his gaze with hers.

Emboldened by the depth of affection she saw in his eyes, she furrowed her brow and feigned confusion. "An answer?"

He cocked his head. "I never thought being coy with me was part of your nature."

"Perhaps it should be. Nevertheless, I'll have your answer for you by my birthday, as promised," she whispered and took his arm. Noting the rain-drenched grass ahead and a mud slick that stretched across the plateau where she'd had a gazebo erected only last year, she was thankful for the security he offered. What would it be like to have the dependability of a spouse again? "Will you come in and warm up before taking the horses back?" she asked as they carefully walked toward the steps that led up to the patio on the side of the house.

Zachary tightened his hold on her arm. "I think it's probably best if—"

Emma somehow lost her footing and plopped down on the slick grass, knocking the breath out of her. Then Zachary's attempts to hold her upright caused him to land right next to her. Together, they slid straight into that mud slick, splattering mud in all directions until they finally oozed to a stop.

Momentarily stunned and thoroughly mortified, Emma clapped her hand to her pounding heart, adding mud to one of the few places on her person the mud had missed. To her horror, mud oozed over the top of her boots and beneath her split riding skirt all the way up to her knees.

Unfortunately, her companion had fared just as disastrously. He was covered with mud from head to toe. "I'm so, so sorry! Truly sorry," she gushed before she dissolved into a fit of giggles that swallowed the rest of her apology. When she finally regained her composure, she shook her head. "I'm sorry. It's just that you're . . . you're quite a . . . a mess." Emma tasted the grit of mud on her lips. She tried wiping it away with her forearm, since her hands were coated with mud, but failed miserably.

Zachary chuckled and held tightly to her arm while he reached inside his slicker to retrieve a handkerchief. "Here. Try this. You took quite a spill. Are you all right?"

"I'm fine. Embarrassed all to pieces, but fine," she insisted as she swiped at the mud on her lips with his handkerchief.

Grinning, he pointed at her face. "You might try wiping the tip of your nose, as well."

Appalled, she followed his suggestion and cleaned the mud from the tip of her nose. When she finished, she glanced down at her mud-splattered cape and riding skirt, glanced up at him, and frowned. "I don't suppose there's any way we could get cleaned up before we get to the house and Mother Garrett sees us, is there?"

"I doubt it. We'll be fortunate to get back to our feet without falling again," he cautioned as he stabilized his footing before reaching down to help her up from the mud.

"You're probably right. I've never been able to get away with a single thing where Mother Garrett is concerned," she grumbled as he helped her get to her feet.

"Easy. Don't try to do more than keep your balance at first."

"I'm terribly, terribly sorry I pulled you down into this mud," she said when she felt confident that she would not fall back down again, at least not right away.

"You don't have to apologize. If there's any fault to be found, it's mine. I should have been able to keep my footing so I could have prevented you from slipping in the first place," he insisted.

"Look at the bright side," Emma suggested.

He cocked a muddy brow.

She grinned. "Mother Garrett might forget to say, 'I told you so,' because she'll be too busy making sure we don't get more than a step or two into her kitchen—if we even get that far," she warned.

During the many years that Emma had operated the General Store and now Hill House, Mother Garrett had always reigned supreme in the kitchen, much to Emma's relief, since she was as untalented at the stove as she was with a sewing needle. Mother Garrett also protected her domain with a fierce combination of pride and ability that few dared to question, and Emma loved her dearly.

"I will consider myself fortunate indeed if she lets either one of us inside," he said as they tentatively mounted the steps to the patio.

Once they reached the top of the steps, they crossed the patio together. Fortunately, the double doors to the dining room were unlocked. She let them into the house, surprised that Mother Garrett was not there to greet them, if only to keep them both from venturing into her kitchen. The boardinghouse itself was quiet, although with no paying guests expected until May, that was not all that unusual.

"If we keep to the floorboards instead of the carpet, it will be easier for Liesel and Ditty to clean up the mud we're tracking inside," she suggested before she remembered that it was late Saturday afternoon. Both of the young women who worked for her at Hill House had already left to spend the rest of the weekend with their families. Since they would not be returning until Sunday night, Emma would be doing all the cleaning up, which probably was more fair than not.

Side by side, they squished their way past the dining room table on their right, where as many as twenty guests at a time had gathered for one of Mother Garrett's meals. To their left, four high chairs Emma had borrowed sat waiting for Emma's grandchildren to arrive. When they reached the door that led to the kitchen, she took a deep breath and offered Zachary a smile of encouragement. Bracing herself to face Mother Garrett, she opened the door and led him into the kitchen.

Oddly, there wasn't a pot or anything else bubbling on the cookstove, nor more than a weak fire in the hearth. Mother Garrett was not there, although Emma's relief was short-lived.

Straight ahead, a slight young woman she had never set eyes on before was sitting at the head of the worktable.

Not on a chair.

On top of the table itself!

With her legs swinging, she was balancing a tin of crullers on her lap with one hand and holding a half-eaten cruller with the other.

Emma gasped. "Who . . . who are you?"

The young woman grinned. "I'm guessing you'd be the proprietress of Hill House, but as for me, let me simply say that I'm probably the biggest surprise you've had for a good long while."

Emma stared at the young woman, hard. But the young woman did not even blink. She did, however, continue to swing her legs back and forth while she polished off the rest of her cruller.

"Surprise indeed," Emma muttered under her breath, convinced with each passing minute of this miserable day that surprises were most definitely overrated.

2

E VEN COVERED WITH MUD and with Zachary by her side, Emma easily slipped out of her role as a woman being courted and back into her position as the owner of Hill House. "I am indeed Widow Garrett, the proprietress of Hill House, and this is my lawyer, Mr. Breckenwith. And might I add that a young woman, however much of a surprise she might present herself to be, usually has a proper name and she definitely does not sit on top of a table instead of using a chair."

Although Emma used the same tone of voice she had always reserved for any one of her three sons while they were growing up and needed to be reminded of their manners, this young woman did not even have the decency to blush with embarrassment.

"My name is Wryn Covington," the young woman replied with a toss of her head that could have easily knocked off the chip of defiance resting invisibly on one of her shoulders. She did, however reluctantly, slide from the tabletop to her feet, defiance neatly intact.

Standing but an inch or so over five feet tall, the young woman had a slim, almost waif-like build. Her thick, wavy brown hair had been tied at the back of her neck. Above the dark cloud of freckles that stretched across her cheeks, deep doe eyes stared right back at Emma. Behind the challenge in Wryn's gaze and the fierce determination in her stance, Emma sensed a lifetime of deep hurts and disappointments that would take a miracle to heal.

Emma, however, was shy of patience at the moment, let alone a miracle.

Why this particular girl was in her mother-in-law's kitchen, if not the boardinghouse itself, concerned her most. "Are you here with your family as a guest?" she ventured, wondering if the inclement weather might have forced some travelers to take shelter at Hill House while Emma had been on her ill-fated outing.

Wryn shook her head. "No, I'm not a guest. I'm family—of sorts. Do you always wear so much . . . mud?" she asked, her eyes flashing with amusement.

Emma clenched and unclenched her jaw. "As a matter of fact, I don't. Are you always so flippant when speaking with adults?"

"Not usually. At least not with strangers, but since we're family—"

"Exactly how are you related to Widow Garrett?" Zachary asked as he took a step forward to stand closer to Emma.

Wryn put her finger on the tip of her chin for a moment. "Hmmm. Legally, I'm not sure exactly how I'm related to her. I suppose she might be my . . . what? Grandmother, maybe? Or my great-aunt? It's all very confusing to me, but since you're a lawyer, maybe you could tell me."

"As confusing as it is, try your best to enlighten us," Emma said. Certain that this young woman was not any part of her family at all, she directed Wryn's attention away from Zachary and back to herself.

"I'll try. Let's see if I can explain this right," Wryn began.

"Uncle Mark is my uncle, of course, because he's married to my Aunt Catherine. I'm related by blood to her because she's my mother's sister. I'm just confused about how I'm related to you since you're Uncle Mark's mother. If you were Aunt Catherine's mother, you'd be my grandmother, of course. But since—"

"Mark? And Catherine? They're here?" Emma exclaimed, stunned to learn that her youngest son and his family had apparently arrived more than two weeks earlier than she'd expected.

"Yes, they're here. We're all here. As we speak, Uncle Mark is upstairs with Aunt Catherine. The twins needed their naps and poor Aunt Catherine was completely tuckered out from our travel, so she's napping, too. By the time Uncle Mark had unloaded our trunks from the wagon and lugged them upstairs, he said he needed to rest awhile, as well. It's been a nasty few days of traveling, especially with today's weather, but I don't suppose I have to tell you that, do I?" she asked, eyes dancing.

"Obviously not," Emma snapped. At this point, the mud was making her skirt and cape awfully heavy. She was dirty and tired and cold. She could still taste the grit of the mud on her lips, and she had little patience left for dealing with this little snip. "I don't suppose you could tell me where I might find Mother Garrett, could you?"

Wryn fished another cruller out of the tin and nibbled off the end. "She went into town."

"Alone? In this weather? Why on earth would she do that?"

"Since we arrived a little earlier than you all expected us, Mother Garrett said she needed some supplies from the General Store," the young woman explained. "But she didn't go alone, if that's what is putting you into a bit of a stew. She went with a man. Mr. . . . Oh, I forget his name. Anyway, he was here visiting with her, so he drove her into town. I'm sure you know who he is. Since he seems to be smitten with her, he's probably been here a lot. You do know who I mean, don't you?"

Emma noticed her jaw was clenched again and prayed this new habit would not be an integral part of her relationship with this young woman. Obviously, Widower Anson Kirk had stopped by to see her mother-in-law. He had moved into Hill House for several months this past winter after his family's home had been one of those destroyed when the match factory exploded, and he eventually set his sights on Mother Garrett.

Although her mother-in-law was decidedly outspoken about her refusal to ever marry again, she did seem to enjoy being courted, albeit unofficially, by the widower Mr. Kirk, who seemed impervious to her repeated rejections.

Staring at Wryn, who seemingly had no sense of what was proper for a young woman to discuss with her elders, Emma tried to remain calm. After raising three sons, she had always felt confident dealing with young men. Handling young women was quite another matter, as her initial difficulties supervising Liesel and Ditty had proven in the past. Unfortunately, this young lady offered a challenge far beyond Emma's experience and well beyond her interests at the moment.

Zachary cleared his throat, which broke the tension of the standoff between the two women. "I'm certain you'd like to freshen up before reuniting with your son and his family. Since you're safe and sound inside now, I think I should get the horses back to the livery," he suggested.

Emma looked up at him, noted the hint of amusement in his gaze, and frowned. "Are you sure you wouldn't want to wash up a bit here first?"

"I think I'll wait. I still have to cross that mud slick to get to the horses again, remember?"

"Then be careful. And thank you for today. For everything," she murmured.

He smiled. "I'll see you at church in the morning. If the weather improves, we might try finishing our outing in the afternoon, although you're probably more inclined to stay home with your son and his family."

"Yes, I am. Perhaps we might go later in the week on Wednesday. Would the same time suit you?"

"I don't have to leave on business until Thursday. I'll bring the horses at one o'clock on Wednesday," he agreed and took his leave.

Emma closed the door to the dining room again, ready to pose a host of questions to Wryn, but the young woman took the initiative.

"Is he really your lawyer? Or is he a lawyer you know who also happens to be interested in you, which was very apparent by the way he—"

"He's just my lawyer," Emma replied, more annoyed at herself for answering Wryn's question than she was at Wryn for having the audacity to ask it. Without offering any further explanation, she tiptoed past Wryn to get to the sink, where she pumped water into a pot that had been resting on the counter.

"Even I can see he's more than just your lawyer, although he isn't a very good one," Wryn stated before wiping her sugared hands on her skirts.

"And after living all of what—fourteen years?—you can tell how good a lawyer he is?" Emma snapped, unable to juggle both her patience and the heavy pot of water she was now carrying to the cookstove.

"Fifteen years. I'm fifteen," Wryn said, completely unaffected by Emma's curtness. "And yes, I can tell he isn't that good of a lawyer, because he couldn't answer my question. Or he didn't want to answer it, which means I still don't know how we're related legally. Mother Garrett had no problem telling me what to call her, but I still don't know what to call you. Would you prefer Grandmother or Aunt?"

"Widow Garrett will do quite nicely for now," Emma insisted, more concerned about how she was going to get washed up than she was about how Wryn might address her. Once she set the pot of water onto the cookstove and set it to heat, she stared long and hard at the water, as if she could will it to heat faster.

With Mark and his family staying here at Hill House now, she could hardly clean up right here in the kitchen. Tracking mud through the rest of the house to get to her room upstairs made no sense. She would only make more unnecessary work for herself, since she could not very well leave it until tomorrow night, when Liesel and Ditty would be coming back.

Instead, once the water had heated, she decided she should carry the pot with her, slip out the back door, cross the yard, and enter her office by using the door that opened on the side porch, which was the same door guests usually used when they arrived to register. Once she was inside her office, she would have the privacy she needed to get out of these muddy clothes and wash up just enough to use the private staircase that connected directly to her bedroom upstairs so she could change.

With her problem solved, at least in her own mind, and anxious to get started so she would be presentable by the time Mark and his family were awake, she returned her attention to Wryn. "As soon as this water is warm enough, I'm going to freshen up and change. In the meantime, I'd like you to go back upstairs. Once Mark and Catherine and the boys are up, you can let them know I've returned and that I'll be waiting for them in one of the front parlors. I assume that Mother Garrett made sure you had a room of your own close to them," she said, confident that her mother-in-law had put Mark and Catherine and the twins in the suite of rooms they had prepared for them on the west side of the house. Hopefully, she had put Wryn into one of the rooms directly across the hall from them.

Wryn shrugged, put the lid back on the tin of crullers, hoisted the tin to one hip, and set a pout to her lips. "I liked one of the rooms in the opposite hall, but I wasn't allowed to have that one." She let out a long sigh. "She made me take that bland, boring room. You must know the one. It's completely beige and without any spirit at all."

"I know it well," Emma replied. She was not surprised that Mother Garrett had refused to be intimidated by this wisp of a young woman, forcing Wryn to take the room directly across the hall from Mark and his family. Emma would sorely have loved being home to watch their encounter, though.

When the young woman abruptly left the room, Emma was tempted to call after her to remind her to store the tin of crullers back in the sideboard in the dining room where it belonged, but decided to let the issue drop. For now. She was too excited about reuniting with Mark and his wife and seeing her two grandsons for the first time to worry about an ordinary tin of crullers.

At the same time, Emma was curious to learn why Wryn had come along with them. To put it gently, this girl had a feisty, but abrasive, temperament. Mark and Catherine, however, were both gentle and soft-spoken by nature, and Emma could scarcely imagine them traveling together, let alone living together here at Hill House.

Nevertheless, just thinking about Wryn matching wits with

Mother Garrett for the next several weeks made her smile, especially since she knew who would survive as the winner in the end.

———————

One muddy cape. Two mud-crusted boots. A sodden bonnet. One nearly ruined riding skirt. A pair of riding gloves destined for the trash heap.

"Not bad, considering," Emma murmured as she passed the day's casualties she had piled on the porch outside of her office door on her way back to the kitchen. Grateful that the rain had finally stopped, she paused for a moment in the yard to dump the soiled water from the pot and checked the winter chicken coop near the house. She also made a mental note to have the chickens moved to the coop near the woods as soon as the mulberry trees began to blossom—a sure sign that spring had arrived to stay.

She peered into the coop, looking specifically for one chicken she had named Faith. As she hoped, she found Faith roosting with her charges, safe and sound and dry inside the coop. "We're going to need lots and lots of eggs for my family," she crooned before hurrying off to the kitchen again. Collecting eggs with her grandchildren was only one of the many activities she had missed sharing with them, since they were all growing up so far from Candlewood. Mindful of her many other blessings, however, including the fact they'd all be together very, very soon, she opened the back door and stepped into the kitchen.

Mother Garrett looked up from her place at the cookstove, where she was frying bacon, and grinned. As plump as Emma was slender, the elderly woman wore visible testimony that she was the finest cook in all of Candlewood. "Good. You're back!"

"Barely. I've only had time to slip upstairs to get changed," Emma replied, relieved that she had also had time to rebraid her hair and coil it neatly at the nape of her neck before encountering her mother-in-law. She tied an apron over the dark blue work gown she had changed into and shrugged. "We were gone a bit longer than we expected, I suppose, although the weather—"

"Don't quibble about the weather. Start with your good news first, then I'll tell you mine. Just hurry. Tell me, tell me. I'm about to burst with curiosity. Which one did you choose? The bay mare or the chestnut one?"

"Mare? Did you say mare?" Emma asked, completely perplexed by her mother-in-law's questions.

The grin on Mother Garrett's face sank into a frown. "Just because I teased you shamelessly for the past few weeks doesn't give you license to tease me back. I'm your elder. Unlike some other person currently residing in this boardinghouse of yours, who shall remain nameless at the moment because that's part of my news, you're unlikely to forget that. Save for a rare occasion or two over the years for which I've completely forgiven you," she cautioned before turning back to turn over her bacon.

Emma set the pot into the sink to be washed and joined her mother-in-law at the cookstove. "I'm not teasing you. I simply have no idea what you're talking about," she insisted and snatched a piece of cooked bacon from a platter on a nearby counter. She took a nibble but stopped almost instantly to stare wide-eyed at her mother-in-law when she realized exactly what Mother Garrett had asked her. "It's the secret! It's the secret you've been keeping with Mr. Breckenwith, isn't it? It's a . . . a horse! He got me a mare. He did, didn't he?" she gushed, completely overwhelmed at the very thought she might have a horse of her own. Although riding had been one of the ways they had enjoyed spending time together, she had been perfectly content using the mare he had rented for her from the livery while he rode the horse he kept stabled there.

Mother Garrett's eyes widened. "Please don't tell me you didn't know. I saw you both leave together and—"

"We never got to finish our outing. The weather slowed us down and then got worse, so we had to turn around and come home."

Mother Garrett dropped her gaze and let out a long, sad sigh. "I did it again, didn't I?" she whispered. "I've been trying so hard lately to keep secrets people tell me, but now I just let this one slip out. I didn't mean to do it. I truly didn't, but now I've ruined his surprise for you. I just thought—"

"You just assumed that since I'd been gone so long he must have taken me to see what he'd gotten for me, that's all," Emma said gently, putting her arm around her mother-in-law's shoulders. "You couldn't have known, any more than you could have warned me it was going to hail this afternoon."

"Hail? We didn't have any hail today."

"Perhaps not, but *we* did. Now let's get back to that mare you mentioned," Emma prompted, anxious to know more. "I think you said one was a bay, but I didn't quite catch the color of the other one I could choose from."

Mother Garrett focused her attention on her work. "I don't believe I remember precisely."

"Don't be silly. Of course you do."

"Even if I did remember, I couldn't tell you. It's supposed to be a secret, and I'm still bound by my promise to keep Mr. Breckenwith's secret, although there isn't much left of it now." She paused, stared at the bacon she was frying for a moment, and looked up at Emma. "You won't tell him I blabbed a little, will you?"

Emma planted a kiss on the elderly woman's cheek. "No, I won't. It'll be our secret."

Mother Garrett smiled just a little. "Good. And don't worry—I'll keep this secret for sure. I hope he doesn't wait too long, though. And you have to promise me that you'll act surprised."

"I promise," Emma said, although she doubted she would be able to fool Zachary. He knew her too well. "We're going to try again Wednesday afternoon, weather permitting, of course," Emma offered before she polished off her piece of bacon. "This bacon is delicious, but it's nearly suppertime. Why are you cooking bacon now?"

Mother Garrett smiled. "I need the grease to make those potatoes Mark loves. That's the good news I've got for you. Mark and Catherine and the boys arrived while you were gone. They brought a surprise with them, too."

Before Emma could reply, the door to the dining room burst open. When Wryn charged into the kitchen, Mother Garrett leaned toward Emma. "Speaking of surprises, here she is."

"You've got to help me," the young woman cried, panting for breath. "Please, please help me!"

3

H E'S . . . HE'S MISSING . . . HE'S gone! I've . . . I've looked everywhere, but I can't find him. I've gone into every room upstairs. I've looked under the beds. But he's gone . . . gone! We have to find him. Please, help me. Help me find Jonas," Wryn gushed and wrung her hands together as she gulped to catch her breath. With her face flushed and her eyes filled with panic, she bore no resemblance to the overconfident, defiant young woman Emma had met less than an hour ago.

Emma's pulse quickened with alarm the moment she heard Wryn say the name of one of her twin two-year-old grandsons. "Calm down. Take a deep breath. Now another one," she said firmly. Although Emma had yet to meet either of her grandsons, Mark and Catherine had written enough about them in their letters that she felt as if she knew them. Both boys, according to Mark, were sweet, gentle souls, much like both of their parents. Although he was the younger of the two by all of twelve minutes, Jonas was the leader of the two, so it did not surprise Emma to learn that he was the one who had wandered off.

"Tell me what happened," she said when the young woman was breathing normally again.

Wryn blinked back tears. "I . . . I did what you said. I went upstairs to wait for Uncle Mark and Aunt Catherine and the babies to wake up. About twenty minutes ago, I peeked into their little sitting room to see if anyone was up yet, but they weren't. Except for Jonas."

"Jonas was in the sitting room? By himself?" Emma asked as Mother Garrett moved the frying pan off the stove and began wiping her hands on her apron.

"He and Paul are pretty quiet babies, especially for boys. He must have woken up and wandered out into the sitting room. That's where I found him playing with the latch on one of the trunks Uncle Mark had brought upstairs."

"How did he get away from you?" Mother Garrett interjected.

Wryn gulped. "The door to the bedroom was ajar, and I could see everyone else was still sleeping, so I took Jonas with me back to my room. I played with him for a bit, then I went back again to see if anyone was up yet. I . . . I only left him in my room for a minute. Not even a minute! When I got back to my room, he was gone. Please! Can't we stop talking and start looking for him? We need to find him before Uncle Mark and Aunt Catherine discover he's missing!"

"Mark and Catherine need to know, and they need to help us find Jonas," Emma insisted, less concerned about Wryn having to explain herself than she was about finding her little grandson. "Go back upstairs. Wake them up if you have to, but tell them exactly what happened and have them help you search the upstairs again. In the meantime, Mother Garrett and I will start searching here on the first floor."

"He's only two years old. I don't think he could have made it all the way downstairs by himself. Not that quickly," Wryn argued.

"You'd be surprised how fast a two-year-old boy can move if he wants to, which is why you can't ever take your eyes off of him, not even for a minute," Mother Garrett countered. "I'm sure he's fine, just having a bit of an adventure for himself. He's got to be in the house somewhere, since he couldn't let himself outside. I'll check the front parlors and the dining room. Emma, take the rest of the rooms downstairs. And you come with me," she said to Wryn, ushering her out of the kitchen before the young woman knew what was happening.

Emma closed her eyes for a moment, prayed that they might find little Jonas safe, and followed the others out of the kitchen. She hurried through the dining room and when she reached the center hall, she turned and went directly into the library. Since the door was closed, she doubted she would find him there. Once inside, she quickly looked behind the leather chairs grouped in front of the fireplace and the glass cases of books. No Jonas.

Next, she headed to her office by way of an adjoining door that was also closed, which offered little hope that Jonas could have wandered there, either. When she opened the door and looked inside, however, hope blossomed into sheer joy and her heart sent a prayer of gratitude straight to heaven.

There he was, straight ahead! He was standing on the chair behind her desk, pencil in hand, doodling on the cover of the guest register she kept there, and completely oblivious to her presence, at least for the moment.

Blinking back tears, she gazed at him. With her spirit surging with the deep, deep love that only a grandchild could inspire, she stored the image of her husband's namesake, with his chubby cheeks, dark wavy hair, and intense hazel eyes, deep in the scrapbook of her heart.

Fearful that she might frighten him into tumbling off the chair and that he might hurt himself with the pencil in the process, she held her place just inside the doorway. "Precious, precious Jonas," she crooned, just above a whisper. "Hello, baby. I'm your Grandmother Garrett."

He looked up and grinned at her, wide enough to show off his baby teeth and to deepen the dimples in his cheeks. "Papa!" he said, before turning back to the register to scribble a bit more.

"Papa likes to write, doesn't he?" Emma murmured as she took several slow steps into the room. "Grandmother likes to write, too. Do you like Grandmother's book?" she asked once she was within arm's distance.

He was too intent on his scribbling to reply.

She edged closer, satisfied that if he tumbled now, she would be able to catch him. Ever so slowly, she reached out to put her hand on top of his, hoping to take the pencil away from him, but he yanked his hand away and scowled at her.

"Mine!"

"That's not your pencil. That's my pencil," she said gently. "You're too little to be using a pencil, especially when you're standing up. You could hurt yourself."

His cheeks reddened and he tightened his hand around the pencil to make a fist. "Mine!"

"Typically two," she muttered to herself. She could simply take the pencil away from him, but that was bound to upset him, which was hardly the way she wanted to introduce herself to him. Trying to explain why something was dangerous to a two-year-old was pointless, and she suspected it would simply be easier all around if she was able to distract him, a tactic which worked when she was dealing with her guests.

Smiling, she slipped her arm around his little waist and opened one of the drawers in the desk. "Let's see what's in here, Jonas. Is there something in here you'd like to have?" she asked. She was hoping she could find something in the clutter she kept hidden in the drawers that would be safe enough for a two-year-old to handle, but interesting enough to make him forget about the pencil he was gripping in his fist.

She made an exaggerated search through the papers and other contents in the drawer that was noisy enough to attract and hold his attention while she looked for something he might want more than his pencil. She was tempted to give him one of the candle-wood crosses Reverend Glenn had whittled for guests, but thought better of that idea, since the edges of the wood were too sharp for a baby.

"Oh, look, Jonas!" she gushed as she lifted out one of the handkerchiefs Aunt Frances embroidered for guests at Hill House. Still keeping one arm around Jonas, she used her free hand to drape the handkerchief over her fist to make it into a puppet of sorts. "Hello," she said in a singsong voice. "Would you like to read a book with me?"

Jonas stared at her makeshift puppet and smiled. "Book!"

"Yes, we have lots and lots of books. If we go back into the library, you can pick out whatever book you like," the puppet promised as she hoisted Jonas to her hip. "Let me show you all the books, but you can't take the pencil with you," she crooned.

He dropped the pencil and reached for the makeshift puppet. "Book!"

Holding him close, she laid her cheek atop his head and inhaled the sweetness of this baby boy as she walked toward the door. She was barely back inside the library when Mark came rushing in, with Catherine right behind carrying Paul on her hip. Mother Garrett was close on their heels, but Wryn was nowhere to be seen.

"You found him!" Mark exclaimed.

"I did indeed. He was in my office, trying to register guests, I assume," she said as she handed little Jonas over to his father. "We were just about to pick out a book for him."

Mark hugged his son close. "How did he ever make his way down to your office?"

"We probably don't want to know." Just imagining this little one working his way down the steep staircase from her bedroom to her office made her tremble, but she also gave credit to the angels, who must have been watching over him, for keeping him safe.

"This isn't quite the way I hoped to welcome you all home to Candlewood, but I'm so glad you're here. You look wonderful," Emma offered, pleased to see her daughter-in-law for the first time since she had married into the family.

"Book!" Jonas cried as he struggled against his father. "Book!"

"Yes, you shall have your book," Catherine crooned. "Thank you for finding him for us before he hurt himself, Mother Emma," she murmured. She edged close enough to her husband to be able to lay her hand gently against Jonas' back, as if to reassure herself that he was safe and sound again. Jonas himself seemed to be totally distracted by seeing his brother again and quickly forgot all about wanting a book.

As the parents reunited with their little runaway, Emma studied their images as she slipped her hand into her pocket to finger the keepsakes she kept there. To others, the swatches of cloth she had sewn together over a lifetime would mean little, but to Emma, each bit of cloth represented a special experience or a milestone in her life that she treasured.

She fingered through the pieces until she found the cloth she had cut from the work apron her husband had worn while working alongside her in the General Store, which had been founded by her grandparents before Candlewood had even been established as a town. Jonas had always been a loving father to their three sons, and she knew he would have been very, very proud of Mark and his young family.

Mark was the youngest of her boys and shortest in stature and the most slender of build. He was also the most gentle and quiet. His wife, Catherine, was a shy, timid woman by nature, but when she looked at Mark, even now, her loving gaze revealed how much she treasured the man she had married.

Like his brothers, Mark had never shown any interest at all in remaining in Candlewood, let alone in taking over the General Store. Emma had used some of the wealth she had inherited from her mother and grandmother to set up each of her sons in business. She had been very pleased when Mark had decided on owning and operating a bookstore, a business well suited to both his nature and his interests. She had not been pleased, however, when he decided to open his business far away in Albany, which is where he met and married Catherine.

His profits were not substantial, but he had built a quiet, satisfying life for himself and his family. She wished he had decided to live and work closer to Candlewood so that she would be able to see him and her grandchildren more often, but knowing Mark was happy was all that really mattered to her.

Emma's arms literally tingled with the anticipation of holding her other little grandson for a spell, but Paul, named for Catherine's late father, seemed more interested in the collar on his mother's gown than in meeting his grandmother.

As if reading her mind, Catherine handed Paul over to Emma so she could take Jonas from her husband. "He's a bit heftier than his brother, isn't he?" Emma asked as she pressed a kiss to the top of his head and cuddled his chubby frame against her body. Like Jonas, he had a mop of dark waves on his head, but his eyes were dark brown and his dimples were not as pronounced as his brother's.

Catherine chuckled. "By a good bit."

"You'll be great buddies, the two of you," Emma crooned.

"They're inseparable already," Mark offered with a grin. "I'm surprised Paul didn't tag along with his brother for a little adventure today."

"Give him time. He probably will," Mother Garrett said. "If you'll all excuse me, I'm going to head back to my kitchen. I've got lots of mouths to feed for supper tonight. I'm making that potato casserole you like so much, Mark, and there will be plenty of bacon to crumble on top, assuming your mother hasn't eaten most of it."

"I only took one piece," Emma argued.

Mark laughed. "So far. I'll try to keep Mother out of the kitchen for you, Grams."

Mother Garrett grinned. "I've been waiting a long time to hear one of you boys call me that again."

When she turned to leave, Catherine settled Paul onto her other hip. "I'll come along with you, if that's all right. The boys usually have something to eat this time of the afternoon to hold them over until supper."

"Let me carry one of those little darlin's," Mother Garrett insisted and took hold of Jonas. "While you're having a bit of a snack, maybe you can tell your Great-Grams all about your little adventure today," she crooned as the two women left for the kitchen.

For her part, Emma was grateful to have a little time alone with Mark. "Let's sit together for a moment," she suggested, and they settled themselves in one of the two leather chairs in front of the fireplace. "It's a little damp in here. Would you want to start a fire?"

"No. I'm fine. What about you? Are you chilly?"

"Not really," she replied. "If I'd known you were going to arrive earlier than what you'd said in your letters, I would have been here to meet you," she began, then asked suddenly, "Where's Wryn?"

"Wryn's upstairs in her room, which is where I sent her," Mark replied curtly. He looked down at the floor for a moment before looking up again at his mother. "Wryn is the reason we're here now instead of when you expected us. Under the circumstances, Catherine and I thought it best to arrive a good bit before the others."

Curious to know exactly what those circumstances were, Emma merely nodded.

He drew in a deep breath. "How much do you know about Wryn already?"

"Enough to know she's Catherine's niece. And enough to know she's a troubled young woman."

"True. Very true," he replied.

"What I don't know is why she's traveling with you."

"She's not simply traveling with us. Wryn lives with us now. She only came to us a number of weeks before we left, which is why I didn't bother to write to let you know. I knew we'd probably be arriving before my letter even got here. Little did I know—"

"She's living with you and Catherine and the boys? Why?" Emma blurted.

He stretched out his legs and let out a sigh. "It's a complicated tale, I'm afraid. You knew Georgina, Catherine's sister, married again last fall, didn't you?"

"I believe Catherine wrote to tell me, but—"

"Did you know that it was the second time she'd buried a husband?"

Emma pulled back in her chair. "No. I didn't."

"She had Wryn with her first husband, John Covington. She had two other children, as well, but both of them died, along with their father, in the same wagon accident."

"Poor woman!"

"Indeed," he said. "From what Catherine tells me, after their deaths, Georgina moved back home with Wryn to live with Catherine and her parents. She eventually remarried several years later. I believe Wryn was six or seven years old by that time. Anyway, Georgina had three boys with Daniel Robinson. He died from some sort of infection in his leg, leaving Georgina with little more than the four children, the food in the pantry, and the clothes on their backs."

Emma shuddered. "How awful."

"By then, Catherine's parents had passed on and Georgina had no place to go and no place to live. We offered to let her stay with us temporarily, even though we hardly have enough room for ourselves, but she chose to quickly remarry, instead. James Gordon is her new husband. Apparently, he'd been raising his two daughters on his own for some time before he met Georgina. He seems decent enough, and Georgina seems settled again. She's expecting another child in late fall."

"Any man willing to take on the responsibility of raising

another man's child, let alone four of them, qualifies as decent to me," Emma noted. "But if Georgina is settled again, why is Wryn living with you and Catherine?"

"You've obviously met her."

"I have."

"Then you know she can be . . . difficult," he ventured.

"Yes, I'm sure she can be, but I still don't understand why Wryn isn't living at home with her mother and her stepfather."

Mark sat forward in his chair and squared his narrow shoulders. "Because Wryn's behavior is so disruptive and so manipulative, James gave Georgina an ultimatum: either she found a home elsewhere for Wryn or he was going to take his daughters and leave."

"How decent of him," Emma said, quickly reversing her opinion of the man.

"Decent or not, after living with Wryn for a matter of weeks, I'm not quick to condemn the man or to question his word. Not where Wryn's concerned."

Emma leaned forward in her seat. "Wryn is a child. She's only fifteen years old. What could she possibly have done that would justify such an ultimatum?"

Mark shook his head and sighed. "James claims Wryn is responsible for the constant bickering between his two daughters. Some of their little trinkets have even disappeared, which he blames on Wryn, who in turn constantly twists and turns everything he has to say to her into another heated argument. She even ran away. Twice. When she finally refused to speak to him or to obey anything he or her mother told her to do, that's when he gave Georgina his ultimatum."

"If the man felt he was forced to choose between his own young daughters and his new wife and stepchildren, I suppose I'm not surprised he sided with his children. But Georgina did just the opposite, didn't she?" Emma whispered.

"Not completely," Mark argued. "Wryn isn't her only child. She has three other children and another on the way to consider."

Emma stiffened her back. "No mother should ever sacrifice one child for another. There's simply got to be another way."

"If there was, she couldn't find it and neither can we. If Wryn's not in her room pouting, which almost seems like a blessing, she's making our lives miserable. She lies persuasively without blinking an eye. We can't rely on her to do a single task for the simple reason that she either finds excuses not to do it or she simply disappears and refuses to tell us where she's been when she finally decides to come home. Frankly, Mother, Catherine and I are at our wits ends, which is why we left Albany sooner than we'd planned. We were . . . that is, Catherine and I were hoping we could make . . . make arrangements for Wryn before Warren and Benjamin get here."

"Arrangements?" Emma asked as her pulse began to rise with one possibility she would rather not consider for more than a single heartbeat. "What kind of arrangements?"

He cleared his throat. "Catherine and I both realize how much we're asking, but we . . . we were hoping that you would let Wryn live here at Hill House with you, because in all truth, you're the only one we think might be able to bring her under control."

4

FLABBERGASTED, EMMA BLINKED HARD in a vain attempt to make sense of what Mark had said. "Here? You want Wryn to live here? At Hill House?"

"We wouldn't ask you unless we really needed your help, but we haven't been able to think of any other solution. You've written about the two young women here working at Hill House, and we thought you might allow Wryn to live with you and work here, too. Unless you have a better idea," he ventured.

Emma had all sorts of ideas lobbing back and forth in her brain, but not one of them involved having Wryn take up residence here at Hill House. After spending less than fifteen minutes with that young woman, Emma had a very clear feeling that adding Wryn to this household would make as much sense as adding a wet log to a bed of embers in the hearth and expecting a good, healthy fire to result.

At this stage of her life, she had neither the patience nor the inclination to battle the sparks of discontent this young woman would ignite here in an ill-fated attempt to be sent back to her mother. Supervising her hired helpers, Liesel and Ditty, had already proven to be challenge enough, and both of those earnest young women were well-mannered and eager to please.

Wryn, on the other hand, had already displayed qualities that would make her troublesome, at best. Based on what Mark told her about Wryn's behavior back in Albany, Emma could only imagine what kind of influence she might have on Liesel and Ditty.

Wryn's taunt that she was possibly the surprise of a lifetime echoed in Emma's mind, and she rejected the very thought. "Does Wryn know you want her to come live here with me?" she asked, hoping there might be another solution to this problem.

Mark dropped his eyes for a moment. "No. She doesn't. We didn't want to tell her anything until we had an opportunity to discuss it with you first," he admitted. "Catherine and I both know we're asking a great deal of you, but if you don't want Wryn here, we're at a loss as to what to do with her."

The look of total desperation in Mark's gaze tugged at Emma's heartstrings. Though reluctant to refuse his request—at least outright—she was even more reluctant to get involved in another family dispute, even if it was her own.

Not after stepping into the middle of one between James and Andrew Leonard only last fall at the request of their eighty-one-year-old mother. Although the two brothers had eventually reconciled and their mother, whom Emma affectionately called Aunt Frances now, had become a beloved member of Emma's extended family, Emma had no desire to involve herself in a situation that was far more complicated and held much less promise of a successful solution.

"What about Wryn's mother? Does she approve of having Wryn come here to live?"

"Honestly, we haven't discussed it with her, either. She's more concerned about her other children."

"Even if I could accept that," Emma argued, "I still can't understand why Georgina didn't have some inkling that there was going to be trouble between Wryn and Mr. . . . ."

"Gordon."

Emma nodded. "Mr. Gordon and his daughters. She must have known there was going to be a problem before she married him, even if he didn't."

Mark shrugged his shoulders. "I suppose you're right, but given her dire circumstances, she probably didn't feel like she had much of a choice. With four minor children at her skirts, she didn't have a long line of suitors at her door."

"Probably not," Emma admitted, struck by the stark difference in circumstances that existed for both Emma and Georgina as they each faced widowhood. The wealth Emma had been blessed to inherit had given her many advantages throughout her life, not the least of which was the security of knowing she would always be able to provide for her children even after her husband died. Her circumstances had also kept her from ever being forced to choose between her husband and any one of her children—a choice no woman should ever have to make.

"Isn't there some way Wryn's mother can broker a peace between her new husband and his daughters and Wryn?" Emma asked.

"She tried. More than once. So did her husband. Pastor Bonn tried, as well. But Wryn simply refused to have any part of it. She claims her two stepsisters are at fault and denies any responsibility for the estrangement within the household."

Perplexed, Emma shook her head. "You told me what Wryn has done with you and Catherine, but do you know why she's been so difficult?"

Mark swallowed hard. "Catherine thinks Wryn is deliberately

misbehaving with us because she thinks we'll be able to force her mother to take her back into the household. Unfortunately, Georgina refused to do that only a day before we left Albany, although Wryn doesn't know that."

He paused and locked his gaze with his mother's. "All I know is that while I can sympathize with Wryn's situation, she simply cannot live with us any longer. She needs a firmer hand than either Catherine or I can give her," he admitted. "With Catherine carrying a new babe, I simply can't allow Wryn to continue to upset her."

"Catherine's teeming again? Truly?" Emma exclaimed.

Mark's broad smile eased the tension that had tightened his expression. "We expect to have a new brother or sister for our boys in September," he whispered. "Obviously, we haven't told Paul or Jonas yet. We haven't told anyone. Not even Wryn knows."

"I'm so happy for you," she whispered back as her heart leaped. Learning she had another grandchild on the way was one joy she had not expected to be part of her reunion with her sons and their families, but agreeing to take on the responsibility of a troubled fifteen-year-old was not something she had expected, either. As much as she did not want to disappoint Mark or Catherine, Emma could only envision the chaos Wryn was bound to bring to Hill House with her.

As it was, life at Hill House for the past few months had proven to be uncommonly chaotic. The quiet months of winter usually gave Emma and her Hill House family an opportunity to rest and recover from the hectic pace of operating a boardinghouse during guest season, which lasted from May to October each year, when the canal was open.

Just this past January, however, Emma had opened Hill House to several families whose homes had been damaged or destroyed after an explosion at the match factory in town had unleashed a fire that had quickly spread. After nearly twenty people had left, Emma had scarcely had time to prepare for her sons' visits. Since there would be no time at all for anyone here at Hill House to rest up before paying guests began to arrive in early May, Emma was hardly prepared to consider taking on the responsibility of a troubled young woman.

Emma also had to consider how this young woman's presence in her life would complicate her plans for the future. Zachary Breckenwith had asked her again only today to marry him, but she suspected he might reconsider his proposal if Wryn became part of Emma's household.

"I've upset you," Mark ventured. "I didn't mean to—"

"What? No. No, you haven't upset me," Emma replied and realized she was wearing a frown. "You know I'm always here for you and Catherine to help you any way that I can, but . . . but I'd have to give this a lot of thought before I could agree to have Wryn live here with me. I also have to consider your grandmother. I couldn't take on a responsibility like this without discussing this with her first. And, well . . . I hadn't planned on telling you this until your brothers had arrived with their families, but . . . but I'm considering getting married again."

Mark's eyes widened. "You are?"

"Yes, I am."

"But you never mentioned anything about getting married in any of your letters," he argued.

"No, I didn't, and I haven't actually agreed to marry him yet. I've only allowed him to start courting me this past month or so, and I've promised to give him my answer once all of us have had an opportunity to spend time together for my birthday," she explained. Pausing, she carefully studied the expression on his face for any hint that he might find the prospect of his mother getting married again to be problematic.

To her gracious relief, his gaze softened, and he reached out to take her hand. "Does this very intelligent, very wise man who's decided to pursue my mother have a name?"

"He does," Emma murmured as her cheeks flushed. "How can you be certain he's either intelligent or wise?"

"Because he chose you," her son replied as he squeezed her hand. "What's his name?"

"Zachary Breckenwith. He's the nephew of my previous lawyer. You do remember him, don't you?"

"Of course. He came by the General Store quite often."

"Yes, he did. Initially, Mr. Breckenwith came to Candlewood to help his uncle with his law practice when he took ill, but that was right around the time you were getting ready to leave for Albany, so the two of you never met. After his uncle passed on, Mr. Breckenwith decided to move here permanently to help his aunt Elizabeth. He's living in their house on Main Street, as it turns out, which he purchased after his aunt passed on last year."

"So he's been your lawyer?"

"For about five years now," she replied without bothering to mention that Zachary still insisted she needed to retain another lawyer to represent her while they were courting.

"Then you know him well."

"Yes."

Mark smiled. "And he knows you well."

Her cheeks got warmer. "Yes, I believe he does. Would you . . . I mean, how would you feel if I decided to marry again?"

"I think I'd be relieved, as well as disappointed."

She caught her breath for a moment. Although she appreciated the fact that he was as honest with her now as he had always been, she was still taken aback by his reply. "Disappointed?" she prompted, upset by the thought she would disappoint any of her sons, especially her youngest.

"Yes. I'm disappointed that you would think I wouldn't approve of anyone you chose to marry, but I am truly, truly relieved to know that you will have someone by your side to love you and care for you, just as Father always did."

Tears welled and she blinked them back while she tried to swallow the lump in her throat. "Thank you, Mark."

"I'm sorry," he said, shaking his head. "It appears that we couldn't have brought this problem of ours to your doorstep at a worse time. The last thing you need in your life right now is to take on responsibility for Wryn. Forget I asked. I'll talk to Catherine tonight. We'll simply have to find another way to—"

"No. Please don't. Not yet. You're my son, Mark, and I love Catherine like she was my own daughter simply because she's your wife and she loves you. She's also given me two darling grandsons I am looking forward to spoiling for the next few weeks, as well as the promise of another grandchild come fall. We're family, and if we can't count on our family to help us when we have a problem, then we can't count on anyone," she insisted as she got to her feet. "Let me pray for a few days about what we might do for Wryn to help her the very best way we can. In the meantime, there are two little ones in your grams' kitchen I'd like to cuddle a bit."

He laughed as he got up from his chair. "If they're having a snack like Catherine suggested, now might not be the best time to cuddle them," he cautioned. "They're still a bit messy with their food, despite our best efforts."

"And you weren't?" she teased as they headed out of the library into the center hallway to the kitchen.

"Was I messy?" he asked, as if troubled by the very thought.

"Not really," she admitted. "You were never a messy child. You were as quiet and deliberate at mealtimes as you were when you were doing most anything because you were never very far from the books you loved then and love even now."

"Mark?"

Emma looked up to see Catherine coming down the center staircase with a worried look on her face.

"What's wrong?" her son asked as he hurried to meet his wife at the bottom of the staircase.

"It's Wryn. I went up to her room to let her know that we'd found Jonas and to see if she wanted something to eat, but she's not there. She's gone."

"She's probably upset that she was sent to her room and wasn't allowed to help look for Jonas. She couldn't very well come downstairs, since we were all here, but she may have wandered up to the garret, where Liesel and Ditty have their rooms. I'll check there for you," Emma said.

Catherine let out a sigh. "You can check, but I doubt you'll find her there," she insisted before Emma could start up the stairs. "Her cape is missing, along with her reticule. I think she may have run off."

5

VENTURING OUTDOORS AGAIN to look for Wryn, after spending hours riding in the rain, was about as appealing to Emma as eating a warm hunk of bread without a thick layer of butter on top.

Wearing Mother Garrett's rain cape that was too big for her, an old pair of boots left behind by a previous guest that were too wide, and a pair of gloves that were too tight did not help Emma's mood, either. She held on to Mark with one arm as they made their way through the drizzle down the steep hill to Main Street.

The cobblestones beneath her feet were slick, and her feet slid from side to side inside her boots as she walked, making her feel clumsy.

"If Wryn has no coin, she won't get very far," Emma said, hoping to ease the worry from her son's face. "She couldn't leave Candlewood even if she did. The stage doesn't come through for a few days yet, and the canal won't be open again for a few weeks."

Mark let out a sigh. "To be honest, I'm less worried about Wryn leaving Candlewood than I am about having her stay here.

From what I could see when we drove down Main Street earlier today, there are far too many ways for a young woman like Wryn to get herself into trouble."

"Once the weather warms a bit more and the canal opens, the town will be brimming with strangers and all sorts of dangers, perhaps, but not now," Emma countered, hoping to ease his concerns. "Candlewood has grown a great deal since you've left. There are more people living here now and the business district is filled with all sorts of new businesses, but I can't see how any young woman could get into any sort of real trouble here, even Wryn."

"That might be true for most young women, but not her," Mark countered. "You have no idea, no idea at all, of the trouble she can get herself into."

When they reached the bottom of the hill, they turned south on Main Street and walked past a number of smaller cross streets, including the one where Zachary lived and worked, which she pointed out to her son. Eventually, they reached the planked sidewalk that lined the business district, which had mushroomed since the building of the canal. Area products could now travel to the East Coast by way of the Erie Canal, and new goods were introduced in return, as well as a huge influx of workers and their families who now called Candlewood their home.

Main Street itself held little traffic, which was not unusual for late on a Saturday afternoon. Emma assumed that the dreary weather had probably kept most shoppers at home, though she could not really see through the misty drizzle more than a square or two ahead of them to determine if anyone else was out and about.

Emma patted her son's arm and smiled. "You have every right to be concerned and you have every right to be upset with Wryn, but please don't worry. I'm certain she hasn't gotten into any trouble yet."

An hour later, after Emma and her son had followed Wryn's trail from one shop to another down one side of Main Street all the way to Emerson's Hotel at the far end, Emma was no longer smiling.

Neither was Mark.

In point of fact, Mark was coldly silent when they left the hotel and headed for the General Store.

"It's not your fault," she said. "At least she didn't register at Emerson's, too."

"If she had, she would have insisted on a suite. You can be sure of that," he gritted. "We should never have brought her here. Never. We should have left her at home. She can cook better than women twice her age, and she's proven she's certainly old enough to be able to fend for herself otherwise for a few weeks."

"That may be true," Emma replied. "But if you had left her home, how much debt do you think she could have accumulated in your name while you were gone?"

"I'm not certain, but at least it would have been in my name instead of yours," he grumbled. "I'm so embarrassed that she's done this to you. I'll . . . I'll find a way to pay you back. I will. It may take some time—"

"It's not your fault," Emma repeated more insistently as they started to cross the street. She paused for a moment until they made their way around a rather large puddle of mud, since she had already enjoyed the dubious pleasure of sliding into one earlier today. "It's not your debt, either," she continued when they had put the mud puddle behind them. "It's Wryn's debt, which means *she'll* have to pay me back, not you."

"And just exactly how do you expect a fifteen-year-old girl to pay for a new bonnet from the millinery, not one but *two* boxes of Belgian chocolates, a French lace shawl of some sort, and a . . . a beaded reticule?" he charged.

"She'll have to work it off," Emma stated as they mounted the steps to the planked sidewalk in front of the General Store.

He threw one hand up into the air. "Work it off? She'll be thirty years old before she could possibly work off the sum she owes you."

"At least," Emma quipped.

He stopped just outside the door to the store and shook his head. "I still don't understand why all those shopkeepers let her put her purchases on your account."

"Since we haven't passed a single other soul so far, I'd venture to say it's been a very slow day for most of the businesses. Wryn was probably but one of a handful of shoppers today, which means the shopkeepers would have been anxious for any kind of sale."

"Still—"

"Candlewood isn't Albany, Mark," Emma continued, anxious to get into the General Store to see what kind of damage Wryn had done there to her account. "The town may have changed a lot since you've been gone, but it's still a small town. Everyone here knows Hill House, and they know me. Most everyone has heard by now that you and Warren and Benjamin are all bringing your families home for a visit, too. Even if you hadn't driven down Main Street earlier with her today, they wouldn't suspect Wryn wasn't who she said she was—part of our family."

"The gossipmongers are still as ravenous as ever, I suppose."

She chuckled. "That much hasn't changed, but like I've warned you all along, Wryn's little misadventure today isn't something I'd like to have them chew on. That's why I want you to act as if everything Wryn has bought here at the General Store is perfectly legitimate, just like you've done at the other shops. How or why Wryn decided to go on a little shopping adventure without permission is something we'll handle privately, within our family," she said, even though she considered Wryn to be part of Catherine's family, not her own.

He scowled. "I'd like to send her, bag and baggage, straight back to her mother where she belongs, whether Georgina likes it or not. Georgina got herself and Wryn into this predicament of theirs, and I have a good mind to let them get themselves out of it."

"We may eventually have to do that," Emma said. "In the meantime, let's go inside. Maybe this time we'll find Wryn hasn't left yet."

"Unless she's hurried off and moved on to the stationery store we passed on the other side of Main Street. Wryn has an obsession of sorts with writing," he grumbled while he opened the door for his mother, setting off the bell.

"Good. Then she won't mind writing a very sincere, very lengthy letter of apology. One for each of us," Emma suggested.

Once Mark followed his mother into the store and shut the door behind him, he stopped for a moment and took a long look around. "It hasn't changed. Not one bit. The tables are just as neatly stacked with goods and the glass in the display cabinets is just as clear. Even the curtain behind the counter is the same. I can almost see that old cash box right on the middle shelf below the counter where you always kept it," he murmured.

Emma smiled. "It's still there. Or it was just a few months ago," she replied.

Indeed, it was only last fall that Mr. Atkins had purchased the General Store from the man Emma had sold the store to some four years ago. A single man with limited business experience, he had been overwhelmed by his new responsibilities.

The store had quickly become a disorganized mess, as well as a haven where less-than-honest travelers, canal workers, and factory workers learned how easy it was to pilfer what they wanted instead of paying for it. Emma and Mr. Atkins had had a rough start to their own relationship due to a misunderstanding between him and Mother Garrett and Aunt Frances, but she now considered him to be a friend.

Since then, much to Emma's chagrin, as well as his own, he had also become the focus of matchmaking attention for Mother Garrett and Aunt Frances.

To the surprise of nearly everyone in Candlewood, including the two determined matchmakers, Mr. Atkins had married Addie Doran last week after a very short courtship. A young widow with three young daughters, she had gone to work for Mr. Atkins in the General Store after the man he had hired to help him, Steven Cross, left to take a job at the piano factory with his brother.

When the curtain parted and Addie stepped behind the counter, she greeted Emma with a broad smile. "I didn't expect to see you today, but I did so enjoy meeting your niece. Wryn is a lovely, lovely young woman," she offered as Emma approached the counter with her son. "Mark? Is that really you?"

Mark smiled. "It's me. How are you, Widow Doran? Mother wrote to tell me about your troubles. Please allow me to extend my condolences," he said gently.

"Thank you, Mark, but I'm doing very well. And it's Mrs. Atkins now," she said as a blush stole up her cheeks. "How good to see you again. I'd heard you and your brothers were all coming home for a visit. Mr. Atkins just left to deliver the supplies to Hill House that your mother-in-law ordered earlier today," she explained, turning her attention to Emma. "Did Wryn forget to get something you wanted?"

"I'm not certain," Emma replied. "Mark and I were on our way home, and I thought maybe we would stop in to make sure Wryn got everything. Do you have a list of what she purchased in the account book?"

Smiling, Addie reached under the counter to get the account book, set it on top, and opened it up. "Here is it," she said and pointed to the center of the page. "She didn't get all that much. Just two tins of sweets and some beef jerky. A bone-handled knife, which I wrapped up real good for her, and some needles and thread," she said before looking up again. "Was there anything else you needed?"

"Only Wryn," Emma muttered under her breath. "I'll be back early in the week to settle up the account," she promised.

Addie closed the book. "That's fine. How long will you be staying in Candlewood, Mark?"

"For a few weeks."

"I'm looking forward to meeting your wife and your boys."

"I'll be sure to stop in with them. Did . . . did Wryn happen to mention before she left if she was heading back to Hill House?"

"With all those packages she was carrying, I thought she would be, but she said she still had a few stops to make. I offered to let Mr. Atkins take her packages to Hill House for her when he left to take the other supplies, but she insisted on keeping them with her."

"Thank you for offering to help her," Emma said before departing. Amazingly, they found that Wryn had made only one other stop along Main Street, at Carson's Stationery Store, where she had purchased a day book and several writing tablets.

Unfortunately, her trail ended there.

Standing at the corner of Hampton and Main Streets with her son, Emma was cold and exhausted. She also knew that if she didn't get these boots off soon, she would be sporting a whole family of blisters on her feet. "It's still a long walk back to Hill House," she said as a shiver raced down her spine. "I'd dearly love to warm up with a cup of tea."

"If you like, I can take you back to the hotel, where you can have your tea while I go back to Hill House and get the wagon to take you home."

"I don't want you to go to all that bother."

"After all the trouble I've brought home with me, it's the least I can do," he said. "I don't mind. Truly."

"I know you don't, but . . . wait. I think I have a better idea," she said after rejecting any notion of stopping in at Zachary Breckenwith's. He had not been supportive, at first, when she had taken in Aunt Frances. He was the last person she would expect to support her when it came to taking in Wryn, especially once he found out about the young woman's shopping adventure today.

Emma did, however, know where she and Mark could get the advice they both needed. "I know exactly where we could both warm up in front of a nice fire with a good strong cup of tea," she said as she urged him to turn around. "Remember when I wrote to you and Catherine about Reverend Glenn getting married and working again as our assistant pastor?"

He nodded. "We got the letter just before we left."

"Well, his cottage is only a few squares away. I know he would love to see you and introduce you to Aunt Frances. With the weather as it is, it's not likely they've had a single visitor today. Besides, I haven't been to check up on them for almost a week now, and I want to make sure they're faring well on their own."

"But what about Wryn?" he asked as they started back the same way they had just come.

"She's probably made her way back to Hill House and hidden all of her booty by now. If she has, then Mother Garrett will be sure to keep a close eye on her. If she hasn't, then we're both going to need to warm up before we walk back to Hill House and get the wagon to start searching for her again."

Emma and Mark arrived at Reverend Glenn's new home within five minutes. The cottage itself was small but boasted four small rooms instead of two, as Reverend Glenn had originally thought. The moment she stepped inside, however, she knew she had been wrong about a number of her assumptions today.

First, Reverend Glenn and Aunt Frances did not have a single visitor. They had two.

Second, any hope she had of trying to decide what to do with Wryn without involving Zachary Breckenwith was futile, since he was right there sitting next to Reverend Glenn.

Third . . .

She let out a sigh. She was too tired to think anymore. She simply smiled and wondered how unkind it would be to wish that the young lady who was sitting on the settee next to Aunt Frances might simply disappear.

6

WITH FIVE PEOPLE and one very large, very ungainly dog cramped together in the small parlor, there was little room for anyone to move about, let alone escape.

After introducing and reintroducing her son to everyone, Emma settled down in a chair across from the fire, where she could see that the doors to the two tiny bedrooms had been closed shut. Mark sat next to her in the other of the two chairs he had carried in from the kitchen. Fortunately, her son had shown the same quiet self-control as his father by not exploding into a diatribe the moment he saw Wryn. Emma suspected, for now at least, that Mark was more interested in studying the man who was courting his mother than he was in confronting his wayward niece in front of the others.

Butter, the aged mongrel who had become Reverend Glenn's constant companion, slept at his master's feet. Zachary sat in a chair on the other side wearing the closed expression he usually reserved for handling his clients, although the amusement she detected in his gaze was most definitely reserved for her.

Between them all, Aunt Frances sat with Wryn on a small

settee. The two, both unusually small and finely boned, offered a striking vision of the opposite ends of the life cycle. Both set of cheeks were also bright pink. Emma assumed Aunt Frances' cheeks were flushed with the excitement of having so many visitors at one time, but she hoped Wryn's cheeks were flaming with nervous embarrassment, if only to reassure herself that the young woman possessed any sort of conscience.

After sharing a few pleasantries, Emma smiled. "What a lovely shawl you're wearing, Aunt Frances," she said, anxious to have her suspicions about the source of her shawl confirmed or denied.

Aunt Frances reached up to touch the exquisite lace and smiled. "It's a bit more delicate than I'm accustomed to, but I can truthfully say that I've never owned anything quite as beautiful. Wryn gave it to me just before you arrived. She's as sweet and thoughtful as you are." She patted the girl's hand.

Smiling demurely, Wryn turned her hand over to clasp Aunt Frances' hand. "You're very kind."

"Apparently, you've been very, very busy today," Mark said calmly to his niece.

The blush on Wryn's cheeks flamed red. "But I wasn't too busy to stop and introduce myself to Reverend and Mrs. Glenn," she countered, addressing her uncle before turning her attention back to her hosts. "Uncle Mark and Aunt Catherine told me so much about the two of you while we traveled here. I could hardly wait to meet you both."

"We're very, very pleased that you did," Reverend Glenn noted, pausing for a moment from rubbing his left arm, which had been weakened by his stroke. "You shouldn't have come bearing so many gifts," he added, looking down at his contented dog. "Butter here hasn't had a hunk of beef jerky like you brought for him without being chased out of Mercy Garrett's kitchen for a good, long spell."

"I put the rest of the jerky away and hid it right behind the crock of butter where it'll be safe," Wryn said without looking at either Emma or Mark.

Emma smiled and saw Reverend Glenn and Aunt Frances do the same. Unless Aunt Frances had had the butter stored high, the beef jerky might have disappeared already, courtesy of an old dog who had a peculiar fondness for butter, hence the inspiration for his name.

With the lace shawl and beef jerky accounted for, Emma suspected Wryn had given the knife she had bought to Reverend Glenn for his whittling. Wryn's generosity, however, did not change the fact that she had purchased her gifts for the Glenns under false pretenses.

Reluctant to settle the matter of Wryn's outlandish behavior here and now in front of the others, Emma turned her attention to Zachary. "What brought you back out into this awful weather again today?"

"Widow Ellis made a pot of soup for the Glenns. Rather than venture out into this weather, she decided I should deliver it for her, which I was only too happy to do," he explained. "And you?"

"Just to visit," Emma replied carefully to avoid telling an outright lie.

Aunt Frances got to her feet. "Wryn set some water to boil for tea. Come along, Emma. You can help me in the kitchen."

"I'll help, too," Wryn suggested and stood up.

Aunt Frances urged her back into her seat again. "You've already done enough. You stay right here with the menfolk and keep the conversation going until we get back."

Emma noticed the frown on Wryn's face before the young

woman caught herself and smiled. Following Aunt Frances through an open doorway into the kitchen, she shut the door behind her. The kitchen was twice the size of the cozy parlor, but she did not expect to see how much the room had changed in the course of the week since she had last visited.

Aunt Frances' kitchen now had a corner cupboard and a pantry sitting on either side of the original larder built against the outer wall. Although both were obviously quite old, they appeared to be sturdy and serviceable. The two rocking chairs now rested side by side atop a braided rug instead of bare floorboards in front of the fireplace, along with Aunt Frances' sewing basket.

Three mismatched chairs, similar to the two Mark had carried into the living room, kept company around a square table. The pot of soup from Widow Ellis was simmering on the cookstove, along with the kettle of water Wryn had set to boil. The sink now had two narrow tables on either side which served as counters.

"What a difference a week makes," Emma noted with surprise.

"Faith and friends make all the difference in the world," Aunt Frances replied. "There's a blue teapot in the corner cupboard. If you get that out for me while I get the tea ready, then you can pour the water for me."

She opened the door to the larder to get the tea while Emma headed for the corner cupboard. "Between James and Andrew, we'll never want for foodstuffs."

"I shouldn't think you would," Emma said as she lifted the well-used but attractive teapot out of the cupboard. Both of Aunt Frances' sons farmed together now on the old family homestead they had inherited from their father. They had been very generous while their mother had been living at Hill House and more recently when Emma had provided so many with a place to live after the tragic explosion and fire.

"Widow Ellis' soup smells awfully good," Emma murmured, hoping Aunt Frances could not hear her stomach growl.

"She's a fair cook, but not as good as Mercy," Aunt Frances commented. "Would you like a little soup to tide you over till supper?"

"No, thank you. The tea will be enough for now."

"I haven't had to cook much myself until now. People kept sending something over when we first moved in, but not so much anymore," she said as she filled a tea ball before adding it to the teapot Emma had set onto the table. "Members of the congregation have been so generous in other ways, too. I brought this teapot from home, but the kettle came from Addie Atkins just the day before yesterday. She said she had an extra one after setting up housekeeping with Mr. Atkins."

Emma plucked a heavy cloth from a peg, picked up the kettle, and poured the boiling water into the teapot. "Are you feeling any better about Addie now?"

"I never thought poorly of the woman in the first place. If you're referring to whether or not I've had my feelings hurt because Mr. Atkins chose to marry her instead of listening to my suggestions or Mercy's, then there isn't a doubt in this old head of mine that he made a better choice. And a kinder one," she added thoughtfully. "As we both know, it isn't always easy for widows as they grow older, or for single women, for that matter. Orralynne Burke had that cookstove sent over. She's sold the house she inherited from her brother, you know."

"No, I hadn't heard," Emma replied. "Then I take it she's going to live with the Masseys permanently," she suggested. She was pleased to think the friendship between the lifelong spinster, some ten years younger than Emma, and the young couple who had celebrated the birth of their son at Hill House, had deepened—yet another blessing that had come after the tragedy this past January.

"She seemed to think so," Aunt Frances replied. "She's been a great help to them, and they're being very good to her, too. I believe she said young Matthew Cross and his brother bought the house. Now that their father has passed on, there's no need to stay in that old place where they'd been living. Besides, it's too far from town for them to keep an eye out for their mother while they're working."

"Matthew and Steven are good, solid young men. They'll make good husbands one day," Emma suggested, hoping the two young men she had met shortly after they had moved to Candlewood would not be tempted to court either Liesel or Ditty away from Hill House anytime soon.

Aunt Frances peeked into the teapot and frowned. "Needs another few minutes. You know, Emma, I was very blessed to have a good man like Reverend Glenn welcome me into his life. What about you? Have you decided to marry Mr. Breckenwith yet, or are you following in Mercy's footsteps and simply enjoying the chase?" she teased.

Emma chuckled as she left to remove seven mugs from the cupboard to a tray Aunt Frances had set on the table, along with a crock of honey and a pitcher of cream. "Poor Mr. Kirk. No matter how hard he tries, he just can't seem to get Mother Garrett to accept his proposal."

Aunt Frances countered with a grin. "Heaven knows that woman is as likely to accept a proposal from him as she is to let someone commandeer her kitchen, although she does seem agitated now that she has a serious rival. Widow Cates has given up, but

Widow Franklin is still vying for Mr. Kirk's attention, you know, but I wasn't asking about Mercy. I was asking about you and Mr. Breckenwith."

Emma let out a sigh. "I thought I'd decided to accept his proposal, but with the boys coming home and now with Mark arriving several weeks early, my life's a bit too complicated at the moment to sort through all the issues that need to be resolved before I can agree to marry him."

Aunt Frances placed her hand on top of Emma's. "One of those complications wouldn't happen to be named Wryn, would it?"

Emma sighed again. "I only met that young woman a few hours ago, but calling her a complication is probably the kindest way to think of her at the moment. When I first met her this morning, she was sitting on top of the kitchen table gobbling down one cruller after another and being rude. At the time I thought she was an irreverent little snip. But you wouldn't believe me if I told you half of what she's managed to do since then," Emma grumbled, still reluctant to spoil the pleasure Aunt Frances and Reverend Glenn had received from the gifts Wyrn had given to them.

"On the contrary," Aunt Frances said. "I think I might. That young woman's got a heart full of hurt tucked deep inside of her and acting out is just her way of trying to bear it. I suspect you already know that, don't you?"

"Yes, I suppose I do, but—"

"But you're not the one who has to heal that girl's broken heart. Only God can do that, Emma. Be His instrument. Nothing more. He's brought Wryn into your life for a purpose, but you have to trust Him to guide both of you along the path He's set out. Don't let her complicate your life to the point you forget that He's happiest when we accept all the gifts He's brought to our doorstep—

including the love and companionship of a caring spouse, which I think Mr. Breckenwith is offering to you."

Reminded yet again of how precious this woman was and touched by the wisdom she was sharing, Emma blinked back tears. "I've missed having you and Reverend Glenn with me at Hill House so much," she whispered.

"We've missed you, too, but this is where we want to be and where we need to be. Reverend Glenn and I aren't very far away from you at all, and we're always here to help you." Aunt Frances caressed the back of Emma's hand.

"Thank you," Emma replied, glancing at the lace shawl lying across the back of Aunt Frances' rocking chair.

Aunt Frances followed her gaze and let out a sigh. "But right now, you're troubled by something a bit more immediate. Maybe it would help if I told you that I've been terribly careful handling the shawl. I don't think you'll have much trouble returning it to Mrs. Delaney's Boutique."

Emma's eyes widened. "Why would you suggest . . . ? But how could you know . . . ?"

"I'm eighty-one years old, Emma. I may have only been stitching on cotton and linen with these old hands of mine for most of those years, but I can surely recognize expensive imported lace when I see it. I also know Wryn couldn't possibly afford to buy that shawl for me, along with the rest of the gifts she had for us, as soon as I laid eyes on it. I'm not certain how she managed to get her hands on those things, but I do know that even if she saved every coin she could earn for herself for the next fifteen years, she still wouldn't have enough to pay for them."

"Unfortunately, you're not the first person today to reach that conclusion," Emma said.

"Maybe not, but I can make it easier all around if I just return everything to you. I don't want to hurt Wryn's feelings, so once you all leave, I'll wrap up everything she gave us real good so it'll be ready for you to take back whenever you decide. Except for the beef jerky. I'm afraid Butter found it and devoured it, along with half a crock of my butter, which is why he's fast asleep on the floor right now. He's so full he can't move."

Emma laughed out loud, picked up the tray, and nodded toward the kitchen door. "If and when I decide what to do with Wryn's purchases, I'll let you know. In the meantime, maybe you could open that door for me so I could carry the tea into the parlor."

When Emma followed Aunt Frances into the other room, however, Butter was the only one still in the same spot. Reverend Glenn and Zachary had both donned coats, hats, and gloves and stood by the door, about ready to leave. Mark and Wryn, however, were not there at all.

"Where are Mark and Wryn?" Emma asked.

"Where are you going with Mr. Breckenwith?" Aunt Frances asked her husband, almost simultaneously.

Reverend Glenn smiled. "While you two ladies were busy in the kitchen, Mark grew worried about leaving Catherine alone with the babies for too long, and he didn't want her to worry about Wryn. So he decided they should head back to Hill House. On their way out, they met Mr. Hooper, who stopped on his way to fetch the doctor. It appears Mrs. Hooper has taken a turn for the worse. I promised to meet him back at his house since Mr. Breckenwith offered to see me there and back again," he explained, answering both women's questions.

"What about your tea?" Emma asked as she set it on a side table.

"I'm sorry you both went to all that trouble, but I really shouldn't dawdle, especially since I don't walk so fast anymore.

The two of you can likely finish off that pot of tea by yourselves," he teased.

Aunt Frances took the cape Emma had worn from a peg near the door and handed the garment to her. "Don't worry about the tea. I know how anxious you are to go home and spend time with Mark and his family. We'll visit together again soon."

"Don't you want me to stay to keep you company?"

"No, Emma dear. Reverend Glenn could be gone for hours. I have my stitching to keep me busy," she said and caught Zachary's gaze. "If Emma walks along with you now to the Hoopers' to make sure Reverend Glenn arrives safe and sound, will you walk her to Hill House, as well? You'd still be back to the Hoopers' again long before Reverend Glenn is ready to come home again."

"Even if I'm ready sooner than we expect, I'll simply wait for you," her husband added.

"Then I can't see any reason why I shouldn't take Mrs. Glenn's suggestion, can you?" Zachary asked, gazing directly at Emma.

Hard pressed to think of a single logical reason why she should not leave now and let Zachary escort her home, she smiled in response and slipped into the oversized cape. Avoiding Zachary's questions about Wryn was unavoidable.

Besides, if Wryn's visit to Candlewood thus far was any indication, Emma might expect Sheriff North eventually to show up on her porch looking for Wryn. When he did, she had no doubt she might need a lawyer . . . which made marrying one sound like a very good idea.

After Emma and Zachary had Reverend Glenn safely delivered to the Hoopers', she had the opportunity to speak to Zachary alone and broach the subject of Wryn. By the time she had recounted her conversation with Mark and detailed Wryn's misadventure along Main Street, they were starting up the hill toward her boardinghouse.

Anxious to learn his reaction to her news, Emma drew in a long breath and studied him carefully. As she expected, his expression had hardened, but she was not prepared for the coldness of his response.

"I should expect you told your son that taking on responsibility for this young woman is out of the question."

She stiffened. "Actually, I told Mark I would consider it."

He paused, forcing her to stop, as well. "You'd consider it," he repeated, as if he could scarcely believe he had heard her correctly. "When you were talking to your son, did you happen to mention that you're considering a proposal of marriage and that you might be starting a new, very different life for yourself?"

She swallowed hard. With his squared shoulders and determined gaze, he made it very clear to her that Wryn's presence in her life might make him reconsider his proposal. "Of course I did," she managed, barely able to hear her own words above the pounding of her heart. "I haven't given Mark an answer yet simply because I haven't had time to talk with Catherine or Wryn yet—and I'm not convinced Wryn needs to remain here at all. But if she did, I wouldn't even consider taking any responsibility for her, even temporarily, without talking it over with you first."

"Would you be discussing it with me as your lawyer? Or as your future husband?"

"Both," she admitted.

Apparently satisfied, if only for the moment, he nodded and started them toward Hill House again without saying another word. But Emma sensed they were no longer walking alone.

Wryn now walked between them, as surely as she had walked between her mother and stepfather, and Mark and Catherine.

7

I DIDN'T RUN OFF, and you should have known I didn't run off, because I didn't leave a note. I always, always leave a note because that's how it is done. When you run away, you must leave a note."

With a toss of her head, Wryn folded her arms across her chest and let her words echo in the library. With her lips pursed, she sat straight and stiff, with her back to the fireplace, where a softly burning fire chased the early evening chill from the room. Framed with the glow from the fire, she appeared almost angelic; hardly the image that suited her at the moment, considering her behavior for the day.

Seated a fair distance to Wryn's left, Emma held silent, as well, which was no small accomplishment for her. As proprietress of Hill House, she was not accustomed to relinquishing authority when confronted with disagreements between guests, but Mark and Catherine and Wryn were not guests. They were family, although Wryn's relationship to Emma was dubious.

Still, she was careful to keep to the boundaries she had set for herself as merely an observer before this family meeting had begun. Unless Mark asked her a direct question or specifically asked her to intervene, she was not going to say a word. Mark was no longer a child. He was a grown man, a husband and a father, and she needed to allow him to exercise his authority as the head of his family, particularly where Wryn was concerned.

"Forgive me for jumping to an erroneous conclusion that you had run away," Mark snapped, clearly frustrated by the way Wryn had spent the past twenty minutes cleverly twisting his words to suit herself and manipulating the conversation to confuse the very issue that had brought her here. "I wasn't aware there were rules surrounding exactly what a fifteen-year-old was supposed to do if and when she decided to run away."

"I didn't say there were rules. I said that I always leave a note when I run off, which you would have known if you had taken the time to speak to my mother about it. You obviously didn't cover the topic well, which surprises me because you seem to know practically everything else I've done. Unless she deliberately didn't tell you, which wouldn't surprise me at all. She's good at hiding things. She's good at lots of things that aren't—"

"Don't be disrespectful when talking about your mother," Mark cautioned in the sternest voice he had used so far.

Catherine placed her hand on her husband's arm and addressed her niece for the first time. "Mark and I were very worried about you," she said gently. "Uncle Mark clearly asked you to remain in your room. When we found you weren't there later, we had no idea that—"

"That I might not have run off and that I might simply have wanted to see the town for myself? Or that I might want to have something to give to everyone here? You were so busy getting ready to come for this visit and to make sure you had something special for everyone, you never once thought that I might want to have something to give them, did you?" Wryn said, once again diverting fault from herself to Mark and Catherine.

"No, I . . . I suppose I didn't," Catherine murmured, clearly as frustrated as her husband.

Emma held tight to the keepsakes in her pocket. Unfortunately, Mark and Catherine were apparently so unaccustomed to handling conflict, unless it was between a pair of two-year-olds, they were falling into the verbal and emotional traps Wryn was setting for them. Emma, however, could see exactly what Wryn was doing, and she did not like it. Not one whit.

Whether it was her status here as an observer, the experience she had had raising her own children, or settling disputes with patrons and guests that gave her the advantage of insight during this convoluted conversation was irrelevant. What mattered most was that Wryn admit to her misdeeds and be held accountable for them, but Emma would not be able to help make that happen unless Mark invited her to do so.

Mindful of Aunt Frances' advice to let God's plan for Wryn unfold, Emma listened and prayed as the conversation continued to stray off course.

"I won't. I won't take back the gifts, and I won't apologize to the store clerks for misleading them. I won't."

"Yes you will."

"No I won't."

"Yes. You must," Mark insisted.

"No I don't."

He glared at Wryn and turned to his mother. "Maybe you can do this better."

Emma noted the flush on her son's cheeks, but when she saw he was clenching his jaw, she knew he had gone as far as he could go without losing his temper, a rarity for this gentle son of hers. She whispered yet another silent prayer, this time for wisdom and guidance, but she knew exactly where to start: at the very, very beginning.

Borrowing from a page in Zachary's book, which she knew only too well because he had gone to that same page often enough when he had first become her lawyer, she nodded to both Mark and Catherine before she turned her attention to Wryn. "I only have a few questions, but I'd like you to be succinct when you answer them. A simple yes or no will do. That's not a negotiable request, but it's a necessary one if we have any hope of resolving what happened today within the privacy of Hill House," she said.

She paused for a moment to get up and turn her chair for a moment to be able to look at Wryn more directly, yet still have eye contact with Mark and Catherine. When she sat down again, she continued. "As a courtesy, when I've finished with my questions, you'll be able to ask questions of your own, and I'll follow that same rule when I give my answers. If, however, you refuse to adhere to this rule, if you're uncooperative or dishonest with me, then you'll give me no recourse but to send for Sheriff North immediately and have you arrested for theft by deception," she warned, hoping she had used the right term to describe Wryn's crimes.

Wryn's eyes widened, and her cheeks flamed with outrage. "But—"

" 'But' is not an answer open to you," Emma snapped, quick to stop the young woman from saying more than a single word. "Yes or no?" she asked sternly. "Will you answer my questions?"

With defiance flashing in her eyes, Wryn pressed her lips together.

"Good. I'll accept your silence as a yes, which means you'll have to speak to me eventually if your answer is no," Emma said and immediately formed a question that would have a response Wryn would have to voice. "Did you deliberately let little Jonas wander off today while his parents and little brother were still sleeping?"

Wryn blinked hard, as if surprised by the question. "No," she whispered, but it was difficult to tell if she was upset by the nature of the question or the fact that she had to answer the first question Emma posed to her.

"Were you upset when Uncle Mark sent you to your room instead of allowing you to continue to look for Jonas?"

Wryn pursed her lips.

"Apparently yes," Emma offered. "Are you sorry that you didn't keep a closer eye on my grandson?"

With a nod, Wryn answered silently, the defiance and wariness in her eyes now beginning to dim just a bit.

Satisfied with their beginning, Emma shifted to more difficult topics. She kept her voice low and even and her posture relaxed. "When you left Hill House earlier today, did you intend to run away?"

"No," Wryn said, reiterating her earlier claims.

"Did you think that Uncle Mark and Aunt Catherine might think you had run off and worry about you?"

Another set of pursed lips. Another flash of defiance in her eyes.

"So you did," Emma said, folding her hands together and resting them on her lap. "Did you ever once mention to them that when you had run away while living with your mother you had always left a note?"

Wryn chewed on her bottom lip for a moment, as if torn between telling the truth, which would deflate most of her earlier argument with her uncle, and lying.

Emma waited patiently, sent a reassuring glance to her son and his wife, and rested against the back of the chair. If Wryn did tell a lie,

Emma may or may not be able to detect it, but she hoped the threat of involving the authorities would be enough to deter the young woman from lying. She also hoped the young woman did not know how reluctant Emma was to involve Sheriff North at all.

Eventually, Wryn voiced her answer, but she was so soft-spoken, Emma could scarcely hear her. "I'm sorry. Would you speak a bit louder please?"

Wryn clenched her jaw again. "No. I said no."

"Then it would be fair to say that neither your uncle Mark nor your aunt Catherine, nor anyone here at Hill House for that matter, leaped to any sort of illogical conclusion when they thought you might have run off because you thought you'd been punished unfairly. Wouldn't it?" she asked, unwilling at this point to let this girl know that Emma had been the one who had rejected the idea that Wryn had run away in the first place.

A long sigh.

"That's a yes," Emma said, closing the issue of Wryn's first mistake today. She quickly changed topics, as well as her tactics. Instead of starting at the beginning of Wryn's misadventures up and down Main Street, she needed to pose a question that went right to what she thought might be the heart of the matter.

A question that might shed light on why Wryn had been so flippant when Emma first met her in the kitchen, and why Wryn was so anxious to turn Emma completely against her.

A question that was difficult for Emma to ask because she was not certain yet in her own mind of what Wryn's answer would be.

Emma took a deep breath. "Did you have all your purchases today charged to my account, which you clearly knew was wrong, because you wanted to make very sure that I would not agree to have you stay here to live with me at Hill House when Uncle Mark and Aunt Catherine returned to Albany?"

Mark's eyes widened.

Catherine paled.

Wryn tilted up her chin. When she answered, her voice was loud and clear, even though her gaze darkened, as if angry that Emma had been able to cut straight through the shell of her defiance to the hurts she kept deep inside. "Yes," she said, turning to her aunt and uncle and narrowing her eyes. "You didn't think I knew, did you? Well, I did. I overheard you. I heard what you both were planning. And I—"

"The fact that we understand the reason why you committed your misdeeds today doesn't mean that you won't be held accountable," Emma said, effectively interrupting the young woman. "Uncle Mark and Aunt Catherine need to discuss that with you, of course," she said and turned to face her son and daughter-in-law. "Would you like to do that now?"

Mark took his wife's hand into his own and shook his head. "I'd like for us to think about that until morning," he replied. "Until then, Wryn, I'd like you to stay confined to your room. While you're there, since you're so fond of writing, I'd like you to write an apology to me and your aunt Catherine and to my mother. You should also compile a list of things you could do to make amends to my mother for what you've done today."

Wryn dropped her gaze.

"Do you understand what your uncle is telling you to do?" Emma asked gently.

Wryn nodded without looking up.

"Good. Before you go upstairs to your room, however, I promised that you would get to ask me some questions, too, assuming you have some," she said.

Wryn looked up, a surprised expression on her face. "You did say you'd have to follow the same rules that I did, didn't you?"

Emma cocked a brow. "That's what I promised to do."

"Just say yes," Wryn cautioned. "I only have one question for you. Will you answer it with just a yes or no?"

"Yes," Emma gritted, wondering if all this word play was necessary if Wryn only had a single question.

Wryn tilted up her chin and, without further hesitation, posed her question. "Didn't you lie to me earlier today when you told me that Mr. Breckenwith was just your lawyer because you didn't want me to know you were being courted?"

Stunned by the audacity of Wryn's question, Emma's spine tingled with agitation, and she wondered why she had offered to let Wryn ask her any questions in the first place.

Until she realized the question was more than either clever or audacious.

Wryn's question was a test, and how Emma answered it held the key to unlocking the tollgate and allowing Emma to continue on the path God had set before her by sending Wryn to Hill House.

Unless Emma answered yes and admitted she had lied to Wryn, she would more than fail the test of wills between them. She would lose any hope of ever gaining this young woman's trust.

Emma held her gaze steady. "Yes," she replied and said nothing more.

Wryn's determined eyes flashed not with satisfaction, but surprise, along with just a tad of respect, and Emma knew she had passed the first of likely many tests that would unfold over the course of the next few weeks.

Still, the journey had begun, inspiring visions of the host of prayers she would need to add to her days just to live through them, especially if Zachary Breckenwith had reconsidered his proposal of marriage.

8

WEDNESDAY DAWNED AND PROMISED to be a perfect spring day. Bright sun, anxious to warm the earth, was like a golden blossom nestled in a sky of bluebells while a wispy ribbon of clouds lay far to the west. A soft breeze invited the trees and evergreens to dance and caressed the tender buds of leaves and flowers that would soon bless the world with color.

Inside Hill House, Wednesday also showered the boarding-house with the joy Emma had anticipated by having her family home with her in Candlewood. With still more happiness to come once Warren and Benjamin arrived with their families, she refused to let Wryn Covington be more than a stubborn wrinkle in her skirts that Emma intended to iron out with patience. Lots and lots of patience.

Except for mealtimes, Wryn was still closeted in her room, where she was working on writing apologies and the list of amends she had been ordered to compile. The rest of the household had fallen into a comfortable routine, especially now that Liesel and Ditty were back.

After enjoying nearly four days at Hill House, Mark took his family for an outing after an early dinner. Once Emma saw Mark and Catherine off, pulling the twins along in a high-sided wagon she had borrowed for them, she headed straight for the kitchen.

Winter curtains had been packed away for another year, and bright sunshine flooded into the room through two open windows. With no cooking smells—since they were having a cold supper—fresh air, lush with the scent of spring and evergreens, filled the room.

Emma was not pleased, however, to find Mother Garrett still there. "What are you doing here? You don't have to do that," she insisted, taking the drying towel from her mother-in-law's hand and the plate she had been drying from the other and setting them both down on the counter with the rest of the dinner dishes waiting to be dried.

"Liesel and Ditty can take care of these dishes when they get back from their errands. Go. Hang up your apron, change, and freshen up. As it is, Mr. Kirk should have already been here by now," Emma cautioned.

Mother Garrett frowned, picked up the towel, and started drying the plate again. "I don't need to freshen up, and I'm dressed perfectly fine for what we've planned to do on our outing. Besides, I'm too old and set in my ways to care overmuch about how I look for any man, most especially Anson Kirk."

Emma decided not to mention that she had noticed the new hairpin her mother-in-law was wearing to hold the braid she had fashioned in her hair instead of the bun she usually wore.

She also did not mention that Anson Kirk was taking her mother-in-law to his brother's farm just outside of Candlewood. The very fact that Mother Garrett had agreed to help him select a pair of chickens from his brother's flock to add to Emma's made little sense, considering Mother Garrett had often said the only chickens she liked at all were the ones in her soup pot.

Emma suspected her mother-in-law had another reason for accepting Mr. Kirk's invitation today, although what that reason might be remained a mystery.

When Emma gently tried to reclaim the towel and plate, Mother Garrett held tight. "You might consider following your own advice, assuming you're still going for your ride with Mr. Breckenwith today. How are those blisters of yours?"

Emma wriggled her toes inside her shoes and grinned. "Much better now, thank you. And he won't be here for at least another half an hour," she countered. Anxious to distract her mother-in-law from revisiting the topic of how she had let Zachary's secret slip out again, as well as her own fears that Zachary might have had second thoughts about his proposal, Emma quickly altered the course of their conversation. "I have my riding skirt and my boots set out in my room, which reminds me that I don't believe I thanked you properly for getting rid of all that mud and those stains for me."

Mother Garrett chuckled. "You should thank Liesel and Ditty for that. They took turns scrubbing out those stains in your skirt. I'm not certain what was more entertaining for them, gossiping about how you got so muddy in the first place or how long it would be before you finally accepted that man's proposal. Frances and I are wondering the same thing, so don't get yourself into a snit."

When Emma's cheeks warmed, she snatched up another towel and started drying a plate of her own. Being pressured by nearly everyone at Hill House to accept the man's proposal was proving to be very difficult, especially now that Emma suspected he might be on the verge of rescinding it. "I'm not in a snit," she insisted and concentrated on drying the dish to avoid looking at her mother-in-law.

"Yes you are. You've got your jaw latched tight again," she said nonchalantly as she laid her dish on the table and starting drying a bowl.

Emma grew still, looked up at her mother-in-law, and narrowed her gaze. "Again?"

"Again. Not that you've had this habit of yours for long. Only since that little surprise landed on your doorstep. Have you decided what to do with all the purchases she made?"

"No. Not yet. Mark and Catherine still want me to return them, but—"

"But what? I can't see what all the fuss is about. Take them back."

"But this isn't Albany. This is Candlewood, and I'm not some nameless patron returning a purchase. Thank you, but I'd rather not inspire gossip between the shop owners."

"Careful. You're doing it again."

"Doing what?"

"You're clenching that jaw of yours all tight. Now that I think on it, I do believe there've been a few moments you might have done that while you were watching Mark and Catherine with those little ones, too."

Deliberately relaxing her jaw, as well as the rest of her body, Emma let out a sigh. Holding silent while watching Mark and Catherine gain experience as parents had not been nearly as frustrating as watching them with Wryn. As usual, however, Mother Garrett had known exactly how Emma was feeling. "I'm trying not to interfere, especially where little Jonas and Paul are concerned, but watching Mark and Catherine handle Wryn over the past few days has been harder than I thought it would be," she admitted.

She cocked her head, struck by the idea that her situation was not unlike the situation Mother Garrett had found herself in when she had joined her son's household years ago. If Mother Garrett had felt just as frustrated watching her son and Emma as they raised their three sons, she had never shown any indication. "In all the years we were together while the boys were growing up, I never had the sense you might have found it difficult at times," she ventured.

"Then I did right," Mother Garrett replied. "I knew my place wasn't to take over or to step in when it came to raising my grand-sons, even though I'd had the experience of raising my own sons and my own ideas about what needed to be done when Warren or Benjamin or Mark stepped out of line. That's not to say it was always easy, especially since I didn't want you to put me out like Allan did," she murmured.

Mother Garrett rarely mentioned her firstborn son, Jonas' brother, who lived in New York City. He had sent his widowed mother from his household to live with his brother here in Candle-wood after a dispute of some kind. Unfortunately, their estrange-ment continued, particularly after he had come to Candlewood trying to entice his mother to return to live with him when he needed to hire a cook for his household.

Emma cupped her mother-in-law's cheek. "Jonas and I would never, ever have done that."

The elderly woman patted Emma's hand. "Bless you both, I always knew you wouldn't, but I always held my counsel until you asked for it because it was the right thing to do," she said and smiled. "After my grandsons were grown and gone, I felt less compelled to hold my counsel with you," she admitted.

"True," Emma teased, although she would not have changed a

single thing about her mother-in-law except to ask that she might be wrong at least once or twice in Emma's lifetime.

"Of course, when the boys were all still at home, whenever I was tempted to step in, I had my licorice root. That helped a lot."

"Licorice root?" Emma exclaimed, curious how Mother Garrett's favorite treat fit into this conversation at all.

"I know you don't favor it. To be honest, I didn't care for licorice root all that much at first, either, but you might want to give it a try. If you're ever tempted to say something you shouldn't, which I wouldn't be surprised would happen fairly often during the course of the next few weeks, pop a good piece of licorice into your mouth. You'll be too busy chewing to be able to say much. Frances said it worked for her, too, when she had to move in with James and Andrew."

Emma wrinkled her nose. "I suppose it's an idea."

"If nothing else, developing a taste for licorice root might save you from clenching and unclenching your jaw. Sooner or later, you're going to crack a couple of teeth, which might make Mr. Breckenwith think twice about his proposal," she teased as she dried her bowl and started on another.

Fortified with a good dose of Mother Garrett's common sense and wisdom, if not her sense of humor, Emma smiled. "I'll see if Mr. Breckenwith would mind stopping at the General Store on our way out of town."

The sound of horses approaching the house made Emma smile. "That must be Mr. Kirk. Time to go," she insisted and snatched the towel and bowl out of Mother Garrett's hand.

Mother Garrett walked over to the window overlooking the side drive, which was used for wagons and deliveries, and poked out her head. "No, I do believe that's Mr. Breckenwith I see, and he's headed straight for the kitchen with your mounts."

Emma dropped both towels and nearly lost hold of the bowl, which she quickly set on the table. "It is? He's early!" she blurted. Encouraged that he apparently intended for the two of them to have their planned outing, she grew hopeful of his intentions for their future together. "Whatever possessed him to ride up the hill to the house instead of waiting for me down by the gazebo? Never mind. It doesn't matter. Keep him busy for me, will you? I need to change!" Without waiting for an answer, Emma rushed up the kitchen service steps to her room on the second floor.

By the time she changed into her riding skirt, laced up her boots, and rebraided her hair, she was out of breath. She took a quick peek into the mirror and sighed. There was nothing she could do about the streaks of white entwined in her blond braid or the years that had added wrinkles at the corners of her blue eyes, but she did not have to worry about pinching a bit of color into her cheeks. They were as pink as the roses that would bloom this summer in the terraced gardens on either side of the patio steps.

"At least something good came from rushing," she admitted, heading downstairs scarcely fifteen minutes after getting to her room.

She entered the upstairs hallway at the back of the house and glanced to her left and stopped abruptly. She was tempted to go to Wryn's room to remind her that even though she was going to be alone in the house for a while, she was still under punishment and was not allowed to leave her room.

When she found herself clenching her jaw again, she hurried straight to the center staircase, but only after she had made a mental note to buy several tins of licorice root—one for each floor of the house.

When she entered the kitchen, however, the room was empty. Lured outside by the open kitchen door, she took only three steps out of the house before rocking back on her heels. Zachary Breckenwith was standing just a few feet away with a look of pure joy on his face—a joy that erased every fear she'd had that he might have changed his mind about wanting to marry her. Mother Garrett was sitting next to Anson Kirk in his wagon, which he had parked just behind the horses Zachary had brought with him.

But Zachary was not holding the reins to two horses.

There were three horses behind him.

Momentarily confounded, Emma glanced from his usual mount, a black gelding, to the other two horses. The closest one to him was a bay mare, but the chestnut mare with a blaze on her forehead was so distinctive Emma was drawn to her immediately.

As her brain started to sort through the images in front of her, she realized the two horses Zachary had brought with him were not from the livery, which meant they had to be the horses Mother Garrett had told her about.

The shock of seeing the horses right here and right now was so real she did not have to feign surprise at all. In point of fact, seeing him here now with his surprise for her in hand could only mean one thing: he still meant to marry her. "Wh-what are you, I mean, why did you . . . B-but how did you . . ." she stammered, glancing from Zachary to Mother Garrett to Anson Kirk and back again.

Judging by the grins on their faces, Emma had no doubt that they had all been part of this plot to surprise her.

Laughing, Zachary handed her the reins to the chestnut mare. "Since you already knew about the surprise I'd planned for you, we thought it only fitting to make sure we salvaged a bit of it. Have I assumed correctly that this is the horse you prefer?"

Blinking back tears, she swallowed hard, held tight to the reins, and stroked the length of the mare's forehead. "She's absolutely beautiful. Thank you," she murmured and hoped her heart would fall back into a normal rhythm before she fainted.

He caught her gaze and held it, then whispered so only she could hear him, "If you'll allow me, pleasing you is but one way I plan to spend my life. I've arranged to have your horse boarded with mine at the livery so we can ride whenever we like."

"Surprised?" Mother Garrett asked, unaware from her vantage point a good fifteen feet away that she had interrupted a tender moment for Emma and Zachary.

Emma readily forgave her, if only to unravel the mystery of how these three people had cooked up their conspiracy against her. "In all truth, I'm completely surprised. Exactly how did you manage to keep this a secret from me?" she asked, realizing that in order to make this happen today, her mother-in-law must have gone to Zachary and admitted she had unintentionally revealed his secret.

Mother Garrett grinned again. "I knew I'd get the opportunity to talk to Mr. Breckenwith on Sunday. After services, you were so busy showing off those grandsons of yours, you didn't even notice we were chatting together for a good while. And this time, I didn't blab a word about this new secret of ours."

Zachary nodded. "After your mother-in-law's most heartfelt confession that she had divulged most of the secret we had shared, I thought I owed her the opportunity to make good. And that she did, for which I am very grateful," he said and tipped his hat to Mother Garrett. "Well done!"

Beaming, Mother Garrett actually blushed.

"So you're responsible for dreaming up this whole scheme today?" Emma asked her mother-in-law.

"I am, although I couldn't have done it without Mr. Kirk's

help. He's promised to take the horse you don't want back to the livery on our way out to the farm so you two can just head off for a nice ride together."

"After all the kindnesses you've shown for me and mine, I was pleased to be able to help," Mr. Kirk added, sitting up just as straight as his seventy-odd years would allow.

"Then you really are going to the farm to get those chickens. That wasn't part of the ruse?" Emma asked.

Her mother-in-law rolled her eyes. "No, I'm afraid not, but if those chickens aren't crated up good before they're even put into the back of this wagon, I'm walking home."

Emma chuckled. "I don't imagine Mr. Kirk would let that happen."

"I surely won't, although there still might be a surprise or two left to the day," he suggested, clearly hoping Mother Garrett would surprise him by accepting yet another proposal of marriage he planned to make today.

Mother Garrett cast him a withering glance before catching Emma's gaze again. "With the weather as fair as it is now, I doubt you'll find much mud today, but be careful anyway," she cautioned.

Zachary nodded. "I promise. I'll take good care of her."

"And well you should, young man. Emma is a precious woman, especially to me."

"And to me," he whispered to Emma. "Are you certain of your choice? No second thoughts?" he asked as he held up the reins to the bay mare.

Emma's heart swelled, but her gaze was focused only on the man standing before her. She had known him and worked with him now for five years, but she had only truly come to know the man he was during their courtship. True, he was a strikingly handsome man, but he was also kind and generous and thoughtful, as well. They were well matched in both intellect and wit, and his fortune was at least equal to her own, as far as she could tell.

Both of them could be persistent, if not stubborn, to a fault. Both of them were also strong-willed. But more importantly, both of them valued family and placed God at the center of their lives.

And at that very moment, blessed with the gift of faith-filled certainty, she knew exactly how she wanted to spend the rest of her life—and with whom.

Always decisive and straightforward in business, she could be no less in her personal life and plunged straight ahead. With her heart pounding, she locked her gaze with his and held out her hand to him. "I am very certain of my choice," she began, "and I have no second thoughts at all. You're the one man whose name I want to carry for the rest of my days. You're the one man I want to care for and love and cherish, and I would be most honored and most blessed if you would allow me to accept your proposal and become your wife."

He smiled tenderly, took hold of her hand, and clasped it tight.

9

STILL FLUSHED FROM THE EXCITEMENT of her day, Emma pulled a chair over from the table in front of Jonas and Paul, who were seated in their high chairs waiting for their supper.

Holding any meaningful conversation was a bit of a challenge with Liesel and Ditty scurrying back and forth between the kitchen and the dining room, Mother Garrett giving orders, and the twins babbling as they gnawed on heels of pumpernickel bread slathered with butter.

Emma positioned her chair sideways so she could keep an eye on the twins and continue talking with Mother Garrett and Catherine, who were fixing platters of roasted potatoes and mashed turnips. Zachary was due back momentarily for supper. Mark and Mr. Kirk were outside taking care of one of this afternoon's developments while Emma tried to settle another.

"Mercy is a perfectly wonderful name," she argued without bothering to hide her grin.

Mother Garrett sniffed. "Not for a horse."

"But this is a special horse, with special memories attached to it. If I name her Mercy, then I'll always be reminded of how hard you worked to keep your secret and how successful you were. If you're that unhappy about it, I can try to think of another," Emma said.

"Star would be a good name," Catherine suggested as she layered slices of cold ham on a platter. "Mark and I didn't get to spend much time with you when you stopped us along Main Street to tell us your news, but the moment I saw how the horse had that dab of white on its face, I thought it looked just like a falling star."

Emma tugged on the heel of bread little Paul had stuck too far into his mouth until she was certain he wouldn't choke. "That's one possibility, but the horse is a mare. Since I never had a daughter, I was hoping to pick out a girl's name for once," she said as Ditty hurried into the kitchen and took the platter of ham from Catherine.

Emma took one look at the young woman's pale face, bolted from her seat, swiped her hands on her apron, and took the platter of ham away. "I'll take care of this. I want you to go upstairs right now and rest," she insisted. She studied the row of four black stitches in the girl's chin, as well as the angry red blotches on her cheek where the doctor had removed several wooden splinters, and shook her head. "You took a good fall today on that sidewalk, and you shouldn't be rushing around like this."

Liesel came into the room while Emma was talking to Ditty and nodded. "Dr. Jeffers told you to lay down for the rest of the day. If you won't listen to him and you won't listen to me, you'll have to listen to Widow Garrett," she said firmly and took the platter from Emma.

Emma cocked her head, reached out to grab hold of the bread Jonas was dangling over the side of his chair before he dropped it, and frowned. "You didn't tell me what Dr. Jeffers told you to do."

Ditty's eyes filled with tears. "I didn't want you to be mad at me. With your family here, I know how much you need my help, but I didn't mean to trip up the steps to the sidewalk and I didn't mean to hurt myself and I didn't mean to start feeling so queasy and I don't know how I'm going to pay Dr. Jeffers because my family needs my wages. . . ." Quaking, she dissolved into tears and covered her face with her hands.

Emma dropped the greasy bread onto Jonas' tray, wiped her hands on her apron again, and put her arm around Ditty's shoulders. "Accidents happen, Ditty, and all I want you to worry about right now is getting some rest so you can help me tomorrow. Can you do that?"

Ditty nodded and winced as she wiped her tears from her cheeks.

"Good," Emma murmured, took the platter back from Liesel, and nodded to her. "I'll set this on the table if you'll see that Ditty gets back to your room and into bed. I don't want her going up all those steps to the garret by herself."

Liesel took Ditty by the arm. "Widow Garrett's right. You'll feel better in the morning," she said soothingly as she led Ditty toward the staircase that led to the hallway on the second floor. "I'll bring you up some food later."

"I'll take that to the dining room for you," Catherine said and took the platter from Emma's hands. "I need to go upstairs anyway to get something. I'll be right back," she promised and slipped into the dining room.

Mother Garrett shook her head. "I don't believe I ever saw so many hands on a single platter of ham before it reached the table. Then again, I haven't been proven wrong twice in the same day, either."

Emma chuckled as she sat down with her grandsons again.

"Did you hear that, little ones? Big Grams admitted she was wrong not once, but twice today, and if you're good little boys, she might tell us all why," she crooned as she wiped first one mouth and then the other. Out of the corner of her eye, she glanced at Mother Garrett to see if the name the twins had given to her was sitting any better.

"Big Grams," Mother Garrett mumbled. "If the two of those boys weren't my great-grandsons, I might have a word or two to say about what they're calling me," she said in a whisper, as if making sure Catherine would not overhear her.

Emma smiled at the twins and their innocence as they continued to babble to each other while smearing their trays with the slobbery bread. At two, although they were becoming quite verbal, they had quickly given up on trying to say Great-Grandmother and Grandmother. Instead, relying on the physical difference between Mother Garrett, who wore a wide girth, and Emma, who was slender, they had substituted Big Grams and Little Grams all on their own.

"I think it's adorable and very clever of them. I also think they're finished eating for now," she added, watching the two of them playing with the remnants of their snack. At this point, both of the boys had butter and bits of gooey bread smeared from their foreheads to their chins and from their hands to their elbows, but they were happy and content, which was all Emma needed to see.

"Maybe you're right," Mother Garrett said as she hefted a tray of pickled condiments from the table. "It'll just take some getting used to, although I might ask you to reconsider naming your horse for me. And while you're at it, you might want to come up with some names for those three new nanny goats. After I set this out, I'm going to the patio to call the menfolk in to eat. Let's hope Mr.

Breckenwith gets here by then," she added with a twinkle in her eye before turning to head into the dining room.

Emma groaned, thinking of her return from her afternoon ride. Instead of finding two new chickens in the winter coop next to the house, she had found three young nanny goats in the summer pen, where she intended to move her chickens any day now.

"You can't leave yet!" Emma argued.

Her mother-in-law looked back at her over her shoulder. "Why can't I?"

"You said you were proven wrong twice today. I was wondering how."

"First, I was wrong to trust Anson Kirk. He fooled me into thinking we were going out to the farm for chickens when he knew well and good he was going to fetch those goats. Not that it wasn't a good idea," she admitted. "Those goats will keep the grass trimmed around the gazebo just fine, and we won't have to worry about hiring some strapping young man to come out here to cut it back. He'd likely have one eye on Liesel and Ditty while he was working and wind up hurting himself like that Anderson boy did last spring. I can't imagine what might happen if Wryn stays to join them."

"Neither can I," Emma replied. She also did not want to think about her dream birthday celebration and how it might end up more of a nightmare if that young woman did not change her ways. "What's the second way you were proven wrong?" she prompted, anxious to distract herself from her thoughts.

"Ditty. I've said all along that the poor clumsy girl would grow into her feet someday, but I was wrong. She was just born clumsy and she'll die clumsy. In between, let's hope she finds a man who can keep her safe from herself," she said and left the room.

Laughing, Emma turned her attention to her two grandsons.

"Come on, babies. We've got to think of some names. Ridiculous, outrageous, and silly come to mind. Do you like those names for the goats Mr. Kirk brought to Little Grams?" she crooned.

Jonas' eyes widened and he grinned, showing off his baby teeth. "Goats! Goats!" he exclaimed.

Paul clapped his hands, splattering Emma with bits of buttered bread. "Goats! See goats!"

Emma chuckled. "Not now, boys. Maybe tomorrow. Your father and Mr. Kirk are busy making the pen stronger so the goats don't run away," she said, although the prospect of finding the goats gone in the morning was rather appealing. When both boys puckered their lips, she tapped on their trays. "Look! You still have bread. M-m-m-m-m. Good," she said and pretended to take a nibble.

Giggling, both boys picked up their smashed bread and began decorating their trays again.

"Jonas! Paul! What are you doing?" Catherine asked as she returned to the kitchen and set a small package on the table. "You mustn't ever, ever play with your food." Although her voice was soft, her frown was stern. Both boys cried when she reached in front of Emma to take the remains of their snack away.

Stung by Catherine's rebuke as well, Emma took a deep breath, got up from her seat, and went straight to the larder, where she had stored one tin of the licorice root. She popped a piece into her mouth and grimaced, but tolerating the odd taste was but little price to pay for holding her counsel.

"I'm sorry," she offered. "I wouldn't have let the boys—"

"Forgive me." Catherine blushed. "I didn't mean to imply you were wrong to let them smear their trays, but Mark and I—"

"You and Mark have your own ideas about raising your babies, which is the way it should be," Emma offered, grateful for the wisdom Mother Garrett had shared with her. She tucked the licorice root on the inside of her cheek. "Would you like to have help cleaning up those two cherubs?"

"I'm fine. Why don't you open your package instead?" Catherine suggested as she moistened a pair of washing cloths at the sink.

Emma walked over to the table and stared at the package wrapped in brown paper and held closed with a bit of twine. While she wiped her hands clean yet again, she narrowed her gaze. The package itself was flat and thin, no larger than an ordinary letter, which only made her more curious. "It isn't my birthday yet."

"It's not a birthday present. It's just something little . . . Just open it. You'll see," Catherine promised as she started wiping Jonas' hands.

The moment Emma untied the twine and unfolded the paper, she had to blink back tears as she examined the bits of cloth, each no larger than half the size of her palm. She slipped her hand into her pocket and gently reached for her keepsakes. She had no idea yet what each of the bits of cloth Catherine had given to her represented, but she had no doubt that they were meant to be added to the keepsakes she was holding tight.

Moved by Catherine's thoughtfulness, Emma struggled to find her voice, as well as the words to convey how deeply she was touched by this simple gift. "I . . . I don't know what to say, except that I'm completely and utterly overwhelmed that you would give me some cloth to add to my keepsakes."

"Mark mentioned your keepsakes to me shortly after we married, and I thought it was such a wonderful idea that I've started my own. I'll show them to you a little later and explain what all those bits of cloth mean after I've cleaned off the bread and butter from my hands," Catherine offered before turning her attention from

Jonas to Paul. "I'm afraid I've been so busy with the twins that I never had time to do more than collect the bits of cloth. I intended to send them to you, but before I knew it, it was time to head to Candlewood, so I thought I'd give them to you in person."

"Mama, up!" Jonas cried, stretching his arms high in the air and scrunching up his legs, trying to escape from behind the tray and out of his chair.

"Mama, up!" Paul repeated, following his brother's lead.

Emma laughed. "I think we may have to let the keepsakes wait."

Catherine smiled and shook her head. "Would you mind? I was hoping to let Jonas and Paul toddle off a bit of energy before supper. Otherwise, they're not likely to last through the meal."

"It's still warm enough for them to go outside on the patio or we could take them into the east parlor. I put away most everything there I thought might hurt them," Emma said.

"I'm more worried about what they'll hurt or crack or break." Catherine paused. "Let's try the patio. The fresh air this afternoon tired them out. Maybe more will get them settled into bed for the night a little earlier than usual."

"True, but on second thought, maybe the parlor would be better. If they're out on the patio and hear those goats—"

"Goats!" Jonas yelled. "See goats!"

"Me go, too," Paul insisted.

"No goats," Catherine told them, taking Jonas and Paul out of their high chairs.

Once their little feet hit the floor, the two boys headed straight for the back door. Catherine swooped up one toddler as Emma scooped up the other. Laughing together, they headed through the dining room, where the table was set for supper, toward the parlor. They were halfway down the center hallway when there was a knock at the door.

Through one of the narrow windows on either side of the door, she saw Zachary and smiled. "It's Mr. Breckenwith."

"I'll take the boys into the parlor. If they're anywhere near that front door when it opens, they're bound to slip out," Catherine quipped and ushered both boys away.

Emma stopped in front of the massive oak coatrack to smooth her skirts and check her reflection in the mirror. Pleased that she had decided to change into her favorite winter green linen gown, she opened the door. The moment her gaze locked with his, she could not hold back a smile that came straight from her heart. "You're right on time for supper. Mother Garrett just went out to fetch Mark and Mr. Kirk."

He chuckled. "I take it they're reinforcing the chicken pen down by the gazebo. Does that mean the nanny goats are staying?"

"For the time being," she said while he stored his hat and coat on the rack. When he turned to face her, he handed her a packet of papers. "You might want to put these in your office for now. After supper, we can go over them if you like."

When she furrowed her brow, he straightened his shoulders and set his features into the expression he normally reserved for when they discussed business matters. "Since you've finally agreed to marry me, there are certain legal matters that will need to be settled first. I took the liberty of preparing these documents, and I'd like to discuss them with you before you take them to your lawyer. As soon as you do, we can talk about setting the date for our wedding."

Seeing the package of papers in his hands and hearing him talk about reviewing legal documents reminded her that there was a great deal at stake when they married. At this particular moment, the issues seemed as daunting as finding a solution for Wryn's situation.

Still, she did not regret her impromptu acceptance of his proposal earlier this afternoon, though she was not prepared to act quickly on any of those decisions. But until they made them, they would not be able to set a date for their wedding, and Emma knew this man well enough to know he would not be willing to wait a day longer than necessary to make her his wife.

She sighed and took the papers from him. "After supper, then."

"Don't look so glum," he whispered. "It's not often that a woman gets a horse named after her mother-in-law and a trio of nanny goats on the same day she becomes formally betrothed," he teased.

"You forgot to mention having one of her housekeepers injured."

He nodded. "True."

"And a young woman still confined to her room because she can't seem to write a simple list of punishment."

"Also true," he admitted with a frown.

"Now that you've given me these papers, you wouldn't happen to know if there might be any other facets left to the day, would you?"

"Only one," he murmured, "but I'm not telling you about it until after supper and we're alone."

10

I'VE FINISHED MY LIST of possible punishments and my letters of apology," Wryn announced as she entered the dining room. Her surprising arrival silenced the heartfelt celebration Emma and Zachary had shared with her family during supper, and the troubled young woman slipped into her chair just as Mother Garrett started to dish out hearty servings of bread pudding still warm from the oven.

Emma swallowed hard and avoided Zachary's gaze by focusing only on Wryn, who waved away Mark's suggestion she might want to start with a bowl of the soup that had been taken back to the kitchen. "I'd rather start with dessert," she insisted before looking directly at Zachary. "I assume by now you've had enough time to research exactly how I'm related to Widow Garrett—or is that something I need to ask a lawyer who is more competent?"

Mark scowled and put his hand protectively on Catherine's arm. "Wryn!"

Mother Garrett set down her spoon and stopped dishing out anything but a glare she served directly to Wryn. Before Emma could find her voice, Zachary responded to the little twit.

"It's not entirely an unfair question," he said. "Many lawyers specialize in various aspects of the law, so they are more competent in some areas than others. But to answer your question," he said, turning toward Wryn, "I can tell you without reservation that you have no legal relationship to Widow Garrett, only a social one."

"I believe you're either ill-informed or motivated to give me incorrect information by your own self-interest," Wryn insisted. "I could hear you all celebrating way up in my room. Perhaps now that you're marrying Widow Garrett, your advice is based more on the fact that you're about to establish your own legal relationship to her than on the law itself—"

"That's enough," Mark snapped. "There's no reason for you to be rude to Mr. Breckenwith."

"There's no reason for Widow Garrett to even think about remarrying. Not at her age. But apparently that hasn't stopped her from making a fool of herself by accepting Mr. Breckenwith's proposal, has it?"

Emma's cheeks burned with embarrassment, if not a flash of anger she fought to control.

"Don't bother to send me to my room. I can see I'm not welcome here." Wryn slipped away from the table and waltzed out of the room, leaving an awkward silence in her wake.

After Mark and Catherine left just as abruptly to go upstairs to deal with Wryn, promising to let Emma know later how they fared, Zachary took a deep breath, rose, and nodded toward Emma. "As much as I'd like to sample some of your mother-in-law's bread pudding, I'm afraid I have a lot of work waiting for me at home, and there are a number of matters we still need to discuss in your office," he suggested.

Grateful to make her own escape, Emma preceded him out of the dining room, across the hall, and through the library. Unsteadied by Wryn's outrageous behavior, which had clearly ruined the festive mood at the supper table, she blinked back tears of disappointment. By the time she and Zachary reached her office, however, she had composed herself and led him inside.

As he closed the door to assure their privacy, she turned up the oil lamp she had lit earlier in anticipation of their meeting tonight and swallowed hard. Whenever they had met in her office to discuss legal matters in the past, she had always sat behind the massive wooden desk that had been used by the previous owner while her lawyer sat in one of the two chairs opposite the desk facing her.

Tonight, however, Zachary Breckenwith was more than just her lawyer. He was her betrothed, although she feared he might be ready to change his mind about that, given Wryn's little performance at supper.

She acknowledged their new relationship by handing him the documents he had given her earlier before sitting down beside him. "Please allow me to apologize. Wryn had no cause or right to speak to you the way she did."

"She was more disrespectful to you," he said.

Emma blinked back a swell of tears that threatened again. "I wish I had a simple answer to the question of how to help her, but you obviously saw for yourself that Wryn is a very complicated young woman. She hasn't any manners at all, and she seems utterly resistant to developing any, either." Emma drew in a long breath and gave voice to her fears. "Truthfully, before tonight, with all the disruption she's caused, I was half afraid you'd change your mind about courting me, let alone marry me. Now, after the way she just behaved . . ."

"Let's just hope your son and his wife fare well with her tonight," he said gently. "They promised to come back downstairs to tell you, but even if it turns out that Wryn needs your firmer hand for a few weeks, I'm not overly concerned. I don't believe there's a man, woman, or child you've met who couldn't be persuaded to do exactly what you wanted them to do. It shouldn't take very long for Wryn to discover that for herself, which means she'll be returning to Albany with your son and his wife as a reformed young woman," he said.

Turning toward her, he offered her a reassuring smile. "In all truth, I'd like for the moment to set aside concerns for Wryn in favor of something much more important we need to discuss."

Relieved, she nodded and swallowed the lump in her throat. Zachary sorted the documents she had given him before handing one to her. "You'll probably recognize the format of this document, which is very similar to the one protecting your assets in a separate legal estate when you married Jonas."

Memories of preparing to marry Jonas swirled through her mind as she skimmed the document. She had inherited the General Store, as well as a number of properties in the area in and around Candlewood, from her mother, who had inherited everything from *her* mother. To protect those holdings after she married Jonas, when all that she had inherited would have legally become his, Zachary's uncle had indeed drawn up a document very similar to this one.

With no head for business at all, her dear Jonas had never once questioned the need for a separate legal estate. In turn, Emma had tried never to give him cause to regret marrying a woman with means far more substantial than his own. She was grateful Zachary had no qualms about keeping her holdings separate from his, unlike the devious Mr. Langhorne, who had tried to lay his own claim to her wealth by attempting to court her last fall.

"I took the liberty of compiling a complete inventory of your assets, as well," Zachary noted as he handed her a second document. "You'll want to have your lawyer look at both, of course."

Without bothering to read the second one, she folded the two documents together and laid them on her lap. "I don't suppose I should even attempt to argue that I don't need another lawyer, since I've agreed to marry one," she teased.

Zachary's demeanor, however, remained very formal—indeed, very lawyerly. "Once we're married, I see no reason why I can't continue to protect your legal interests, but not until then. Will you be using Mr. Larimore? He's discreet, as he should be, and he's experienced, which he demonstrated when he transferred title to Hill House from Mr. Lewis to you."

Recalling her previous experience with the lawyer, she wrinkled her nose. "Probably not. I think I'll go see young Mr. Hennings. He's just joined his father in practice, I believe."

Zachary snorted. "That he has. Setting aside their combined legal incompetence, there isn't more than half a whisker of common sense between the two of them."

She chewed on her lower lip. "There's always Mr. Campbell."

"From what I've observed, Mr. Campbell has one foot in the grave and the other in Gray's Tavern most days, if not nights," he charged and narrowed his gaze. "If you think you can change my mind by suggesting one impossible lawyer after another, then I should warn you that—"

"I'm just teasing you," she murmured and set the papers on the far side of her desk. "Since you're so insistent that I must engage another lawyer, I'll see Mr. Larimore. Will you be getting another lawyer for yourself to protect your interests?"

Despite his narrowed gaze, his eyes started to twinkle. "I believe I'm competent enough to protect my own interests, unless you think otherwise."

She grinned. "Obviously not, since I've agreed to entrust myself to you as your wife, but I'm quite curious about the other documents you have on my desk."

He reached for the document farthest away from him and handed it to her. "Before we get married, I think it only fitting that you have some idea of the extent of my holdings, especially since I'm so familiar with yours. I've compiled an inventory for you, but I'd rather you didn't share this with Mr. Larimore."

She nodded, but by the time she finished skimming the four-page document, her head was spinning and her hands were trembling.

In addition to a home in New York City, where he had practiced law before moving to Candlewood, he also had the home in Candlewood he had purchased from his widowed aunt before she had gone to live with cousins in Bounty, the town just north of Candlewood, where she subsequently died. He owned property there, as well as a variety of interests in businesses in each of these cities and towns.

Although she had thought their financial situation was similar, his combined assets were worth more than her own. Decidedly more.

She drew in a deep breath. When she looked up at him, he was smiling. "Now you understand more, perhaps, why I need to travel rather frequently."

"Y-yes. I . . . I had no idea . . ."

His smile broadened. "I've also been blessed to have had parents and grandparents who had a talent for business and investing, although it's typically been the men in my family who were most successful," he added with a grin, finally removing the lawyer mask he had worn during their entire conversation.

Pleased, she cocked her head. "Since you said the Breckenwith men were the *most* successful, then there must have been a capable

Breckenwith woman or two, or perhaps even three, who contributed to acquiring the fortune you now have."

When he captured her gaze and held it, his was simmering with emotion. "I'm sure there has, but you're the only woman I'll ever need in my life, with or without my fortune or yours, for whatever days I may have left in this world."

Unaccustomed to hearing such an open admission of devotion from any man, including Jonas, she stared at the documents on her lap and prayed that the warm blush on her cheeks was not shining as bright as the oil lamp on her desk.

Being married to Zachary was apparently going to be very different than being married to Jonas, who had never been a man to voice his feelings. Instead, he had always shown her how he felt about her with a caring look or a gentle touch of his hand.

Thinking about her first husband, when she was sitting right next to the second man she was going to marry, also inspired a flash of guilt that heated her blush. She assumed it was only natural to compare the two men, but she wondered if Zachary was thinking of his first spouse, too.

She looked up at him again, hoping he would be willing to tell her about the woman he had loved and lost over ten years ago. "I've spoken to you about Jonas quite often, but you've never told me about Jane, other than to tell me her name," she prompted.

His gaze tightened for a moment, then softened. "Jane was my wife for sixteen years. She was an only child, spoiled senseless by her parents, but she was bright and vivacious and laughed her way right through life until lung fever stole her away. After we married, she was perfectly content to spend her days shopping or visiting with friends. There wasn't a thing she truly wanted in this life that she didn't have, except for children. We always wanted children," he murmured.

Struck by how different she was from his first wife, Emma placed her hand on top of his. "I'll be sharing my children with you and my grandchildren, too," she offered before chuckling. "Once they're all here at Hill House for my birthday, you might change your mind about wanting a family or even a second wife, for that matter. Life can get very noisy and very complicated with so many family members living together."

When he turned his hand over and laced his fingers with hers, he was smiling again. "I find the prospect highly unlikely that I would ever change my mind about you, although I claim the right to reserve judgment until I see exactly how Miss Wryn Covington fits into the scheme of things," he offered, although his smile dipped into a bit of a frown that told her he was not entirely pleased at having their plans to marry threatened by the presence of a troubled fifteen-year-old.

When his gaze filled with affection that bordered on desire, he shook his head. "Before I become utterly distracted, which is the primary reason why being your lawyer has become troublesome, I have two more documents I want you to review tonight. That way I can answer any questions you might have before you take them to Mr. Larimore," he said and reached over to the desk to claim the last of the papers he had brought with him.

He handed the first one to her with a wave of his hand. "This is a copy of your will, which I keep at my office, so you're familiar with this one. All that needs to be changed is your name, once we're married."

Emma nodded. Since he had not shown any hesitation about drafting a separate legal estate to protect her holdings, she did not expect that he would object to her will in which all of her assets would be divided between her sons and Mother Garrett, should Emma predecease her mother-in-law.

"Here," he said, giving her the second one. "I'd like your advice on the draft of a will I've drawn up for myself that I want to have ready to reflect my wishes after we're married."

Feeling a bit awkward discussing so many intimate financial details tonight, especially when she realized she was looking at a copy of his will, she moistened her lips. "I'm not sure I have any right—"

"As husband and wife, we won't have any secrets between us," he insisted. "Now that we're officially betrothed, I need to know how you feel about the dictates of my will, especially since it's likely that I will predecease you."

Curious, she quickly read his will. Again. Then again. With her heart pounding, she shook her head in disbelief. Although she was a bit surprised that he had provided so handsomely for her in the event of his death, despite her own substantial resources, she was utterly stunned by the plans he had made for the rest of his estate.

"Y-you can't do this. Y-you shouldn't do this. I–I would never expect you to do this. Y-you haven't even met—"

"I've met your son, Mark, and I'll be meeting Warren and Benjamin soon, so I'm not concerned, and neither should you be. Now that Aunt Elizabeth has passed on, my nephew, Jeremy, is my only close living relative. As you've read, I've provided for him quite nicely, and it would give me a great deal of pleasure to leave your sons the rest. Unless you're totally opposed. If you are, then I'll defer to your wishes and redraft my will accordingly."

She swallowed the lump in her throat. "I'm not certain if I can find the right words. . . ."

He cocked a brow. "Widow Garrett is at a loss for words? I find it hard to believe that would happen not once, but twice in the same evening," he teased. "It's only money, Emma, not the key to all the mysteries of life. Would you prefer that I name your sons as my heirs or not?"

She drew in a long breath. "I'm very, very moved by your generosity, and I thank you for thinking of my sons and in turn, their families. I'd be doing them quite a disservice if I rejected your offer outright, so I'm going to accept the conditions of your will as you've drawn it, but with one proviso."

"Which is?"

She took a deep breath and let it out very slowly. "I wouldn't want any of my sons to know that they're your heirs, to allow you greater freedom if you want to change your will at a later date."

"I sincerely doubt that will happen, but it's a reasonable request. Agreed." He folded up both wills and laid them on top of the other documents on her lap. "Now that the financial issues are settled, we should probably discuss more mundane matters, not the least of which is how soon we're going to get married."

Emma chuckled, and Zachary cocked one brow. "May I ask what you find amusing?"

"I'm afraid it's you."

He cocked the other brow.

"For a man as deliberate and methodical as I know you to be, I find it rather amusing to think you rushed through drafting all these documents so quickly. It's only been five or six hours since I accepted your proposal."

"I carefully and meticulously prepared those documents months ago when I first decided to pursue you. If you'd read them more closely, you would have realized they bore no date."

She gasped. "Months ago?"

"Several," he quipped, exuding his usual confidence. "In point of fact, I prepared them at the very same time I made arrangements for the walking horses to be shipped north and for Mr. Jedson to stable them at his farm for me."

"Oh-h. I hadn't realized how truly overconfident you were that I'd agree to marry you," she managed, although she should not have been surprised. He was so confident about most everything, he might have appeared arrogant to anyone who did not know him well.

He smiled and took her hand. "I was more determined than overly confident, which I've learned sits better with you. In fact, I've brought something with me that I was planning to give you once we were alone to put your mind at ease about my intentions once and for all and to encourage you to suggest a date when we can be married."

Smiling, he reached into his vest pocket to retrieve a small object, which he pressed into her hand. "It would give me great pleasure if you would wear this as a reminder of the high regard and affection I feel toward you," he whispered "and my commitment to marry you and be your devoted husband."

She stared at the dark green velvet, nearly the precise color of her gown, loosely wrapped around an object tiny enough to fit into her palm. With her fingers trembling, she lifted the corners of the fabric to find a small gold pin lying within the folds of the velvet. Delicate strands of gold formed the petals of a rose in full bloom. A tiny but perfectly shaped pearl lay in the very center.

The pin was exquisite and obviously quite old. She thought it might be an heirloom, although she knew very little about jewelry. Ordinarily, she did not favor wearing jewelry, any more than she paid much attention to her wardrobe. Other than making sure she wore clothes made of sturdy fabrics and dark colors because of the work she did every day, she had only a few gowns suitable for church or entertaining important guests.

This small pin, however, held such sentiment that she could scarcely imagine storing it in the trunk at the foot of her bed, where she kept the treasured mementos she had collected during her lifetime. Short of keeping the pin in a safe place while she did her housework, she intended to wear this pin often, if not always.

Blinking back tears, she looked up at him. "Thank you. The pin is lovely. Simply lovely," she whispered.

"It was one of my mother's favorites," he said, confirming that it was a family heirloom.

That he would give her this piece of his mother's jewelry meant almost as much to her as the fact he was giving her something to seal their betrothal, and she told him so as loving thoughts of her own mother wrapped around the joy that filled her heart. "I shall wear it always."

"May I pin it to your collar for you?" he asked.

She nodded. When his fingertips brushed against her hand as he lifted up the pin, her heart began to race, inviting other thoughts about being married again.

"You're only the second woman ever to wear this pin," he explained as he deftly pinned his gift to her collar. "Jane preferred pieces that were more ostentatious, and I gave them away or sold them shortly after she died."

Touched by his explanation, if not his ability to read her very thoughts, she fingered the golden rose and smiled. "Thank you."

He pulled back his head to admire the pin and smiled. "You're welcome. It suits you, just as I knew it would."

"I'll always treasure it," she said, unable to keep herself from touching and retouching the golden petals with her fingertips.

"Would I be rushing too fast to ask if you'd consider setting a date for our marriage tonight?"

Emma blinked hard. "Tonight? We haven't even discussed

where we're going to live. Or how our marriage will affect Mother Garrett. I should think we'd need to settle those before choosing a date to marry." Zachary knew how much Hill House meant to her, and Emma assumed he'd agree that they would live here together as husband and wife, especially if that would mean they would be able to marry fairly quickly.

"I agree. I think it's obvious we should plan to live—"

"Oh my," she cut in. "If I'm not mistaken, those are footsteps I hear coming toward the door. Mark and Catherine must be coming to tell us how they were able to resolve things with Wryn. Would you mind if we stopped for a moment to talk with them, or would you prefer that I ask them to come back?"

He frowned, clearly as disappointed as she was. "Since what they have to say will influence some of our decisions, we should probably talk with them now."

She let out a sigh, got up from her chair, and reached the door just as she heard someone knock.

11

ANXIOUS ON MANY LEVELS to learn how Mark and Catherine had fared, Emma opened the door. As she had assumed, Mark was standing there, but he was alone.

"Isn't Catherine coming down?" Emma asked as she stepped aside to let her son enter.

"She was awfully tired and asked me to speak with you alone," he said as he passed by her. "I hope I'm not interrupting," he said to Zachary.

"Not at all. We were expecting you."

"It looks like Wryn has been busy," Emma observed, noting the host of papers her son was carrying.

Mark eased into the seat behind Emma's desk, tossed the papers on top, and drooped his body against the back of the chair. He looked as defeated to Emma as he'd been as a child when he had lost his favorite book. "I give up. Catherine and I can't do this," he whispered. "We just can't."

"Would you like to speak to your mother alone?" Zachary asked Mark, although he made no effort to rise.

"No. Not at all. Catherine and I need all the help we can get."

Zachary responded with a curt nod, although Emma sensed he already knew what advice he would offer where Wryn was concerned. "What can't you do?" she asked.

Mark groaned. "We can't talk to Wryn. We can't reason with her, and we certainly can't discipline her. Not when she outwits us at every turn. Read some of these letters. No, read them all, and let Mr. Breckenwith read them, as well," he said as he waved his hands over the papers scattered on her desk. "Once you do, you'll see what I mean, and you'll understand how much Catherine and I need your help. I'm quite sure Mr. Breckenwith will agree."

Emma picked up one of the papers on the desk, drew in a deep breath, and let it out very slowly before she began to read it. She may not have known Wryn for very long, but she knew her son. Based on his total exasperation, she was prepared to read almost anything.

Or so she thought.

Once she had skimmed through half of Wryn's letters of apology, which she automatically passed over to Zachary to read, she had to stifle a giggle, but she eventually lost the battle. She was laughing out loud by the time she finished reading the rest—all twenty-two of them!

"If it was ever a wonder before why that young woman needed so much time to write her apologies, it isn't any longer," she noted and held up the last letter. "Look," she said to Zachary. "She even wrote a letter of apology to Sheriff North for, let me see, 'innocently and inadvertently creating a situation that could have required his intervention when his valuable expertise would have been better spent serving the kindly citizens of Candlewood in more judicious ways, such as keeping the true riffraff from entering the shops on Main Street.' "

"The letter to the mayor is cleverly written, too," Zachary noted with a smirk. "According to Wryn, 'the most influential official in Candlewood should be commended for the quality of his leadership, notwithstanding his apparent misunderstanding of how important it is to have a suitable place established for young men and women, far beyond the shadow of adults who would deny the future voters in Candlewood the opportunity to enjoy the discourse of polite conversation with one another.' "

Mark scowled at them both. "Clever or not, Wryn's letters to half the merchants on Main Street and probably every elected official in town make a mockery of the three letters of apology she was told to write. Three. Not twenty-something. She can't seriously expect me to deliver all of the letters she wrote!"

"On the contrary," Emma suggested. "Wryn is relying on her very valid assumption that you won't deliver a single one of them."

"Then why did she write them?"

Emma shrugged her shoulders. "For a number of reasons, I suppose. One would be simply to irritate you and Catherine. Not only did she annoy you both by keeping you waiting day after day for the letters she'd been told to write, but she also found a way to keep the upper hand by overdoing the task she'd been given to such an extent she made the whole punishment seem ludicrous."

Mark ran his hand through his hair. "So she wins again."

Zachary laid the letters he had been reading back on the desk. "Only if you let her," he insisted. "What she's done reminds me of a case I had some years ago before I came to Candlewood. Succinctly put, on behalf of a client, I had to subpoena a number of financial records from a businessman which I needed by a certain date in order to meet the deadline for filing suit. Like Wryn, the lawyer for that businessman tested the court's patience by taking much longer than necessary. And like Wryn, when he did comply with the court's order, he over-responded."

"How did he do that?" Mark asked.

"Instead of the very specific financial records I'd requested, he gave the court meticulously prepared copies of his entire financial records for the year in question."

"But why would he do that?"

"He knew I'd never be able to locate what I needed in the boxes of records he submitted to the court in time to meet the deadline to file the suit against his client. Because I had just won a very important lawsuit filed against one of his other clients, he also wanted to annoy me and prove he could outwit me, which is exactly the way your mother just described Wryn's motives."

Mark let out a sigh. "Which he apparently did."

"Almost," Zachary replied. "I felt exactly the way you do now until I realized that the information I recovered within the first several days allowed me to file a completely different lawsuit on behalf of my client, which we ultimately won, incidentally."

"I'm not convinced there's any great insight into Wryn's character in any of the letters she wrote that would help resolve the problem she presents to us," Mark replied and turned to Emma. "After what Wryn's already done to you and with her continued defiance, Catherine and I believe it would be best if we reconsidered our request to have her stay here at Hill House with you. With you and Mr. Breckenwith planning to be married, you shouldn't have to contend with her," Mark said softly.

Emma noted the look of satisfaction on Zachary's face but tried to keep her focus on her son. "Perhaps not, but can you think of a better way for her to force you to take her back to Albany with you than to make one grand show of defiance after another?"

"No, but—"

"When I questioned her for you the other day, she admitted she'd overheard you both making plans to leave her here, which means she had a good bit of time to make her plans to force you to change your mind," Emma said.

"I suppose so," he grumbled.

"She may have written all those letters to annoy you," Emma continued, "but I think she's deliberately acting out more for my benefit than yours. If her behavior is outrageous enough or annoying enough, she assumes I won't agree to let you leave her here, that I'll demand you take her back to Albany and find another place for her to live."

Zachary nodded. "Despite the way she's chosen to force your hand, I think Albany is where she should be, if only to make it easier for the girl to reconcile with her mother."

"Her mother has made it very clear she won't even consider allowing Wryn to move back home," Mark countered. "Given her behavior tonight, I'm not sure what we're going to do with her," he said, turning to Emma. "But that shouldn't be your concern, Mother. It's mine and Catherine's. Under the circumstances, we'll simply have to accept the fact that we have to take her back with us."

"I'm not certain we can allow Wryn to force you to do that," Emma argued and held up one of her hands when both Mark and Zachary looked at her askance. "I've been around Wryn long enough to know she's the most flippant, disrespectful young woman I've ever met."

"That's an understatement," her son quipped as Zachary nodded his agreement.

"At the same time, however, she also has more gumption than most," Emma continued. "She's highly clever and intelligent, as well. In other words, she's a handful of trouble, which is perfectly understandable," Emma ventured, voicing her thoughts out loud as they came to her.

"In what way?" Zachary asked as he leaned forward a bit.

"In almost every way," Emma argued. "From what Mark's told me, Wryn lost her father and two of her brothers or sisters when she was very young. Since then, she's had two stepfathers and a passel of new half brothers and now stepsisters who seem to have exasperated her troubles. Her life has been one loss or one adjustment after another, but the greatest loss she's suffered is the loss of her mother's love and devotion," she said as she began to fully comprehend, perhaps for the first time, what a difficult life Wryn had led.

Mark shook his head. "It's not my fault or Catherine's fault that Wryn's life has been so difficult."

"Nor is it yours," Zachary insisted, clearly implying Emma had no responsibility to intervene on Wryn's behalf.

"If there's any blame, it belongs to her mother," Mark offered.

Stung by Zachary's lack of support, Emma stiffened her back. "But if Wryn can't rely completely and totally on her mother, which is only too apparent, then who can she turn to for guidance and understanding? An aunt or uncle? A stranger? Tell me, Mark, wouldn't you or Catherine be different people if either of you had grown up in circumstances similar to Wryn's?"

"Yes, I . . . I suppose we would," her son admitted.

Emma smiled. "Of course you would. We can't turn our backs on her, but if you let her think she's won and simply agree to take her back to Albany because of her outrageous behavior, then you haven't a hope that you can help her change her ways and become the young woman she should and can be."

"Which means what, precisely?" Zachary interjected, his eyes flashing with disappointment. Or was it annoyance?

Emma swallowed hard and held tight to the faith that guided

her. "I have to believe that as inconvenient as it may seem to all of us at the moment, there's a reason why Wryn arrived on Mark and Catherine's doorstep just as they were about to leave for Candlewood to visit with me. There's no denying that having her here at Hill House is difficult, but I also have to believe that our lives have become intertwined because God sent Wryn here as part of His plans and to serve His purpose, not ours."

Zachary sat stone-faced, but Mark's gaze was clearly troubled. "What do you think we should do, Mother?"

"Accept the roles God's given us," she murmured, offering to Mark and Zachary the very wisdom Aunt Frances had shared with her. "I know it won't be easy, but I don't think we can simply turn our backs on her, do you?" she asked.

Mark swallowed. "No, and I don't believe Catherine would want to do that, either."

With her heart beginning to pound, she turned to Zachary, fully aware that her future with this man lay in the balance. "How do you feel about it?"

He let out a long breath. "That depends on what you have in mind for her while she's here and, additionally, how long you expect her to remain."

Despite his lack of unquestioning support, she was grateful for his honesty. She swallowed the lump in her throat and tried to be equally honest. "I'm afraid I can't ease either one of your concerns right now. I've only just sorted through my own thoughts about Wryn. I can say that I think she must find her situation here confusing. On the one hand, Mark and Catherine are telling her what to do. On the other, she has to make amends to me for what she did, which makes her accountable to me. Since we're all living in the same household, she has far too many people to worry about pleasing, and no single person has total authority over her."

Mark shook his head and smiled for the first time since he had entered his mother's office. "I'm not certain she's worried about pleasing anyone other than herself at the moment."

"Maybe not," Emma replied. She began to formulate a plan in her mind. "But it's up to us to make sure she does need to please only one person at a time. Starting . . . starting with me."

"But you just said she deliberately wants to displease you so you won't agree to let her stay here," Mark argued.

"Our goal isn't to have her stay here with me. Our goal should be to convince her that it's in her own best interests to please me. If we do, she'll end up changing her behavior, which means she'll be able to return to Albany with you and Catherine and hopefully, reconcile with her mother."

Zachary's gaze narrowed. "What if she doesn't change her behavior? Are you prepared to have her live here in Candlewood indefinitely?"

Feeling forced to choose between marrying Zachary and helping Wryn, Emma's pulse quickened. Instinctively, she reached up and fingered the delicate pin on her collar as she struggled with a question that tugged at her soul: If God had truly set her on the path to marrying this man, why had He also sent Wryn to her?

"I . . . I'm not certain," she ventured. "I think I might have a plan that—"

"Whatever your plan, make sure you leave me out of it," Zachary insisted as he got to his feet. "If you'll recall, I'm leaving at first light on business, and I still have to pack. Hopefully, you and your family will have this matter resolved before I get back. I can see myself out," he offered gently, but abruptly took his leave.

12

No HISTRIONICS. No FLIPPANT remarks. No challenging retorts. Only disbelief and heart-wrenching pain echoed in the parlor the next morning.

"I can't believe you did this. You actually did this to me," Wryn whispered to Mark and Catherine over and over again, her voice quaking, growing softer and softer with each word. Eventually, she collapsed against the back of her chair in the east parlor and let the papers she had been reading slip to her lap.

Wryn's reaction to the document making her Emma's ward tugged at Emma's heart. With Mark and Catherine sitting together in the settee directly in front of their niece, Emma sat off to the side next to Mother Garrett and watched as huge silent tears flowed down the younger woman's cheeks and dripped off the tip of her chin. Her face was as pale as the moonflowers that would soon blossom at night, and she was trembling so hard she had wrapped her hands around her waist.

Indeed, Wryn's reaction was so surprising and so disturbing, Emma was tempted to cancel the plans she had worked out late last night with Mark and Catherine. Emma had never intended to deepen the pain Wryn had experienced when banished from her mother's home and her affection, but she moved quickly to lessen it. "I'm only named as your guardian temporarily," she offered, grateful that Wryn had not noticed that while her mother's name was on the document, her signature was not, which was also true of the judge named on the papers, which Emma had hastily drawn up herself.

Wryn sniffled, blinked back tears, and looked around the room with a dazed expression. As if only realizing now that she was not alone, she wiped her face with her hands, sat up straight, and set her shoulders back, as if setting the chip she carried there back into place. "The document doesn't say that," she challenged, staring hard at Emma.

"No, the document says you'll be my mother's ward until it's no longer prudent," Mark said in a gentle voice.

Wryn turned to stare at Catherine. "Who decides when that will be? You or him or Widow Garrett?" she asked, finding the flippant tone of voice she had lost while reading the document that now lay in her lap.

Emma noted that Wryn had apparently given up trying to use a more familial title for Emma, an early victory that would establish a distance between them, which Emma hoped would be in her favor. She also noticed that Mother Garrett was holding to her own plan to do nothing more than attend this family meeting, watch, and listen.

"Your uncle Mark and I make all our decisions together," Catherine replied. "Although we've tried very hard, we haven't been able to provide you with the guidance you need. Here at Hill House, we believe you'll have that."

Wryn pursed her lips. "Then *she* decides."

"Yes, I do," Emma replied, since Wryn was obviously referring to her, "but your uncle Mark and aunt Catherine will be staying here for another few weeks, and I'm hopeful that I'll be able to allow you to return with them to Albany when they leave."

"And if you won't?"

"Then you shall stay here in Candlewood."

"Here. With you."

"Yes."

"What about Mr. Breckenwith? Since the two of you are getting married, he must have something to say about this. Why isn't he here?"

"Mr. Breckenwith had to leave on business. He'll be back in a week or so," Emma explained, although his refusal to support her still made her heart ache.

Wryn huffed. "I assume he's the one who drew up these papers," she said, glanced down at her lap, and scowled. "Did he also decide what I'm supposed to do when I'm living here?"

"That will be entirely up to me," Emma remarked without correcting Wryn's misassumptions about the creator of the document. "As you know, Liesel and Ditty work very hard for me during the week. When they return home to their families each weekend, the work they normally do naturally falls to Mother Garrett and myself."

"And now it will fall to me?"

"Yes, along with other work you can do during the week as a member of my staff. I'm hoping—"

"Then I'm you're slave, not your ward. I'm not even to be treated as good as those hirelings of yours," Wryn snapped.

"Wryn!" Catherine exclaimed in gentle reprimand.

"Well, it's true," Wryn charged. "Liesel and Ditty have time off for themselves, but apparently I won't, which means I'll be slaving every day of the week. Except to go to services on Sunday morning, of course, although I shouldn't make such an assumption. Despite Sunday being a day of rest, I shouldn't be surprised if I'm forced to work then, too."

"No, that isn't true." Emma silently prayed for more patience. "Before you interrupted me, I was going to say that you'd be a member of my staff and you would be entitled to choose a specific day off during the week for yourself."

Wryn cocked a brow. "I choose?"

"Yes, although we may have to change that day occasionally, should you be here when guests start arriving in May."

Wryn stood up, snatched up the document that had fallen to the floor, and tossed it onto Catherine's lap. "You should keep that as a reminder of how poorly you've treated your own niece," she snapped and cast a glance at Emma. "I'm choosing today as my day off," she announced and started to hurry her way out of the room.

"You're not to leave Hill House without my express permission," Emma firmly stated.

Wryn tilted up her chin. "I'm sure if I violate any of your precious rules, you won't hesitate to call for Sheriff North. But don't worry. If he's busy, you could always call for the judge who allowed Uncle Mark and Aunt Catherine to throw me away, just like my mother did. At least she didn't make me a stranger's ward," she snapped as she passed by Emma with a swish of her skirt and left the room.

The young woman's heartbreaking words echoed in the room and stirred the very depths of compassion in Emma's soul. More than ever, she was convinced that Wryn needed patience and understanding to help her heal, even if that meant causing her pain now.

Once the sound of footsteps marching up the center staircase had faded, Mother Garrett was the first to break the silence in the parlor. "Might I get back to my kitchen now?"

"You still don't approve," Emma ventured, disappointed that like Zachary, Mother Garrett had refused to be part of the conspiracy that was necessary to make Wryn responsible to only one person—Emma.

"No, I don't, but this isn't my house and I don't make the rules, except for in the kitchen—which is where I need to be or the dinner I've got simmering on the cookstove won't be fit for eating. All I've got to say before I leave is . . . Never mind. I'll keep the rest of my thoughts to myself. For now," she announced and traced Wryn's footsteps out of the room.

Catherine's eyes widened, and she rested her hand on Mark's arm. "Oh, dear. I hope we haven't upset your grams, too."

Mark patted her hand. "Grams has her own way of doing things that is much more . . ."

"More to the point," Emma said. "I wouldn't worry. My mother-in-law won't be able to hold back her advice for long. When she does, I'm sure we'll be able to find some common ground."

"I wonder how long it will take for you and Wryn to do the same. She was very, very upset by the document, which didn't stop her from being snippy with you," Mark commented.

Catherine shook her head. "Mark told me Mr. Breckenwith wasn't very pleased when he left last night. I'm so very sorry to impose my family's troubles upon you, Mother Emma."

"You're family, too, Catherine, and Wryn is your niece. I'm more than willing to do what I can to help," Emma said, without admitting she was worried about the way Zachary had taken his leave, too.

While it remained to be seen how Wryn would decide to respond to the plans that had just been set into motion, it was clear she was as intimidated by the document as she had been when Emma had mentioned involving Sheriff North to get Wryn to admit to her misdeeds.

In point of fact, despite all their plans, Wryn could remain outright rude and defiant, in hopes of having Emma give up and force Mark and Catherine to take her home with them. On the other hand, she could decide to undermine Emma's attempts by over-responding, just as she had over writing her letters of apology. Or she could simply give up and change her behavior, which is what Emma prayed she would do, in time to return to Albany with Mark and Catherine.

In any case, the first lesson Wryn needed to learn was that Emma was more persistent than Wryn gave her credit for. With that thought in mind, she offered her son and daughter-in-law a smile. "You did notice how she managed to leave the room without settling the matter of her punishment for her misadventure on Main Street, I hope."

Mark and Catherine looked at each other and shook their heads.

Emma chuckled. "Apparently not, but don't worry. I've got the list right here in my pocket. Since Wryn has chosen today as her day off, I believe I'll let her think she's made me forget all about it. By tomorrow morning when she's back to work, I'll have made my decision about which punishment she must do. In the meantime, since Wryn will be too busy either feeling sorry for herself or plotting ways to undermine me, we can all enjoy a peaceful day together. Why don't you go upstairs and see if those precious grandsons of mine are up from their morning nap and ready to play with their Little Grams?"

With Wryn stewing in her room, peace lasted the rest of the morning and through most of dinner. While Mother Garrett held Mark and Catherine captive through dessert with her tale of how Mr. Kirk had managed to get the three nanny goats caged up to bring to Hill House, Liesel and Ditty were washing and drying the dinner dishes. Little Jonas and Paul were sitting in their high chairs feasting on spoonfuls of warm bread pudding Emma was feeding them.

When Wryn blew into the kitchen, Emma looked up, clenched her jaw, and reached for the tin of licorice root sitting on a nearby counter with one hand while she offered Jonas his bread pudding with the other. Mother Garrett's eyes widened for a moment, just long enough for Emma to see a flash of disapproval that quickly disappeared. Mark's cheeks flushed almost as deep pink as his wife's, while Liesel and Ditty simply froze in place.

Wryn stopped and made a deep curtsy. "I've come to ask my lady for permission to leave Hill House for the afternoon."

Emma popped a piece of licorice root into her mouth and held it between her teeth, just long enough to let the awful flavor distract her from an immediate response while she kept Paul busy with another spoonful of bread pudding. After deciding to ignore the title Wryn had given her in favor of focusing on the outrageous apparel Wryn was wearing, she even managed a smile. "I see you've taken great pains dressing for an outing."

Wryn swirled about to show off her costume. "Yes, thank you, I did. It was kind of you to notice."

Emma nearly choked and tucked the licorice root in one of her cheeks. If Wryn was standing in any of the crowds that had gathered in Candlewood last fall for the fiftieth anniversary of the town's founding instead of the middle of the kitchen, she still would have been hard to miss.

Apparently, instead of spending hours in her room recovering from the shock of being placed under Emma's guardianship, Wryn had used that time to prepare for the first skirmish in the battle of wills Emma had not expected until tomorrow.

The straw bonnet Wryn had worn in her travels now sported the forget-me-nots that once had been sitting on the bird's nest atop Mother Garrett's garish daffodil bonnet before plopping into Reverend Glenn's soup some months ago. She had trimmed the bodice and skirts on the brown muslin gown she wore, as well as the band on her bonnet, with remnants left from the silk brocade costume Aunt Frances had used to fashion a riding skirt for Emma. Wryn was also wearing the ruined leather gloves Emma had worn on her fateful outing with Zachary just the other day.

Determined to be patient and to wear down this young woman's outlandishness and defiance one challenge at a time, Emma chose not to be baited into battle, especially now that Wryn's tactics were clear. If Wryn thought she would force Emma to make her change or embarrass Emma by wearing such a garish costume, Wryn was wrong.

Rather than comment further on the young woman's apparel or ask her how she had found the discards meant for the trash pit, Emma swallowed the last of the licorice root in her mouth and gave each of her grandsons another spoonful of pudding. "Are you going visiting?"

"Or joining the circus?" Mother Garrett muttered under her breath, just loud enough for Emma to hear her.

Wryn swirled about to show off her costume, which gave Emma a peek at the pink laces in her boots. "I'd like to visit Reverend and Mrs. Glenn today, if that meets with your approval."

After Wryn's misadventure on Main Street, there were few places in Candlewood Emma would allow this young woman to go. Fortunately, Reverend Glenn's cottage was one of them. "I think that's a lovely idea, as long as you're home by six for supper. And remember: no shopping," Emma replied. "Are you certain you wouldn't like something to eat before you go?" she asked, pausing to wipe the babies' mouths.

"Thank you, no. While everyone else was busy elsewhere, I had something to eat before you all sat down to dinner. The stew you prepared was particularly good today, but I do prefer a pinch more basil in mine," she said to Mother Garrett before she turned and scurried from the room.

Emma held her breath, waiting for Mother Garrett to say something caustic, but her scowl said it all.

13

At six-thirty, Wryn interrupted supper by poking her head into the dining room. "I know I'm late, but I have a good reason," she announced, standing in the open doorway without joining the rest of the family.

Emma glanced at Mark and Catherine before responding, as if reinforcing her position as the one person responsible for handling Wryn and her behavior. "Whatever the reason, you're still late for supper. If you'll wait for me in your room, I'll speak to you—"

"But I need to speak to you now," Wryn insisted.

Emma cocked her brow. Responding to Wryn's demand and leaving her supper to cool while she dealt with whatever Wryn had to say was not the way she wanted to handle this confrontation, and she remained in her seat.

Wryn shrugged her shoulders. "Fine. I'll wait for you in my room until you finish your supper. You might want to stop by your office before you come upstairs to see me, but for now, I'll just stop there on my way upstairs to let the person waiting for you know that you're more interested in eating your supper than you are in common courtesy," she offered before disappearing from view.

For the second time that day, Emma deferred to Wryn, a pattern to their relationship that she definitely needed to correct before it became the norm. Curious about who might have come to call, she rose, caught Mother Garrett's disapproving glance, and walked out of the dining room.

Wryn was waiting for her at the bottom of the center staircase. "I met someone today on my way to the Glenns' and brought her back to Hill House."

"Why?" Emma asked hesitantly.

"Because she needs help. Legal help."

Emma shook her head. "I'm not a lawyer. Why would you even think I could—"

"I know you're not a lawyer, but you're going to marry one and you could speak to Mr. Breckenwith on her behalf."

"Despite the fact that you think he's 'ill-informed'?" Emma charged, using the very words Wryn had used at supper last night.

"He's apparently competent in some areas, given the document he just drafted on my behalf," Wryn argued. "Besides, he'd be putting his legal experience to good use by helping someone who really needs his help rather than interfering with my life."

"Mr. Breckenwith is away on business, or had you forgotten that fact?" Emma countered, reluctant to involve herself in something she suspected would only widen the estrangement she felt growing between herself and the man she had agreed to marry.

"She doesn't want to speak to him directly, which is why I brought her here. I promised you'd speak to her, but beyond that, I really don't want to say anything more about her predicament.

Do you want me to introduce you to her or do you still want me to wait for you in my room?"

Grateful to be given a choice, Emma nodded. "I'll meet with her and talk to you later. Does this caller of yours have a name?"

"Her name is Morning," Wryn replied with a grin and scooted up the stairs.

Shaking her head, Emma opened the door to her office. Fully prepared to tell the woman that Wryn had overstepped her place by promising her anything, Emma was taken aback when she saw a young woman barely into her twenties sitting in front of her desk and toying with the small canvas bag resting on her lap. She had stored her cape and bonnet on the chair next to her. Dark curls framed her thin face, and her gaze was clearly troubled. "I understand you came to see me, Morning," Emma offered before taking a closer look. "You look familiar. Have we met before?"

"We haven't been introduced, Widow Garrett, but I serve tables at Gray's Tavern. You might have seen me the day you and Mr. Breckenwith came to see Mr. Gray a few months back. My name is Morning Drummond."

Emma nodded as she closed the door behind her. "Yes, I may have seen you there," she said as she took her seat behind her desk.

Morning blushed. "I hope I haven't come at a bad time, Widow Garrett, but Wryn insisted—"

"You met Wryn at the tavern today?" Emma asked as she took her seat behind her desk, worried that Wryn had only used the Glenns as an excuse to gad about town and ended up, quite inappropriately, at a tavern of all places!

"No, not at all," Morning gushed. "I was on my way home from work when I met her. I have a room at Mrs. Sweeney's, but I was hoping to see Mr. Breckenwith on my way home. I . . . I have a few questions about a . . . a problem I have," she said, pausing to swipe at a tear. "I must have walked by his house three or four times, but I didn't even have the courage to stop and knock at the door. I'm afraid I'd gotten myself into a bit of a state. That's when Wryn came along, comforted me, and invited me here to see you. Since you and Mr. Breckenwith are betrothed, she was certain you'd be able to help."

"I'm afraid there's been a misunderstanding," Emma offered gently. "If you have a legal problem, Mr. Breckenwith is the one you need to see. Obviously, I'm not a lawyer. I'm sorry, but Wryn misspoke. I don't believe I can help you, and I'm afraid Mr. Breckenwith is away on business."

When tears welled and spilled down the young woman's cheeks, Morning swiped them away with the back of her hand. "I'm sorry I bothered you. I shouldn't have come. I can see myself out," she whispered and turned to pick up her cape and bonnet.

Touched by the girl's distress, Emma let out a sigh. "As soon as Mr. Breckenwith returns, I'll send word to Mrs. Sweeney's for you to stop and make an appointment with him."

Morning paused and shook her head. "No, please don't. I don't want anyone to know, especially Mrs. Sweeney. And . . . and even if I had enough coins to speak to him, which I probably don't, I'm not even sure I could talk to him or to any lawyer. Not directly."

"But you wanted to speak to me?"

She nodded. "Wryn told me she was living with you now and that you were going to marry Mr. Breckenwith and that you might be able to help someone like me with a legal problem too . . . too delicate to discuss with a man, even if he is a lawyer. I thought meeting Wryn was the answer to all my prayers. Apparently, I was wrong."

Emma swallowed hard and offered a silent prayer for guidance.

Trusting He had led this woman here to Hill House through Wryn, she also trusted He would lead the way He meant for Emma to follow. "I'm not a lawyer, Morning. I couldn't be a lawyer, even though I've always wanted to be one, but I can certainly be a good listener. Sometimes, I think just talking to another woman helps more than anything else."

When Morning managed a smile, Emma knew she had said the very words He had wanted her to say, although it would have been easier all around if He would help her to do the same with Wryn.

Half an hour later, after listening carefully to the young woman tell her tale, Emma drew in a long breath and let it out slowly. "Let me see if I understand this correctly. Your name isn't Morning Drummond after all. It's Josie Matthews. You're not from Candlewood but from Bounty, and you're married, not single, and you want to get married again to someone else," she said, certain no one but Wryn could bring home someone with such a convoluted story.

The young woman blushed. "Yes. When I left Bounty two years ago, I was worried that someone . . . I wanted to leave everything behind me when I moved to Candlewood. I was . . . I was so stupid to agree to marry Thomas in the first place. But his mother had been very kind to me when I was working for her, and since it was her dying wish that her son end his days of bachelorhood, it seemed like the right thing to do. She passed away the following day, and Thomas told me to leave. Since we never celebrated our union as husband and wife in . . . in the flesh, I just assumed the marriage wasn't valid, but now that I've met someone I'd like to marry, I need to be certain."

"How much of this have you told this young man who wants to marry you?" Emma asked.

"Everything, including my real name. But he's the only one who knows the whole truth, except for you, so please call me Morning."

"Your husband, Thomas Harrison, whose name you've never used at all, knows," Emma murmured before she let out another long breath. "I'll talk to Mr. Breckenwith as soon as he returns, but at some point he'll want to speak to you directly so he can tell you exactly how this matter can be resolved," she offered, hoping Zachary would confirm her suspicion that this young woman's marriage would have to be legally dissolved, perhaps with an annulment of some kind, before she would be free to marry again.

Morning dropped her gaze. "When I speak to him, you'll be there, too, won't you?"

"If you want me to be there, I will be," Emma promised.

When Morning looked up again, her eyes were filled with tears. "Thank you. I don't know what I would have done if you didn't offer to help me get my problem resolved."

"You're a bit far away from fixing the mistake you made," Emma cautioned. Intrigued by the legal quandary the young woman found herself in, she opened the top drawer of her desk, took out a tablet of paper, and placed it on top of her desk. "I'm going to the kitchen to fix a pot of tea for us. While I'm gone, I'd like you to write down all the details, including exactly when and where you were married. That way, Mr. Breckenwith will have all the facts at hand when he actually meets with you," she suggested without mentioning the possibility that she might be able to investigate what this young woman had told her on her own.

"How will I know when he's ready to meet with me?" Morning asked.

"I can send word with Wryn to Mrs. Sweeney's," Emma said.

"No, I-I'll get in touch with you next week, if that's all right."

"That's fine," Emma replied and headed to the kitchen. Whether or not Zachary would approve of her getting involved seemed almost irrelevant, given his mood when he left last night. Emma had been far too independent all of her life, however, to be intimidated into changing her nature or her interests by a man who was supposed to love her and cherish her for the woman she was, not the woman he thought her to be.

Unless he was not the man she had assumed him to be after all, which was something she needed to discover before she actually married him—even if it dashed all of the hopes and dreams his courtship had resurrected from the deepest recesses of her heart.

———————

Two days later, blessed with an unusually warm day, Emma left Candlewood at first light with plans to be back home before sunset. To avoid gossip, she chose not to take a packet boat; instead, she chose to ride to Bounty on Mercy, the mare Zachary had given her. The scowl Mother Garrett was wearing when Emma left was still fresh in her mind, but so was the respect she had seen in Wryn's expression when she learned where Emma was going and why. Mark, as always, was supportive, and Emma's only regret was that she was missing a full day with her grandchildren.

Hopeful she would not run into Zachary, if only to avoid facing the possibility of yet more of his disapproval, she arrived in Bounty at midday, tired but exhilarated by the challenge of actually trying to help the young woman Wryn had brought home to her.

Two hours later, with little information that was helpful to Morning, Emma was ready to admit that her trip to Bounty had been a total failure when Mercy added to the day's frustration by throwing her shoe. Due to the local blacksmith being called away to a nearby farm, Emma's horse would be forced to stay overnight in the livery.

Frustrated and upset with herself for not planning on such an ill-fated eventuality, Emma had no provisions for herself to spend the night. With only a few coins in her purse, which would barely cover the cost of having Mercy reshod, Emma accepted the fact that she had no other choice. She had to seek out Zachary Breckenwith and ask for his help, which undermined any hope she might accomplish her goals today without running into him.

Following directions to his home that she got from the blacksmith's wife, she managed to find it easily enough. The single-story house itself was much smaller than his home in Candlewood. A redbrick structure, it was surrounded by towering trees about to burst into full foliage and appeared homey and inviting, although she had no idea of what kind of reception she would receive once he learned her purpose for traveling there.

She set her reticule on one of the benches on either side of the narrow porch, paused to shake the dust from her cape and riding skirt, removed her riding gloves, and wiped her face with her hands before taking a huge breath and knocking on the door. When no one answered, she knocked again. And again. Still no answer.

With no place else to go and no idea how to find him in a strange town, she sat down on one of the benches to wait for him. Rather than waste time thinking about what he would say when he finally arrived home or how worried her family back in Candlewood would be when she did not arrive home tonight, she folded her hands and did what seemed like a much better idea—she prayed.

"Emma? Is that you?"

Startled, Emma turned about in her seat, saw Zachary approaching his home, and waved. "Yes, it's me, I'm afraid," she called, the sight of his striking image causing her heart to gallop.

He quickly covered the distance between them and set down the package he had been carrying on the bench across from her. "What are you doing here? Is something wrong?"

She smiled, hoping to ease his troubled expression. "Other than the fact that Mercy threw a shoe earlier, which forces me to stay in Bounty overnight because the blacksmith can't re-shoe her this afternoon, everything is fine."

"You rode here from Candlewood? All alone?"

She stiffened her back. "I often ride alone, although I much prefer your company on an outing. Might I trouble you for a cup of tea?" she asked, mortified when her stomach started to growl the moment she caught a whiff of something delicious coming from his package and realized she had not stopped to eat anything since she had left that morning.

He frowned before unlocking and opening the door. "Apparently, you need more than a bit of tea," he noted, snatched up his package off the opposite bench, and ushered her into the house. "I don't keep a live-in housekeeper here. Mrs. Lott comes by once a week or so to freshen up the place, so it's always tidy enough. Fortunately for you, I planned on eating at home today instead of taking my meal at the hotel. There's more than enough for us to share. The kitchen is straight ahead. I'll lead the way."

She followed him down a narrow hallway past rooms closed off from view and into the kitchen. Although the room itself was quite small, several curtainless windows offered lots of afternoon light. A yellow-and-white checkered tablecloth on the table added a warm touch, but she was far too nervous about his reaction over why she had come to Bounty to be able to relax.

"There's a peg over by the back door for your cape and bonnet," he offered as he set his package on the table. By the time she had hung up her outerwear, he had laid out two plates and utensils and had a pot of water set to boil on the cookstove.

"What can I do to help?" she asked, impressed by how self-sufficient he seemed to be here.

"Nothing at all," he replied, pulling out a chair for her. "Would it be too much to hope that you rode all the way to Bounty to see me?" he asked as she took her seat.

She drew in a breath and held it for a moment. "Why would you say that?"

He sat down across from her, caught her gaze, and held it. "In all truth, after how poorly I behaved when I left you at Hill House, I wasn't certain what type of reception I would receive from you when I returned to Candlewood," he said.

Reaching across the table, he took her hand. "I'm sorry. I should have been more supportive of your efforts to help Mark with Wryn, but I must warn you that I am not particularly patient when it comes to anything that might interfere with our plans to marry as soon as possible."

Moved by his apology, she swallowed hard and squeezed his hand. "I thank you for your apology, which I accept," she whispered, reluctant to spoil the moment by telling him of the plan she and Mark had set into motion, because she sensed he would most definitely not approve.

"Why did you come to Bounty?" he asked, typically direct as he usually was, before he started opening the package he had set at the end of the table.

"Actually, I came because of Wryn," she admitted. While they shared a hearty portion of the veal stew he had brought home, along with a pot of tea she fixed once the water had come to a boil, she detailed the general purpose for her journey here without mentioning the specific names of the parties involved, including Morning's. "Although I was able to find out that the minister is deceased, I'm afraid I didn't have enough time to learn anything about the man she married," she said in conclusion.

He shook his head. "I'm not certain I understand why you got involved at all. The woman clearly needs the services of a trained, experienced lawyer."

Stung by his words, despite the fact they were gently spoken, she tilted up her chin. "There are some things women feel uncomfortable discussing with a man, especially a stranger," she argued.

"That may be, but a lawyer—"

"Is always a man," she interjected. "That said, I rest my case. In any event, since I'm forced to stay the night, I'm hoping to find the man she married tomorrow. I didn't come here to seek your legal advice on her behalf, at least not yet. Unfortunately, I didn't plan on Mercy throwing a shoe. I only came here to ask if you'd be willing to loan me the funds I need to secure lodging for the night. Obviously, I can't stay here. We're not married yet."

He gave a sly smile. "No, but we could change that easily enough."

She drew in a deep breath. "Without my family here?"

He smiled. "It was worth suggesting."

She did not return his smile. "Perhaps, but I'd rather have had you offer to help me find Mr. Harrison."

"Did you say Harrison?"

She nodded. "Yes, why?"

"Because I came to Bounty on behalf of one of my clients in Candlewood, William Harrison."

143

"Oh," she whispered. "This woman's husband's name was Harrison, too. Thomas Harrison. Do you think they might be related?" she asked as her heart began to race.

Zachary's eyes widened. "Thomas Harrison is, or I should say *was*, my client's brother. He lived in Bounty until he died some months ago."

Stunned, Emma clapped her hand to her heart. "H-he died?"

"After some kind of accident. It's the terms of his will that are at the center of the problem I'm trying to resolve for his brother. I'd been having a difficult time locating the man's widow, until now, it seems. He was married two years ago to a woman named . . ."

"Matthews. Josie Matthews," Emma murmured. "That's the name of the woman Wryn brought back to Hill House, although she calls herself Morning Drummond now. She said she used to work for Thomas Harrison's mother. I think her name was Esther."

Zachary nodded. "Yes, it was."

"Then they are the same. The widow of Thomas Harrison you were looking for is the same woman Wryn brought home to see me. Wait," she said and retrieved the accounting Morning had written down. "This is what she wrote down for you."

She returned to her seat while he read the paper, anxious to know what he thought. "Well? Is Morning the woman you're looking for?"

"Apparently," he admitted, nodding his head.

Emma grinned. "Then Morning's problem is solved. She doesn't need a divorce or an annulment. She's free to marry again, isn't she?"

"Yes, she is, but only if I can confirm everything she's written down, which is what I could have done if she had entrusted this to me in the first place instead of coming to you. Both you and

Morning should leave this now in the hands of a trained lawyer," he noted firmly as he set the paper down on the table.

"I believe we just did," she murmured, without bothering to remind him that she had been able to give him the very information he needed to help his client. Instead, she tucked his rebuke, however gentle it had been, next to her growing concerns that by agreeing to marry this man, she may have made a mistake after all.

14

THREE DAYS AFTER RETURNING home to Hill House from Bounty, Emma walked calmly out of the library and into her office without saying a word to Wryn. She climbed the stairs to her bedroom, opened the tin of licorice root, and popped two small pieces into her mouth.

She sat down on her bed and chewed them very slowly and cringed as the distinctive flavor filled her mouth. One quick glance at the packages sitting in the corner next to the scarred wardrobe that had belonged to Emma's grandmother told her she had another problem. Although Wryn had been tight-lipped about her plans for the remaining gifts, it hardly mattered who was going to receive the two boxes of Belgian chocolates. To get rid of the awful taste of licorice root in her mouth, Emma had managed to eat her way through one box and was nearly halfway through the other.

"If I could develop half the taste for licorice root that I've discovered for chocolate, I would be happy," she grumbled, although she was not sure how she would explain to Mother Garrett what she had done.

Although she was satisfied now that she would be too focused on the unpleasant taste in her mouth to be baited into responding to Wryn's most recent taunt, she resisted the urge to slip a piece of chocolate into her pocket. She returned to the library holding tight to the slim strand of patience she had left. She also tried to keep her concerns about marrying Zachary in the back of her mind. The fact that she expected him to return to Candlewood in the next day or two made that almost impossible, since she knew he would definitely not approve of her making herself Wryn's guardian any more than he had approved of her helping Morning.

Wryn, however, was no longer there.

The ladder she had been using was leaning up against one of the paneled walls. The bucket of water and the beeswax she had been cleaning and polishing the walls with were still there, right where she had left them.

"But she's not here. Again," Emma grumbled, gripping the licorice root between her teeth and marching into the center hall in pursuit of the wayward young woman. When she reached the center staircase, she met Liesel, who was just getting to the bottom of the steps carrying a basket of soiled bed linens, and tucked the licorice root behind her cheek. "Wryn didn't pass by this way, did she?"

Liesel blushed. "I didn't see her, and I'm . . . I'm sorry, Widow Garrett. I know I should be using the back stairs, but I was so preoccupied I was halfway down the steps before I realized where I was," she gushed and shifted the basket from one hip to the other.

"Please don't give it a second thought," Emma replied, hoping her answer would ease the frown on Liesel's face. Although Liesel was only a year older and perhaps an inch or two taller than Wryn, they both had the same slender build, but they were direct opposites in temperament. Liesel was hardworking, anxious to please, and always respectful, which was how Emma could only hope Wryn might be someday.

When Emma's response did not ease the frown on Liesel's face or completely erase the guilty look in the younger woman's gaze, she cocked her head. "Is there something else bothering you?"

Liesel's eyes darted around the hallway at doorways leading to the two front parlors, as well as the dining room. "I know how busy you are, but I was hoping to speak to you. Privately," she whispered, still looking about as if worried they might be overheard.

"I think we're alone, so you can speak freely now, unless you'd rather come into my office," Emma whispered back.

"No, I . . . I suppose here is fine," she murmured and leaned closer. "It's just that . . . I don't mean to tattle, but Ditty and I both got ourselves in trouble last fall because we were lying to you and . . . and even though Ditty doesn't think this would be a lie exactly, she thinks . . . that is, we both think we should tell you so we don't get in trouble again."

Emma immediately took a slow chew on the licorice root. "Tell me what?"

Liesel surveyed the hallway one last time. "Four or five nights ago, while you were away in Bounty, Wryn started sneaking up to the garret to our rooms to visit with us late at night. We didn't invite her. That's the honest truth, but we were afraid if we tried to make her leave or to make her stop visiting she'd cause a scene and . . . and . . ."

"And she'd manage to convince me it was all your idea and you and Ditty would be in trouble again."

Liesel nodded and blinked back tears.

Emma smiled. "Thank you for telling me. Thank Ditty, too."

Liesel nodded again. "It's not like we don't want her to come. Sometimes young people just like to be with other young people.

Wryn's got a trunk full of troubles, and she's awful lonely, Widow
Garrett. Me and Ditty . . . we wouldn't mind if she came up to
visit with us, if you said she could."

"That's very kind of you both. I'll see if I can't find a way to
let her know that she's free to visit with you and Ditty without
letting her know we had this conversation. In the meantime, I'll
let you get back to your work," she suggested.

With her face still troubled, Liesel hesitated. "Me and Ditty
are real happy for you and Mr. Breckenwith. You're not planning
on selling Hill House, are you?"

"We haven't discussed it at all, but I can't imagine I would,"
Emma said to assuage the young woman's unspoken fears that she or
Ditty might lose their positions if Hill House changed owners.

Wearing a smile now instead of her frown, Liesel bounced off
to the kitchen, leaving Emma with yet one more item to discuss
with Wryn. She was making so little progress with Wryn, she hoped
she had made the right decision to let the three young women visit
with one another without any adult supervision. "Not that my
decisions lately have proven to be very wise," she muttered and
swallowed the last bit of licorice root.

Emma realized that taking Wryn's suggestion that she clean
and polish the paneled walls in the library as the first way she
would make amends for her shopping spree had been Emma's big
mistake.

Anxious not to make another poor decision, she hurried to
the kitchen. She spotted the basket of laundry sitting on the floor,
but Liesel was not there. Neither was Wryn, which surprised her,
since this was where she had found the young woman twice already
today. Emma walked over to Mother Garrett, who was sitting at
the table dicing turnips while she had a pot of beef bones simmering on the cookstove.

"I see Liesel was here," Emma noted as she walked over to her mother-in-law. "Is that pumpernickel bread in the oven that smells so good?"

"Two loaves, but they won't be good and done for a spell, so don't plan on waiting for a hunk. Liesel went back upstairs to help Ditty finish dressing the beds. If you wouldn't mind, you might grab a knife and get started on those carrots or the potatoes. I need to get these vegetables added to the soup or it won't be ready for dinner."

"I came looking for Wryn," Emma replied. More reluctant to deny her mother-in-law's request than she was to delay searching for Wryn, she sat down and picked up a knife. "Why isn't Liesel helping you?"

"Because she's helping Ditty. Doctor Jeffers just took out those stitches yesterday afternoon, and Liesel wanted to make sure Ditty didn't hurt herself again, since she's tripped a few times on bed linens. Not that she's particular. Planked sidewalks will do. So will stairs."

Emma grinned and started peeling a potato. "You could have asked Ditty to sit with you and chop vegetables. At least she'd be off her feet."

"But likely to lose a finger or two. I know vegetable soup is Mark's favorite, but I highly doubt he'd be pleased knowing it wasn't all beef that flavored his soup."

"Oh, Mother Garrett, that's a gruesome thing to imagine." Emma shuddered. "You wouldn't have any idea where I could find Wryn, would you?"

Mother Garrett pointed to the back door with the tip of her knife. "She's hanging up the cleaning rags she rinsed out again."

"That's the third pair of rags she's used today, and it's only midmorning."

"How many did she use yesterday?"

Emma sliced the potato in half, laid the pieces flat on the table, and cut each piece into quarters. "Sixteen," she admitted and slipped a sliver of raw potato into her mouth.

"How many walls has she finished cleaning and polishing so far?"

"One and a half."

Mother Garrett used the back of her knife blade to slide the turnip pieces out of her way before tackling another. "At that rate, she should be finished by my birthday, not yours."

Emma grimaced and swallowed the raw potato. "Your birthday isn't until August. I don't think I'll survive living with Wryn that long."

"If the good Lord is willing, I'll actually be here to celebrate my seventy-seventh birthday, which gives me a good twenty-five years more experience than you have. I know you haven't asked for my advice this past week, but since Mr. Atkins has run clear out of licorice root, I'm going to give it to you now. Before you do anything else, forget chewing on that licorice root."

Emma's eyes widened. "But you said—"

"Forget what I said. It's not working for you, at least where Wryn's concerned."

Emma set her knife down and tilted up her chin. "I'm sure I can develop a taste for it, but it's taking a little longer than I thought it would."

Mother Garrett chuckled. "That I can see with my own eyes. You might learn to favor it eventually, but in the meantime, for every bite of licorice root you take, you've been eating other things to get rid of the taste," she argued and nodded toward Emma's gown. "If I'm not mistaken, wasn't that a piece of raw potato you were just munching on? Must mean you've eaten your way through both boxes of those fancy chocolates that Wryn charged to your account."

Emma's eyes widened for a moment before she stiffened her back. "There's still half a box left."

"I've only got one more thing to say," Mother Garrett cautioned and covered Emma's hand with her own. "You raised three fine sons and you've been good with Liesel and Ditty, even though you've made a mistake or two. I've watched you accommodate the fussiest guests, but you've always had the upper hand and you didn't need some kind of legal paper to keep it," she said gently.

She offered Emma a smile. "Instead of trying so hard to be patient with Wryn, you need to trust in yourself more. Regardless of what Pastor Austin preaches now and again, I've lived long enough to know patience isn't always a virtue. Sometimes it's a trap. I've tried to explain that often enough to Mr. Kirk when I tell him not to keep asking me to marry him again. But he's just bound and convinced that if he's patient enough, I'll change my mind—which I won't."

"Poor man. He has no sense at all of how stubborn you can be when you set your mind to it," Emma teased.

Grinning, Mother Garrett picked up her knife again and quartered a turnip with two quick slices. "No, he doesn't, but you know how stubborn Wryn can be because you've seen it with your own eyes. She still does everything her own way, and she's still defiant. Being overly patient with her hasn't done you a bit of good, but you'll notice she hasn't put as much as a toe into my kitchen unless I'm here. Not after I told her straight out that I'd see she go without a nibble of food for a good week if she did."

Emma let out a sigh. As much as she did not want to admit it, Mother Garrett was right. "I know Wryn's just as defiant as ever, but at least she's been less disrespectful since I got back from Bounty," she offered.

"She's got a long road to travel yet before she'll be the kind of young woman she should be," Mother Garrett argued. "And what about you? You haven't left the library for days and days because you insist on staying with her to make sure she doesn't slack off. You haven't been able to play with your grandsons as much as I know you want to. You haven't been to see Frances or Reverend Glenn since you and Mr. Breckenwith stopped to tell them your news about accepting his proposal, either. So who's being punished in the end, Emma? Wryn or you?"

"You're right. I do feel like I'm being punished more than she is, but you saw how upset she was when we told her I was taking over her guardianship and—"

"Upset? Did you ever worry about upsetting those three grandsons of mine when you or Jonas were disciplining them?"

Emma stiffened her back. "No, I didn't."

"That's right. You didn't, and neither did my son, but you've let your pity for that young woman override your common sense. She's got your brain so twisted up, like those pretzels I make, that you've forgotten who you are. You're not her friend, and you're not her pastor. You're an adult, and you're supposed to be her guardian now. It's time you acted like it."

Emma glanced around the room to make sure they were alone. "But I'm not her guardian. Not legally," she argued in a hushed voice. "You know I drew up the papers we showed to her that named me as her guardian, but I could never file them with the court. They're not legal," Emma countered defensively, shoving aside all thoughts about what Zachary would say when he found out what she had done.

Mother Garrett narrowed her gaze. "Wryn doesn't know that now, does she?"

"No, but—"

"Stop dillydallying around. Do what needs to be done with that little snip. Stop giving in to her all the time in the name of patience. Stand up to her, before Mr. Breckenwith gets back from his trip to find out the woman he plans to marry lost her backbone while he was gone."

Stung by her mother-in-law's final criticism, Emma felt the blood drain from her face. She was tempted to defend herself again, but Mother Garrett's plainspoken words sliced right through her excuses as deftly as her knife had cut through those turnips.

Unwilling to share her concerns about marrying Zachary at all, given his obvious belief she had far too much backbone for her own good already, she felt a wide band of tension tighten across her forehead. She tried to rub it away with the tips of her fingers, to no avail. "You're right. I've been wrong. Using patience to wear down Wryn's behavior instead of confronting it head-on has been foolish. I just thought . . ."

"You just thought that with Mark and Catherine and those little ones here, you didn't want to cause a commotion, and with Warren and Benjamin due here any day, now that the canal is open again, you don't want anything to spoil their visit. Am I right?" her mother-in-law asked gently.

She let out a sigh and nodded her head. Although Wryn's presence at Hill House might very well be only one of the reasons her plans to remarry might change, she had not realized that she was even more concerned about having her there once her other sons arrived with their families. Not until Mother Garrett forced those thoughts from the back of her mind. "Yes, of course you are. I've waited so long for the boys to all be home for my birthday, I just don't want anything to ruin it," she admitted. "You're always so . . . right. Will I ever see the day when you might possibly be wrong about something as important as this?"

Mother Garrett chuckled. "You've missed a few times over the years, but I imagine I have a few good mistakes left to me, including my assumption, I'm afraid, that Ditty will ever grow into her own feet."

Emma brightened. "Wait. I've thought of one. I could remind you that you were wrong about the woman Mr. Atkins eventually married."

Mother Garrett scowled. "Or you could go outside and let Wryn know that her time to rule this roost is over."

15

OUTSIDE IN THE BACKYARD, Emma found bright sun, the heavy scent of woodsy pine, a flock of chickens sunning themselves, and Mark's wagon, which he had parked at the far end of the side drive. Six cleaning rags flapped side by side on the wash line next to the chemise Emma had spent days looking for.

Irritated that Wryn had actually gone into her room to take the chemise, Emma cupped her hand at her brow and scanned the rear of her property. There! She saw a flash of white before Wryn's aproned skirts disappeared into the thick woods. She grinned. "I think I know exactly where you're headed," she murmured and immediately retraced her steps.

When she reentered the kitchen alone, Mother Garrett looked up. "Is she gone again?"

"She's slipping down to the back woods to get to the gazebo, but I can be there before she is if I cut through the house to get to the patio," Emma answered on the run. She hurried through the kitchen to the double doors in the dining room and slipped outside. She stopped at the high stone wall and waited until she caught sight of Wryn climbing down the steep hill at the rear of her property. She had a good climb and a decent walk through the woods ahead of her to reach the gazebo sitting on the small plateau where Mark had tied up the three nanny goats.

With time to spare, Emma glanced above the tree canopy to glimpse the canal. Once again, the land wore a ribbon of blue water that carried freight and travelers to and from Candlewood, including her son Warren and his family. Rays of sunshine reflected on the distant water and danced on the bronze roof of the gazebo just below her. The bright sunshine, however, did little to ease the guilt that shadowed her heart, and she bowed her head.

She had been so busy trying to match wits with a fifteen-year-old, she had forgotten that Wryn was not an adult but merely a girl on the verge of womanhood. Indeed, Emma had been so consumed with winning, she had been able to convince Mark and Catherine to go along with her plan. And she had been so determined to hold on to her dream of having all of her family together in Candlewood for her birthday and so worried about how Wryn might somehow ruin everything or interfere with her plans to be married, she had forgotten what Hill House had been meant to be—a place of hope and contentment for all who dwelt there.

The truth was not pleasant to see, but she did not turn away from it. She had been very wrong, and she had been selfish by not doing what she should have done in the first place: accept Wryn as part of her family. Worse, she had not even treated Wryn as well as she always treated her guests, however finicky or demanding they might be.

Why or how she had stepped off the path she believed He had set before her mattered little now, and she prayed for His forgiveness, as well as His guidance.

Refreshed and renewed in spirit, she picked up her skirts with one hand, let herself through the gate, and secured it behind her in case Mark and Catherine allowed the boys to wander about the patio. She reached the gazebo moments later and sat down on one of the side benches built along the railings to wait for Wryn to arrive. Although the air here in the shade was chilly, she warmed herself with the hope she was about to start a new relationship with Wryn.

When she saw Wryn finally leave the woods and head to the gazebo, her heart skipped a beat.

Halfway there, Wryn stopped in midstride and glared at Emma. "You're here."

"Yes, I am. We need to talk," Emma said gently and patted the seat beside her. "Come and sit with me."

Wryn tossed her head and marched slowly toward Emma as if approaching the gallows. The dazzling sun lent rays of highlights to her dark hair that made her appear fragile, an image Wryn dispelled when she clomped up the two steps into the gazebo, plopped down on the seat across from Emma, and set her lips into a pout. "I was hoping for a moment's peace, but you've ruined it."

"Members of my family, as well as my staff, never speak disrespectfully to me or to anyone else. I suggest you keep that in mind, young lady."

"Or what? You'll call the sheriff?" She paused to slap her forehead. "Oh no. How could I forget? Lady Garrett has a judge at her beck and call. What will you do if I don't? Have him put me up for bid to another family or send me off into some asylum for the criminally unwanted?"

Emma swallowed hard, quite deserving of this young woman's disdain. "You're here at Hill House because I want you to be here . . . because you're part of my family," she said with bated breath.

"That's not what you said before, and Mr. Breckenwith agreed with you. He said—"

"We were both wrong. I was wrong. Very wrong, and I'm sorry."

"What about those legal papers that made you my guardian?"

"They're worthless," Emma admitted. "If you'd looked closely enough, you would have seen that your mother hadn't actually signed them. Neither did the judge, because he couldn't sign them. Not without her signature. But more importantly," she added, "they're not legal papers at all. Mr. Breckenwith didn't draw them up as you assumed. I did. In all truth, Mr. Breckenwith has no idea those papers even exist."

Wryn's gaze darkened. "You lied to me! You all lied to me," she charged and leaped to her feet. "Uncle Mark lied and Aunt Catherine lied and—"

"Yes. We lied. At the time, I thought—"

"I hate you!" Wryn screamed and covered her ears with her hands to block out anything Emma might say. "I hate you! I hate you all! I hate you! I don't want to hear any more. You're a liar! A liar!" she cried and stomped her feet with each exclamation, tears falling.

When Wryn finally collapsed onto the bench, she turned away, laid one of her arms along the top of the railing, and presented her back to Emma. "Go away. Leave me alone," she rasped.

Stunned by Wryn's outburst, Emma had not expected to feel as hurt as she did, but she held steady to her purpose and moistened her lips. "I can't change the fact that you and your mother are estranged. I can't change the fact that she sent you from your home to live with your aunt Catherine and uncle Mark, either, any more than I can change the fact that your impossible behavior disrupted their lives to the extent they found it equally impossible to live with you," she murmured gently.

No response.

"Mark and Catherine are sweet and gentle people who are almost as young to marriage as they are to parenthood," she continued. "You knew that and you used it to your advantage, hoping they'd give up and take you back to your mother. Instead, they brought you to me because . . . because they had no other choice . . . because your mother won't allow you to come home."

Still no response.

"I'm so sorry, Wryn. But you can't go home. Not yet," she added, trying her best to provoke some response from Wryn.

When Wryn's head perked up just a hair, Emma drew in a long breath. "As sad and as heartbreaking as it might be, you may never be able to reconcile with your mother. But if you're willing to listen, I'd like to tell you how you can try to make that possible."

Wryn edged in her seat to be able to see Emma without turning around completely. Though her cheeks were still glistening with tears and her eyes were red from crying, her gaze was steady.

"Do you enjoy eating pumpernickel bread still warm from the oven?"

Apparently caught off guard by the odd question, which Emma had hoped she would be, Wryn replied almost automatically. "Yes, I suppose I might favor it, but I can't see what that has to do with—"

"What would you do if you accidentally drizzled vinegar on top of the whole loaf of bread instead of butter?"

Wryn wrinkled her nose and scrunched up her face. "I'd toss it away!"

"The whole loaf? Why?"

"It'd be ruined!"

"You can't just lop off the crust on the top?"

"Hardly," Wryn snapped. "The vinegar would have gone through and flavored the entire loaf of bread."

"Exactly so," Emma replied. "Flippant remarks and defiant or outrageous behavior are much like vinegar, Wryn. They seep from our mind and our lips to our hearts and souls, where we've buried our most awful hurts until our entire lives and the lives of the people around us are destroyed. You haven't any hope of reconciling with your mother unless you change your behavior."

Wryn dropped her gaze.

"That means you can't lie to people anymore. You can't talk back to adults or try to provoke them by exaggerating whatever punishment you've been given. You can't take things that don't belong to you, either." Emma drew in a long breath. "Everyone here at Hill House wants to help you. Me. Your aunt Catherine and uncle Mark. Even Mother Garrett. But you can't go on the way you have."

Wryn let out a sigh. Nothing more.

"I know it won't be easy. But if you can change your ways, which I'm very confident you can do, I promise that I'll do what I can to help you and your mother to reconcile. If I fail, or if we both fail to accomplish that, then you'll be welcome to make your home here with me at Hill House or back in Albany with your aunt Catherine and uncle Mark. On that you have my word. But ultimately, wherever you live is entirely up to you."

When Wryn looked up at Emma, her gaze darkened. "What about after you get married?"

"Nothing will change what I've just discussed with you," Emma promised, knowing that if Zachary objected, he would not become her husband and would not have any say in the matter at all.

"Everything will change," Wryn whispered.

Emma swallowed hard, all too aware of how Wryn's life had changed after each of her mother's marriages and unsure of how to convince her it would not happen again.

"Even if I did believe you, which I don't after what you did to trick me, how do I know you're not lying to me again?" Wryn asked.

"You don't, but I'll try very hard to regain your trust. I kept my promise to help your friend Morning, didn't I?"

Wryn nodded.

"From now on," Emma continued, "I promise you that I'll always be truthful with you."

"Completely truthful?"

"Yes."

Wryn pursed her lips. "Did you really eat all those chocolates I bought?"

Emma sniffed. "I don't suppose you have a proper excuse for being in my room in the first place, which you can't deny, since I saw my chemise drying on the line. You have no right to go snooping about other people's rooms or taking things that don't belong to you."

Wryn cocked a brow.

"No, I didn't eat all the chocolates. Only most of them, I suppose."

Wryn grinned. "Not quite. I ate a few, but I think I like the licorice root better."

Chuckling, Emma shook her head. "Good. I have a few tins you can have, as long as you promise not to go into my room or anyone else's room without permission," Emma cautioned and held back a smile. "There's also something you need to understand."

Wryn narrowed her gaze again.

"Mother Garrett just warned me that having too much patience can be as much of a mistake as having too little, and . . . and I'm afraid I'm inclined to agree with her. From now on, since I'm the proprietress here at Hill House, I'll decide if and when you should be punished if you don't change your ways. If you're disrespectful or misbehave, you'll be punished immediately by being sent to your room, with no writing tablets or books to entertain you. You'll also lose the privilege of joining the rest of the family for meals. I'll have them brought to your room. You could also lose your privileges to leave Hill House. I have no objection if you'd like to visit with Liesel or Ditty at night after supper, but that's also a privilege you could lose."

"What about the list of punishments I wrote for having my gifts put onto your account?"

"Considering how I've treated you, along with the fact that I've—that *we've* eaten through most of the chocolates, you can tear it up or toss it into a drawer, which is what I did with all those clever letters you wrote. We still have to decide what to do with the rest of those ill-gotten gifts you bought, though."

When Wryn looked away, Emma understood she had said enough for now and stood up. "I don't expect you to change overnight, but I do expect you to try. You may stay here and think about what I've said for as long as you like, although I hope you'll join us for dinner. If there's anything else you'd like to say to me later, I'll listen," she promised.

She took a step to leave but stopped abruptly. "In the future, I'd prefer not to be addressed as or referred to as Lady Garrett. You may call me Widow Garrett for the time being, although I'd be pleased if you might want to choose a more familial term later. Just so you know, I'll be introducing you to others as my niece," she offered before leaving Wryn alone.

Emma left the gazebo and headed toward the patio steps

whispering a prayer to thank God for helping her. Although she was tempted to see what Wryn was doing now, she did not look back; instead, she tried to keep her focus on the days ahead and slipped her hand into her pocket. When she found the strips of cloth from Catherine that she had added to her other keepsakes, she smiled and hoped one day to have one there for Wryn, too.

With one burden lifted, her steps were a bit lighter now. The moment she spied Zachary watching her from the patio, she smiled, hopeful she might resolve her doubts about marrying him as easily as she had cleared much of the tension between herself and Wryn. She held on to her smile as she mounted the steps and walked through the gate he had opened for her. "You're back!"

Without returning her smile, he nodded. "Just now."

"Were you able to confirm everything Morning claimed to be true?"

"Both of my clients should be pleased. Just be sure to have Morning make an appointment with me so I can discuss it with her directly," he suggested. "How's the war with Wryn going?"

"It's over, or at least I'm hopeful it's over," she replied. Anxious to make a clean sweep of her mistakes, she quickly explained the plan she had set into motion with Wryn that was now defunct and apologized for involving him, albeit by innuendo, in the first place.

His gaze grew more distant. "Where is she now?"

"She's still sitting in the gazebo, so I don't know what she'll do for certain, but I feel much better and I hope she does, too."

"I hope you made it very, very clear to Wryn that I had no part in this foolish little scheme of yours."

Emma blanched. "I told you that I did."

He shook his head. "Yet you waited until now to tell me how you planned to keep that young woman under control, even though you had ample opportunity to tell me when we were together in Bounty," he said, using the same tone of voice he reserved for when he challenged one of her business decisions, like selling the General Store or purchasing Hill House.

"I may have had the opportunity, but given your suggestion that Morning Drummond's interests would be better served by a formally trained lawyer, I had no reason to believe you would be either supportive or understanding of what I'd done in regards to Wryn," she countered. She had never let him intimidate her in the past when he was strictly her lawyer, and she refused to do so now that he was her betrothed. "I did what I thought was right for her at the time. Perhaps if you hadn't left so abruptly when Mark and I were discussing what to do, you would have been able to offer a more suitable plan. Or perhaps if you'd spent even a few words acknowledging that I was right to try to help Morning Drummond instead of reminding me more than once that I wasn't a lawyer and I should leave her concerns to a properly trained lawyer, I might have told you," she said, unloading the disappointments she had kept bottled up inside of herself, including the very real fear she had sorely misjudged the man who had claimed her heart.

"It's never been my intention to be anything less than supportive or understanding, with the possible exception of setting a date for our marriage," he replied.

"Choosing a date to be married is not a simple matter. It's something we need to discuss at length," she argued, not quite satisfied with his apology.

"You're right, but the sooner we do discuss it, the sooner we can both agree and the sooner we can be married, although I'll grant you one thing: It may take some time to find a suitable buyer for Hill House."

16

STUNNED, EMMA DROPPED BACK a step. "You don't want to live here at Hill House?"

"It isn't practical. Setting aside the fact that my clients would be greatly inconvenienced by it, there's little sense in either one of us remaining here."

Emma could only stare at him. She was scarcely able to hear him over the throbbing in her ears. Disbelief unleashed so many questions in her mind she grew faint—for the first time she could ever remember.

"You're uncommonly pale. Apparently, we should have reserved this discussion for a later time," Zachary noted with concern. Taking her elbow, he guided her to one of several pairs of outdoor chairs that had been set up on the patio. He helped her into her seat and then turned the chair next to her so when he sat down, he was facing her. "Would you like a glass of water?"

Trembling, she shook her head. "No. I . . . I'm fine. Just . . . surprised," she admitted, although she was touched by the concern for her that etched his features.

"More than a bit, judging by what I can see. A white linen sheet has more color than you do at the moment."

She dropped her gaze and folded her hands together on her lap to keep them from shaking. Unable to comprehend how he could expect her to walk away from the home she had worked so hard to make for herself and her guests, she was determined to continue to be as forthright with him as she had been during this entire conversation. After drawing in several long breaths, she looked up at him. "You're right. I am very surprised and deeply disappointed. I just assumed . . . that is, I thought you understood how much Hill House meant to me."

"When you finally accepted my proposal and agreed to marry me, I assumed that I had come to mean more." He took one of her hands in his own. "Are you saying now that I haven't?"

She managed a smile. "No, I'm simply saying that you and I apparently have very . . . very different visions of what our lives together would be like."

"Perhaps we do," he said, tightening his hold on her hand.

She cleared her throat. "Could you tell me why you want me to leave Hill House? Succinctly," she added, making the same request he had so often made of her when they had discussed her legal affairs.

"Succinctly put," he said, "if I can assume you've planned to set aside a specific room at Hill House for my office, I'm afraid my clients would find it most tiresome to traipse up and down the hill to meet with me."

"I truly didn't think far enough ahead about where your office would be, except that it would be here. My office is obviously too small for you and I'd still need it for myself, but I should think the library would be suitable. From what I've seen of your office, the room would be large enough, although we could make whatever alterations you think are necessary," she offered. "We'd need to add an outside entrance, too, so your clients wouldn't have to pass by my guests, who would be using the front parlors or the center hall. I realize there are times when discretion might be paramount."

"Regardless of how you alter Hill House, accommodating my clients by remaining in town is important, but it's not my first priority," he cautioned. "I travel more often now, and I was hoping that I wouldn't have to travel alone once we're married."

"If I travel with you, I'd be gone too often to effectively run Hill House and accommodate my guests. Is that what you think?"

He cocked a brow. "Am I wrong?"

"No," she admitted. "I need to be here, especially in the warmer months, although I might occasionally arrange for someone to take my place. I'd be much freer to travel in winter when the canal is closed and we rarely have guests, but the weather wouldn't be very accommodating, and opportunities to travel then are limited."

He grinned. "Especially when we have snowdrifts taller than I am."

"Travel is easier in spring and summer. . . ."

"Which is precisely when you're busy with the guests who travel here to Candlewood to stay at Hill House, and when I travel more often, as well," he interjected. "Obviously, when I have business in New York City, we'd travel by canal for comfort's sake. When I have business in Bounty, I was hoping we might ride there together. We'd also have time to visit your sons and their families."

Her eyes widened with new understanding about the gift he had given to her. "That's why you had Mercy shipped north for me instead of purchasing an ordinary horse here."

"A walking horse has a different gait, so you can ride Mercy literally all day and still be comfortable, which you no doubt discovered traveling to and from Bounty," he said defensively.

"Then your gift held yet one more surprise for me. Perhaps

if you'd mentioned why you'd purchased a walking horse for me at the time, we could have had the conversation then that we're having now," she argued and gently removed her hand from his. "Why didn't you tell me then? Was it truly an oversight? Or did you deliberately not tell me?"

"Did you think to ask? Or were you so taken with my gift that it didn't matter at all?" he countered.

She swallowed hard. "In all truth, I was so enthralled with your gift and with the prospect of marrying you that I didn't press you to know why you'd gone to the expense of bringing Mercy here. At the time, I thought you were being an overzealous suitor, although I probably should have known otherwise."

He cocked his head. "Have I been overzealous?"

"Only occasionally," she murmured. Determined not to be distracted from his insistence they could not make Hill House their home, she pressed him on the issue. "Other than what you've already told me, have you any other objections to living here at Hill House?"

His gaze hardened. "Only the most important one. Even if you did arrange for someone to take your place from time to time so we could travel together, living here would mean that we would be constantly surrounded by your guests, as well as any number of staff members. I'm a selfish man, Emma Garrett. I prefer to have my wife to myself when I'm at home, although I wouldn't mind sharing her with family members or guests from time to time," he added.

A blush of heat rushed from the tips of her toes to her cheeks, but his words also unleashed a host of objections of her own. "What about Wryn?" she argued without giving any thought to organizing her protests into any sort of order by importance. "I just told her that if she changed her ways and wanted to live here with me at Hill House, she could."

"If and how Wryn changes her ways shouldn't be your concern, although I understand why you've taken charge of her for the limited period of time she's residing at Hill House between now and your birthday. After that, she's Mark and Catherine's responsibility, and I daresay the goal for everyone involved should be to return her home to live with her mother. That said, I suppose I could agree to reconsider allowing Wryn to remain living here in Candlewood in our home, should that become the only alternative."

Barely mollified, Emma stiffened her back before voicing her most important concern of all—one that wrapped itself around her heart until it ached. "What about Mother Garrett? I always promised she could live with me. If you expect me to sell Hill House—"

"I expect your mother-in-law will make her home with us, wherever we are. My home is large enough that she would have a room to herself on the second floor."

"I was thinking more about a room on the first floor, specifically the kitchen," Emma countered. "In the five years we have known one another, you could not have overlooked the very real and significant fact that I cannot cook well and that Mother Garrett has always, always ruled my kitchen."

He laughed, breaking a bit more of the tension between them. "Then I shall relinquish the kitchen in my own home to her very capable hands."

Still not convinced his plan to move the three of them into his home would work, Emma offered another objection. "What about your housekeeper, Widow Ellis?"

The smile on Zachary's face disappeared. "Oh."

"Precisely my reaction. With two, possibly three people moving into your house, Widow Ellis would have enough cleaning and laundry to keep herself busy, but putting those two women together in the same house would be like flicking a lit match onto a bale of hay. Your house withstood the fires that spread through town after the match factory exploded, but I wouldn't expect the same to happen twice."

"You're right, but firing Widow Ellis presents a whole host of new problems, since I was the only one to offer her employment after her husband died."

"But you'd have to let her go if you moved into Hill House, although I daresay she'd find the reason for her dismissal a bit more understandable," she offered, sensing that their conversation had finally turned in her direction.

"Even if you're right and I did agree we could live at Hill House, that wouldn't alter the fact that I want to offer you more than just a different life as my wife. I want you to have a better life. One where you don't have to spend every waking moment of every single day working to accommodate your guests, which is precisely what would happen if we lived here together."

He gentled his words. "I know how much the boardinghouse means to you and how committed you have been to making Hill House a haven where guests receive much more than just a meal or a place to sleep. But giving it up doesn't mean you have to stop helping other people. Living in town should give you ample opportunities to do that."

He paused and captured her gaze. "I love you, Emma Hires Garrett, with my whole heart. Promise me you'll think about the life I'm offering you, the life we can share together."

Moved by his deep affection for her, she blinked back tears. "Yes, I promise," she whispered, praying she might be able to make one of the most difficult decisions of her life—to leave Hill House to become his wife . . . or to stay and spend the rest of her days alone as a widow.

17

DRESSING FOR DINNER after Zachary left, Emma settled for wearing the first gown she had tried on after twice changing her mind. The rose pin she wore as a symbol of her betrothal looked best against the winter green color, and she paused for a moment to trace the delicate gold petals, wondering if she had made the right decision to remarry at all.

With Reverend Glenn and Aunt Frances arriving with Zachary soon for dinner, however, she set aside worrying about the difficult decisions she had to make, considering the conditions Zachary had added to his proposal of marriage. She pinched a bit of color to her cheeks and slipped out of her room into the hallway. She tiptoed to the center staircase to avoid disturbing Mark and Catherine or waking the twins, who were napping, and continued quitely until she got to the bottom of the stairs.

Resuming her natural step, she checked the dining room and smiled when she saw the two high chairs pulled up to the table, which had already been set for their midday meal. Satisfied, she followed the luscious smells into the kitchen, where Liesel was busy at the table filling a platter with cookies. Two loaves of pumpernickel bread sat cooling on the table, too. Since the bread had not been sliced, Emma snatched a molasses cookie, took a bite, and closed her eyes to savor the hearty flavor.

"They're my favorite, too," Liesel offered as she started adding sugar cookies to the platter.

Grinning, Emma moistened her lips to catch a few crumbs. "Where is everyone?"

"Mother Garrett went upstairs to freshen up before dinner after she sent Ditty into town on an errand. There! That should be enough, don't you think?" she asked, pointing to the virtual mountain range of cookies.

Emma swallowed the last bite of her cookie. "I should hope so," she said and walked over to check the soup simmering on the cookstove. "After what happened to Ditty last time, I'm surprised Mother Garrett sent her into town alone."

"Oh, I guess I forgot that part. Wryn went with her, just to make sure she didn't fall again," Leisel said as she picked up the platter. "If you wouldn't mind watching the cookstove, I'll be right back. I want to set this on the sideboard, and I promised Mother Garrett I'd make sure there were enough chairs on the patio in case we decide to have dessert outside."

"Go ahead."

"I won't be long," she promised, nudging the door open with her shoulder and backing into the dining room.

Emma took a deep breath, thought about the trouble Wryn and Ditty could get themselves into, and headed for the tin of licorice root she had hidden in the cupboard. "It can't be gone," she grumbled as she poked her head into the cupboard and used her fingers to search behind a stack of crockery bowls, nearly knocking them over in the process.

"If you're looking for the tin of licorice root, it's not there."

Startled, Emma knocked the top of her head on the edge of the first shelf and inadvertently sent a couple of bowls crashing to the floor. "Ouch!"

"I didn't mean to sneak up on you. Did you hurt yourself?" Mother Garrett said when Emma turned to face her.

Emma gently patted the top of her head. "No, I'm fine. Just irritated. How did you know what I was looking for?"

"Because I just found that tin of licorice root this morning. I didn't know it was yours. I thought maybe I'd just forgotten that I stashed it there," she said and grabbed a large knife. Skirting the broken pieces of crockery on the floor, she headed for the bread. "I have the tin up in my room. I'll get it for you."

Emma sighed. "No, you keep it. I'm giving up. If I tried until I was ninety, I'd still detest the taste."

"And you might have all your teeth intact," Mother Garrett quipped as she started slicing the bread.

Emma bent down and started picking up the largest pieces of the broken bowls. "Liesel said Ditty and Wryn went into town on an errand for you."

"You didn't want me to send Ditty alone, did you?"

"No," Emma replied as she walked past Mother Garrett to set the pieces she had gathered up into a bucket on the floor by the sink.

"You wanted me to send Wryn into town alone?"

Emma grabbed the broom and started sweeping up the finer pieces. "No. I suppose I'm just a little worried."

"I thought you said you talked to that young woman and got matters set straight."

"I did, but—"

"Widow Garrett?"

Emma turned about and saw Liesel standing there, a puzzled look on the young woman's face. "Yes, Liesel?"

"Weren't the goats supposed to be tied up to graze down by the gazebo?"

Emma's heart dropped, and she tightened her hold on the broom. "Of course they were. I saw them there just a little while ago."

Liesel cringed. "They aren't—"

"They aren't tied?" Emma cried.

"No, they aren't there at all."

"Mark must have put them back in the pen instead of moving them like he said he was going to do," Mother Garrett remarked.

"I looked. They're not there, either. They're just . . . gone."

Emma shook her head. "I knew something like this would happen. I just knew it," she groaned. "Those three nanny goats probably ate right through that rope. I wouldn't be surprised if they're munching their way down Main Street right now," she remarked and looked at Mother Garrett. "I'll take over slicing the bread for you. You'll need to take Liesel with you, too, and you can recruit Ditty and Wryn, since you'll probably pass them on their way home."

Mother Garrett brandished her knife. "Me? I'm not hunting down those runaway goats."

Emma huffed. "They're your goats, not mine. You brought them home with you, or was that a different woman I saw sitting in the front of the wagon with Mr. Kirk that day?" she charged, hoping to spark Mother Garrett's ire a bit by referring to her rival.

"As if Widow Franklin would deign to put her dainty self in a farm wagon!"

Emma flashed a victory grin. "Then you did bring those goats to Hill House, which makes them yours."

"No, Mr. Kirk brought them here as a gift to you. I've got no claim on those goats at all, which means I'm staying right here to fix the rest of dinner, and so is Liesel, unless you want dinner to be late."

"No, but—"

"You might want to take that broom with you to scoot them home, and I wouldn't mind if you borrowed my umbrella. Makes a good poking stick."

"Fine. The two of you stay here and fix dinner. Even though I'm dressed for company, I'll look for the goats. But the next time Mr. Kirk comes to call, I'll need the entire contents of two tins of licorice root to keep me from telling that man he's a . . . a nuisance in my life!"

Mother Garrett shrugged. "I couldn't put it any better myself."

Emma held on to her broom and stomped her way to the patio. She peeked over the high stone wall, hoping to get a glimpse of the goats, but she only saw the pegs in the grass and an empty pen. "Horrid creatures," she gritted and charged down the steps. As soon as she reached the plateau, she marched to the closest peg in the ground.

Oddly enough, the rope had not been chewed through, as she had suspected. In fact, the entire rope was gone, which meant someone had removed it and taken the goats.

She laughed out loud, almost giddy with the joyful prospect someone had stolen the three nanny goats—until she heard a distinctive bleating sound behind her. She looked up, spied the three nanny goats now tied to the gazebo, and gasped. Benjamin, her middle son, was standing right next to those goats, and inside the gazebo, his wife, Betsy, was standing in back of their three little children, who were all standing on the bench waving to her.

"Surprise!" they cried.

She dropped the broom and clapped her hand to her heart to keep it from leaping straight out of her chest as her son charged forward and swooped her off her feet. "Benjamin Michael Garrett! Put me down!"

He ignored her protests and swung her around.

"What are you doing? Benjamin!"

"I'm making up for the last six years," he teased and wrapped her in a bear hug. "I've missed you."

She hugged him back. "Oh, how I've missed you, son. You're as ornery as ever, though, aren't you?" Now a strapping man in the prime of his life, he had features weathered by the sun and muscles hardened by heavy work on his farm. She was struck by how much he had changed since he had married Betsy and moved to Ohio with her family to farm, but his zest for life was still shining in the depths of his blue eyes.

He grinned back at her and released her. "I do my best," he said and studied her. "Were you expecting company?"

"Why?" she said as she caught her breath and straightened her skirts.

"You're not wearing your work apron, and I don't believe I've ever seen you wearing jewelry before. Is that a new pin or one I've simply forgotten?"

She fingered her pin and smiled. "It's new. A gift from a friend," she ventured, reluctant to tell him within minutes of arriving that she was planning to marry again.

He cocked a brow and crossed his arms over his chest. "A friend?"

"His name is Zachary Breckenwith."

"Your lawyer."

"He was," she replied and realized Benjamin was not going

to be satisfied until he had the full story. "He's proposed, and I've accepted his proposal, although we haven't set a date yet to be married," she told him. "He'll never take the place of your father, Benjamin, but—"

He placed a finger to her lips for a moment. "You have a right to be happy again," he offered. "When do I get to meet him?"

She smiled. "He's coming for dinner."

"Good," he announced and tugged on her hand. "Until then, there are some grandchildren waiting to meet you, and Betsy and I want a grand tour of Hill House, assuming you'll let a bunch of ordinary farm folks into that mansion sitting up there on the hill."

"It's just a boardinghouse," she argued. She took his hand and walked with him toward the gazebo, wondering how she could ever have all of her children and grandchildren for a visit if she lived in Zachary's much smaller home.

"Those three grandchildren you're staring at don't sit still much. I hope the house is good and sturdy."

Emma heard him but kept her gaze and her thoughts locked on the three little faces staring back at her. She stopped in front of them and looked up at her daughter-in-law. "Oh, Betsy. They're all so sweet, and you look so well. Being a farmer's wife certainly agrees with you."

Betsy smiled at her husband. "Being this farmer's wife does."

"And who do we have here?" Emma asked and scrunched down so she was at eye level with the little boy and his two sisters.

"I'm Teddy. I'm a five-year-older, and I'm the biggest," the boy said proudly.

She smiled. He had that same hint of orneriness in his eyes as his father. "Yes, you are. I'm your grandmother Emma, and I understand that you like molasses cookies."

He nodded and nudged his sister with his elbow. "Sally's a girl. She doesn't like molasses cookies."

Sally pouted. "Yes I do," she insisted and tossed her head, setting ringlets of auburn hair dancing.

"But I'm a girl, and molasses cookies are my favorite," Emma said.

Teddy shook his head. "You're not a girl. You're a grandma. Do you have any molasses cookies for me?"

"Don't be impolite," Betsy cautioned.

"As a matter of fact, there's a whole plate of cookies for dessert, but we have to eat dinner first," Emma replied and turned to the youngest child. At eighteen months, she still had baby-fat cheeks. Two blue ribbons held her dark, wispy hair out of her face. "Hello, Winnie. Did your mama put those ribbons in your hair for you?"

The toddler's bottom lip started quivering, and she turned and immediately reached up to her mother.

"I'm sorry. She's a bit shy around strangers," Betsy whispered. The moment she lifted Winnie into her arms, the little one buried her face against her shoulder.

"We won't be strangers very long, sweetie," Emma crooned and felt a tug on her heart. She would not have been a stranger to any of her grandchildren if her sons had not moved away from Candlewood, but she felt blessed to be with them now and only wished Jonas could have been here with them, too. She was also struck by Zachary's suggestion that if she did not have to work day and night to accommodate guests here, she might be able to travel to see them as often as she liked, which certainly tilted her thoughts in his favor.

She stood up, set those thoughts aside, eased the kinks out of her legs, and smiled down at the children. "I think your cousins

Jonas and Paul might be up from their naps by now. Let's go see, so you can meet them."

"Not before we get these goats back in their pen," Benjamin argued.

"Can't you just tie them up again and let them graze?"

He laughed. "Not unless you want to go searching for them. That pen's too small for them, too. You'd be better served to fence in this whole area."

"Or get rid of the goats," Emma grumbled.

"I'll get them into the pen for now. I've got our wagon parked just off the main road, but I'll worry about that later."

Teddy and Sally scrambled off the bench and ran out of the gazebo to help him. When the goats were secure again, they all made their way to the steps.

"Then Mark's here?" Benjamin asked.

"He and Catherine arrived a bit earlier than we'd planned. They've brought Catherine's niece, Wryn, with them."

"What about Warren?"

"He should be here tomorrow or the next day, at the latest," Emma said, then stopped abruptly when she realized Benjamin's surprise would have been ruined if Mother Garrett had been the one to go searching for the goats. "Did your grandmother have anything to do with surprising me today?"

Benjamin shook his head. "No, that was all our idea."

Betsy chuckled. "No, it was all your *son's* idea."

"Then why don't you surprise her, too?" Emma suggested.

Benjamin grinned. "Grams still rules the kitchen, I assume. Where's that?"

"At the top of the steps, you'll reach a patio. The double doors will take you into the dining room. The kitchen is right through the second door to your right."

Before she could say anything more, he was bounding up the steps. By the time they reached the patio, following after him, she heard Mother Garrett squealing. Emma smiled and tucked yet another precious memory deep into her heart.

18

DINNER HAD HELD as many joys as it did disappointments. Although Zachary had joined them, as expected, Reverend Glenn was feeling poorly and Aunt Frances had stayed home to watch over him. Surrounded at the table by so many of her loved ones, Emma's contentment could only have been more complete if Warren and his family had been there.

Wryn's absence at the table, however, still troubled her.

Emma played hide-and-seek with her grandchildren on the patio until the children were tuckered out and everyone dispersed. Betsy and Catherine took the three youngest children upstairs for their naps while Benjamin and Mark took Teddy and Sally with them down to the plateau to decide how best to accommodate the three nanny goats, who were still nameless. Once Mother Garrett shooed Liesel and Ditty back to the kitchen, Emma finally had a few moments alone with Zachary.

She stood beside him, hand in hand, at the stone wall overlooking the rear of her property watching her sons and grandchildren. "I think that might be Wryn sitting in the gazebo."

He nodded. "She might come around faster if I talk with her."

"Would you do that?"

"I think I have to," he murmured. "From what you and Mark have told me, her situation at home worsened each time her mother remarried, which means she sees me as yet another threat. I need to make it clear to her that while I support her in her attempts to reconcile with her mother, I have no objections if she needs to make her home with us, albeit on a very, very temporary basis."

"When did you plan on talking to her?" Emma asked, grateful for the support he was offering.

"I may as well take the opportunity right now, unless you had something else in mind for the afternoon," he suggested.

"Actually, I was hoping I could stop and see how Reverend Glenn is faring. If I wait for you, we could go together."

Zachary shook his head. "I'm not sure how long my conversation with Wryn might take. Why don't you go see the Glenns and meet me back at my house? Since you haven't seen anything other than my office, I'd like you to take a tour of the house before you make your decision to sell Hill House," he said, tightening his hold on her hand.

Determined to be fair, she could not think of an excuse to put off the inevitable. "If your conversation with Wryn doesn't last very long, come to the Glenns', but if you're not there by the time I finish my visit, I'll meet you at your house," she promised.

———

Emma lugged the goodies from Mother Garrett into Aunt Frances' kitchen. The late afternoon sunshine brightened the room, but it also shined doubt that Aunt Frances and Reverend Glenn were going to be able to live there on their own.

"Just set your bag on the table, Emma dear, and don't mind the muss," Aunt Frances said as she followed Emma into the room.

"With Reverend Glenn feeling poorly today and with my bones aching something fierce off and on, I haven't been able to keep up with my housekeeping."

Emma took a quick glance around as she walked toward the kitchen table, kicking up a bit of dust and dirt along the way. Several pots on the cookstove needed scrubbing, and a pile of bed linens on the floor waited to be laundered. There were no dishes in the sink, but judging from the dishes stacked on the side tables, Aunt Frances had not stored her clean dishes away for several days.

She was dismayed by how quickly it had become apparent that Aunt Frances and Reverend Glenn were not going to be able to care for themselves, as well as the cottage, on their own. Not without help.

By the time she'd set the canvas bag on the table, Aunt Frances was standing on the other side, her face bright with anticipation. "I don't mean to slight the good folks who sent a few meals over when we first took up housekeeping here, but I don't think I've had a really good meal since I left Hill House."

Emma lifted out the tin of cookies on top and handed it to Aunt Frances and smiled, although she was disappointed to learn that the generosity of the members of the congregation had already waned. "I'm not sure how Mother Garrett managed to hide a few cookies from those grandchildren of mine, but she did."

Aunt Frances peeked into the tin. "Molasses cookies!"

"There are sugar cookies in this one," Emma said, then lifted out a good chunk of pumpernickel bread and a crock of vegetable soup. "This is what we had for dinner today. You and Reverend Glenn might enjoy this for supper."

Aunt Frances moistened her lips. "We surely, surely will. Would you have time for a cup of tea? Reverend Glenn shouldn't be napping for much longer, and I know he'd be very disappointed if you left before you had a chance to visit with him, too."

"No, thank you. But if you'd like some tea—"

"Not particularly. I'd rather just sit and chat. I have a few things I'd like to discuss with you," Aunt Frances replied. She looked around the kitchen and frowned. "Why don't we go into the parlor, where there isn't so much muss?"

Emma slipped out of her cape and draped it across the back of one of the chairs. "Why don't you sit and rest while I tidy up a bit?"

Aunt Frances dropped her gaze and ran a finger round and round the rim of the tin of cookies she had just set back onto the table. "Did you ever make a mistake, Emma? I mean a really terrible mistake that kept you up at night, every night?"

Emma's throat tightened. The defeated form standing across the table from her bore little resemblance to the feisty woman who had shown up on her doorstep at Hill House last fall. Reluctant to admit, even to herself, she may have made a mistake by accepting Zachary's proposal before she knew of his expectations about their life together, she gripped the back of the chair in front of her. "I'm sure I have."

When Aunt Frances looked up, her eyes were filled with tears. "I'm such an old fool," she whispered.

Emma walked around the table and put her arm around the elderly woman's shoulders. "Now, why would you say something like that?"

"B-because it's true and because I just don't know what I'm going to do if Reverend Glenn finds out he's married to a . . . a foolish old woman who should have had better sense. . . ."

"You've got more good sense in a single hair on your head than most people, including me," Emma said. "What's wrong?"

"If I tell you, you can't tell anyone. Not a soul," Aunt Frances whispered. "Promise me you won't."

"Not even Mother Garrett?" Emma asked, doubtful that Aunt Frances meant to exclude her mother-in-law, considering the strong friendship between the two elderly women.

Aunt Frances dropped her gaze for a moment. "Mercy's been so busy lately, she hasn't been to visit us, but I think she has an inkling of what's happening here. We talked about it some before I left Hill House, and you can tell her. But no one else. No one."

Emma swallowed hard, anxious to get to the root of the trouble in Aunt Frances' life. "I promise."

Aunt Frances let out a sigh. "If you want to know what's wrong, just look around. Have you ever seen such muss in your life? Do you think Reverend Glenn ever had to live this way when he was married to Letty or when he lived with you at Hill House?"

"When Reverend Glenn was married to his first wife, they were both much younger than either of you are now. And there isn't any muss at Hill House because I have two very strong young women who help me keep it that way, not to mention that I don't have to worry about cooking because Mother Garrett takes care of all our meals. You're just feeling a bit overwhelmed, that's all. You haven't had your own home for a good many years."

"No I haven't, which is for the good. I can see that now. My sons were right, you know. I was too old to live on my own, and I should have realized that instead of being resentful when I had to live with them. And I should have realized that when Reverend Glenn asked me to marry him and live with him here. I don't have the energy to cook and clean for him like I thought I would, and I don't know what I'm going to do about it."

"The first thing you're going to do is sit down right over here," Emma insisted as she guided her aunt-by-affection to her rocking chair. She pulled Reverend Glenn's rocking chair in front of Aunt Frances and took her hands in her own. "Have you talked about this with Reverend Glenn?"

Aunt Frances blinked back tears. "No, I haven't. I can't, you see. He can't live alone, and the only reason he was able to accept the opportunity to become assistant pastor was because I agreed to marry him and keep house for him."

"No. He asked you to marry him because he had developed a great deal of affection for you. He wanted a helpmate and a companion, not a housekeeper. Are you happy together or not?"

"Yes, we're happy with one another, but that's not always enough. Not when there are meals to cook and rooms to clean and laundry that needs washing," she said as she looked down at her sewing basket and sighed. "I haven't threaded a needle since we moved here, either."

Emma drew in a long breath. "You and Reverend Glenn are always welcome to come back to Hill House, which is what I promised you both many times, remember?" she asked, mindful of another reason why she would be reluctant to part with Hill House.

Aunt Frances squeezed Emma's hands. "I know we are, but moving back there wouldn't do anything but invite gossip about the foolish old woman who couldn't properly care for her husband. Living at Hill House again would put Reverend Glenn too far from the center of town and the members of the congregation who need him here."

"Then the answer is simple. We need to get someone to come in each day to help you."

"I—we couldn't do that."

"Why not? I have help. Why shouldn't you?"

"Because the expense would be too great, and don't say you'll bear it for us, because I won't let you do that and neither will Reverend Glenn. And you can't spare Liesel or Ditty every day, either, which means there is no answer," she replied. "While I'm thinking of it, though, I've got that pretty shawl Wryn gave me right over there," she said, pointing to the corner. "I've wrapped it up in an old sheet, along with the knife she gave Reverend Glenn. Be sure to take them with you so they can be returned."

Aunt Frances' request suddenly opened the gate to one of the paths Emma had been searching for. "Actually, I think there might be an answer," she whispered as Wryn came to mind. "There just might be."

"Well, look at this. I take a bit of a nap and wake up to find Emma sitting in my rocking chair."

Emma looked up to find Reverend Glenn standing in the doorway with Butter right by his side. "I wanted to make sure you were feeling better," she said and got up from her seat.

The elderly minister was perhaps a bit pale, but he walked over to join them as steady as he ever was at Hill House. "Can you chat with me awhile, or do you two ladies need time alone?"

"Sit and chat with us," Emma urged.

And chat they did. By the time Emma left them, it was nearly dusk, and she was anxious to get back to her family at Hill House. She hurried toward Zachary's house to ask him if they could postpone their plans to tour his house, although she did want to make time to learn how he had fared talking with Wryn.

She turned off Main Street onto Coulter Lane and was a square away from his house when she saw him coming out the front door.

He waved and met her halfway, but she had to wait until a wagon passed to cross the street to meet him. "I'm sorry. I stayed much, much longer than I planned."

"It's not a problem. I was going to apologize to you. I had an unexpected meeting with a client and only finished up ten minutes ago. Do you have time to come back to the house now, or would you rather wait until tomorrow?"

"If you wouldn't mind, I'd rather stop tomorrow. I'm hoping Warren will be arriving in the morning, so I'm planning on getting down to the landing by eleven. If I left earlier and stopped on my way, say at ten o'clock, would you be free then?"

"I would. I'll try to send Widow Ellis out on an errand by then, too, although I may have to go with her to get her to leave. The front door will be open, so just go in if I don't answer your knock. May I walk you home?"

"I was hoping you'd offer. I have something I'd like to discuss with you," she replied and took his arm. "I have an idea, but I'd like your advice before I do anything about it."

He stiffened. "No legal advice, remember?"

"Of course, I remember. If I need legal counsel, I'll see Mr. Larimore, but for right now, I need some commonplace advice. I have an idea for Wryn and the Glenns that just might turn that young woman around faster than anything else so she can go home with Mark and Catherine to Albany."

That brought a smile to his lips.

Hers, too.

19

Emma never accepted weariness as an excuse when faced with an important task.

At the end of this very tumultuous day, with everyone else either abed or preparing for bed, she was sorely tempted to simply plop into her own and postpone her last task until morning. She climbed the stairs from her office one slow step at a time, more to accommodate her own tiredness than to be careful in the weak glow of light coming from the lamp in her bedroom at the top of the stairs. Learning Zachary's expectations for their lives together after they married, including his refusal to live at Hill House, had been a shock. Benjamin's arrival with his family had been a much more pleasant surprise, but learning about Aunt Frances' situation was still very troubling.

She slipped into her room, shut the door, and leaned back against it. Compared to the more elaborately furnished rooms she offered to family and guests, her room was small and simple with a single bed covered with a quilt, a battered old wardrobe her grandmother had brought with her to Candlewood, and a trunk where she now stored precious mementos from her life instead of baby clothes. The pale green walls were soothing to her spirit.

Covering a yawn, she took the packages out of the corner of her room and set out the purchases Wryn had made on her bed. Or what was left of them. She put the empty box of chocolates, as well as the half-eaten one, on top of her pillow. She couldn't very well hold Wryn accountable for those, since she wouldn't have eaten a few if Emma hadn't opened the boxes in the first place.

She left the bonnet in the box without bothering to look at it and set it in the middle of the bed. Next, she found the delicately beaded reticule and laid it next to the bonnet. When she untied the package from the General Store, which had obviously been tied and untied before, she found a few sewing needles, two spools of white thread, and two tins of licorice root.

Emma shook her head. "When Addie told me Wryn had gotten two tins of sweets, I never imagined these are what she meant. She and Mr. Atkins must think we're serving this stuff for meals. No wonder they ran out of it," she muttered and laid the purchases on the other side of the bonnet. Convinced that not all of Wryn's purchases were accounted for, she paused for a moment to recount what she could remember was missing. "Butter ate the beef jerky, but the knife she gave to Reverend Glenn is downstairs, along with Aunt Frances' shawl."

Letting out a sigh, she retraced her steps, returned to her office to retrieve the package, and carried it back upstairs to her room. She then laid the knife and shawl out on the bed next to the needles and thread.

Now that she had everything set out, she sat down on the trunk at the foot of her bed to wait for Wryn. According to Zachary, he and Wryn had had an open, frank talk with each other, although he had not provided her with any specific details. Since Wryn had come to the table for supper, as she had promised Zachary, Emma hoped the young woman would keep her promise to meet with her here tonight.

She slipped her hand into her pocket while she was waiting, felt for the new keepsakes she had added only yesterday, and smiled. Catherine had cut small pieces of soft flannel from the sheets used to soften the bottom of the cradles where Jonas and Paul had slept as newborn babes. In turn, Emma had cut them again and sewn them side by side to make a single piece. She had done that, as well, to the pieces of cotton cut from the blankets that had swaddled her precious grandsons.

Although her keepsakes helped to remind her of her blessings, she remained confused and troubled about God's will for her future. After praying that she might follow the path He had chosen for her to follow with Wryn, she asked Him to guide her, as well, to make the right decision about whether or not to agree to sell Hill House and marry Zachary Breckenwith. Is that what He truly wanted for her? And if He did, what work did He want her to do for Him? Or had she made a mistake? Did He want her to remain here at Hill House, as she had always thought?

She had scarcely finished her prayers when she heard a soft rap at the door. "Come in."

Mother Garrett poked her head inside. "I know you're expecting Wryn, but I just wanted to say that I've had time to think about what you told me . . . about Frances . . . and I was wondering if I could talk to you about something."

"Of course you can." Emma stood up and ushered her mother-in-law into the room. "I'm afraid there isn't any place for us to sit together on the bed, but you can use the trunk."

Mother Garrett glanced at Wryn's booty on the bed. "Don't bother holding her accountable for that licorice root. I'll take those, and you can just put something on my account to cover the cost."

Emma chuckled and handed the two tins to her mother-in-law. "Done, although I'm not going to worry about the cost of these."

Mother Garrett nodded. "It's a bit awkward to say this, Emma, but we've never let things fester between us and I don't want that to happen now."

Emma's heartbeat pulsed in her veins. "If it's about my getting married again and how that will affect you, I thought I—"

"No, it's not that. I know I have a place with you," Mother Garrett argued. "You've already made that clear."

Relieved, Emma felt her heart slip back into a more normal rhythm. "What did you want to talk about?"

"I've been thinking a lot about Frances and Reverend Glenn, even before you told me what she'd said this afternoon. Even though she's a good bit older than I am, I'm still not as young as I used to be. As long as we're here at Hill House, I'd like to make a change or two in the way we do things."

Emma swallowed hard. "If you need more help in the kitchen than Liesel or Ditty can give you, I've told you before that I would hire someone new."

"You may have to do that, but it's not because the work is too much for me. I want to get some time each week just to myself without worrying about what meals need to be prepared."

Emma's cheeks flushed with guilt for not insisting when they had moved here that her mother-in-law had time off from her work. Mother Garrett was usually frank, if not outspoken, and Emma was surprised she had not brought the matter up before now. "You can have as much time for yourself as you need. What did you have in mind?" she asked.

"If I had my druthers, I'd like to do what Liesel and Ditty do and have Saturday afternoons and Sundays free, except I'd be home to sleep here Saturday night. But since that isn't likely to suit—"

"We'll make it suit. I'm only sorry we didn't talk about this sooner. I hope it hasn't been troubling you for very long."

Mother Garrett shrugged. "Don't be too sorry. The thought just occurred to me this afternoon."

Emma nodded. Now she understood. "Since I talked with you about Aunt Frances?"

A long sigh. "The older I get, the more I realize there are only two, no, three—things that truly matter in life. Following the Word is the most important, but family and friends matter more than anything else. I haven't had a friend like Frances. Ever. She needs me, Emma, and I want to be able to help her and Reverend Glenn. But I know you need me, too. I know it wouldn't be easy for you not to have me here on weekends, but I could make some meals ahead and see if that works."

Emma wrapped her arms around her mother-in-law and hugged her close. "You've been a blessing to me since the day you came into my life, and I wouldn't be half the woman I'm trying to be if I didn't share that blessing with Aunt Frances. She's family, too. As a matter of fact, I'd like you to start enjoying your free time this weekend," she said and quickly outlined her plans for Wryn. "Assuming she agrees, which I hope to find out tonight, Aunt Frances will have help all week long and then you'll be there on the weekends."

Mother Garrett hugged her back. "What about your birthday? That's only a week or so away. Shouldn't we wait till then?"

"My birthday falls on a weekday this year, which means you'll be here. We'll invite Aunt Frances and Reverend Glenn to spend the day with us, so that means Wryn would be here, too. There's only one slight hitch," Emma ventured.

Mother Garrett cocked a brow. "You're gonna need Wryn's help in my kitchen, aren't you?"

Emma laughed. "We both know her faults, but from what Catherine tells me, Wryn knows her way around the kitchen especially well, considering she's only fifteen."

"Which is more than you can say for yourself."

"Very true."

Mother Garrett sighed. "I suppose Catherine and Betsy wouldn't mind stepping in to help while they're here, but come May, there are your guests to consider. They wouldn't be likely to return for another visit if you prepared the meals while I'm gone."

"Also very true," Emma admitted, reluctant to tell her mother-in-law about the possibility that Hill House might have a new owner by May.

"Then I suppose I'll have to agree. For Frances' sake and for Reverend Glenn's sake," she relented. "But if I come back here Sunday night to find my larder in disarray, there won't be a safe place for that young lady to hide."

"Very, very true," Emma replied, planting a kiss on her mother-in-law's cheek and ushering her to the door. "Go get your rest. I'm expecting Wryn any moment." When she opened the door, she saw Wryn coming down the hall.

Mother Garrett slipped the tins of licorice into her apron pockets and leaned close. "Come see me after she's left. I won't say my prayers until you do, just in case I have to add a few to ask the good Lord to send a few strong angels to stand guard over my kitchen when I'm not there," she whispered.

Still trying to absorb her conversation with Mother Garrett, Emma welcomed Wryn into her room. The young woman's expression was guarded, although her demeanor was just as reserved as it had been through supper—until she saw the items displayed on Emma's bed.

"Holding court tonight?" she quipped as she walked over to the bed.

"No. Discussing family matters," Emma said. "Would there be an apology forthcoming for your flippant remark or do I have to—"

"No, I'm . . . I'm sorry," Wryn said.

"Good. I accept your apology," Emma replied, then waved her arm over the bed. "I need your help. Between the two of us, we need to decide what to do about these."

Wryn stiffened. "Am I supposed to offer to humble myself and beg the shopkeepers to take them back?"

"That's one option, but before we talk about others, I'm curious. I know what you gave to the Glenns, but I was wondering if you'd be willing to tell me who you had in mind to receive each of the other gifts."

Wryn shrugged. "I suppose so."

Although Emma was tempted to prompt Wryn to say more, she waited. And waited.

Eventually, when the silence grew as thick as a heavy fog that threatened to cloud their meeting together, Wryn pointed to the two chocolate boxes. "I bought those for Aunt Betsy and Aunt Anna. I thought they could share them with their families, since I don't know them very well."

Emma cringed. "Oh. That's a problem now, isn't it?"

A smile tugged at the corners of Wryn's lips. "Only if you decide to let me give them their gifts."

"What about the needles and thread?" Emma asked quickly to change the subject.

Wryn shrugged. "They were for me."

"So not everything you bought were gifts?"

"Obviously not. What happened to the licorice root? Did you eat that, too, or were those bulges in Mother Garrett's apron what I think they were?" she snapped, blushed, and moistened her lips. "I mean . . . no, they weren't," she added in a tone of voice close enough to respectful that Emma could not find fault.

"I gave the licorice root to Mother Garrett, which means, in all fairness, that it won't be tallied up to you. The same applies to the boxes of chocolate. And you don't have to worry about the beef jerky, either. Butter ate it all."

Wryn nodded and pointed to the box holding the bonnet. "That one was for you. I figured you needed a new one, since the one you were wearing the morning I met you got ruined in the rain."

"It isn't ruined, just a bit broken in," Emma argued.

Wryn cocked her head.

"I can still wear it when I'm working around the yard," she added. "Since you picked out a bonnet for me, would you like to show it to me?"

As Wryn was untying the ribbon holding the lid to the box, Emma held her breath, since she had no way of knowing this young woman's taste. With images of the garish costume she had fixed for herself the other day, she held out little hope the bonnet would be anything she might have picked out for herself.

Until Wryn lifted the bonnet out from the box.

Instead of choosing a fancy bonnet Emma would wear to Sunday meeting or other special occasions, Wryn had picked out a plain wide-brimmed straw bonnet with wide, dark green ribbons that would tie into a simple but striking bow when she wore it.

"I was going to give it to you for your birthday. You need a bonnet that won't fly off when you're riding, and the lady at the shop said the color of the ribbons would match your cape," Wryn offered as she handed the bonnet to Emma.

"Yes, they would. It's perfect, although I'd have to make certain it wouldn't rain when I wore it," Emma murmured. She smiled and reluctantly handed it back to Wryn. "Be careful when you put it into the box again."

Wryn frowned. "I suppose I'll have to return this one."

"Put it in your room for now, along with the shawl and the knife you bought for the Glenns, although I wouldn't expect you to keep the bonnet in the end," Emma replied. "If you'd still like to give them as gifts, there's a way you could work off the cost."

Wryn set the bonnet back into the box very carefully, replaced the lid, and started retying the ribbon to hold it closed. "Is that the other option you wanted to discuss?"

"It's the only one I have at the moment, although I'd be willing to listen if you have another one."

When Wryn shrugged, Emma noticed the usual chip on her shoulder was not there, at least for now. "You've been to visit Aunt Frances and Reverend Glenn," she began.

"Quite a few times. They're nice to me. Why?"

Emma chose her words carefully to avoid breaking Aunt Frances' confidence. "I'm concerned about them. They're up in years and living alone has presented certain challenges."

"Like keeping the cottage clean?"

Emma lifted her brows.

Wryn rolled her eyes. "What? Was that too flippant?"

"No, merely more insightful than I expected," Emma admitted.

When Wryn's posture relaxed, Emma continued. "We consider Aunt Frances and Reverend Glenn to be part of our family. Since Liesel and Ditty are able to give me the help I need here to keep

Hill House operating smoothly, I wanted to ask you if you'd be willing to do chores for me at the Glenns' to work off what you owe me for the purchases you made. I'll explain to them that this is an arrangement we've made between the two of us. I don't want their feelings to be hurt. Understood?"

"Understood. Would I live there, too?" Wryn asked, her gaze troubled.

"No, you'd still live here with me. After breakfast each day, you could go to the Glenns' and do what chores needed to be done. I'd expect you to be home by suppertime, and you'd have your evenings to yourself."

"What about the weekends? Would I still be off, like Liesel and Ditty?"

Emma drew in a long breath. "No. Mother Garrett is getting on in years now, too. Starting this weekend, she'll be off. I suspect she'll be spending a lot of time visiting Aunt Frances and Reverend Glenn, but she'll be back here each night, just like you will. That means I'll need your help here."

Wryn's eyes sparkled. "You need me to help cook?"

"Yes."

"In Mother Garrett's kitchen?"

"Yes."

"Then I'll do it, but I won't need your help. I can cook the meals by myself," Wryn pronounced, almost gleeful.

Emma stifled a chuckle, although she suspected there would be more than an occasional outburst between her mother-in-law and this young woman. "You'll keep in mind that Mother Garrett will still be in charge of the kitchen. She won't tolerate coming home to find her kitchen a mess."

"And I won't be happy if she leaves me a mess, either. Did you want me to start in the morning?" she asked as she began to gather up the gifts to take back to her room.

Emma slid the boxes that had held the chocolates under her bed. "No, I need to see Aunt Frances and Reverend Glenn first to see if they'd be willing to let you come each day. If they are, you can start the following day."

She noticed the beaded reticule as Wryn gathered it up. "We never talked about that. Are you planning on returning it?"

Wryn fingered the beads. "No, not yet."

"Can you tell me who it was for?"

"My mother," Wryn whispered and slipped out of the room carrying her gifts and a piece of Emma's heart.

20

AFTER A FITFUL SLEEP, Emma dressed for the day and stood at
her bedroom window at first light the following morning
to watch the sun begin to chase the night away.

She rested the side of her head against the window frame and
stared out at the canal slicing through the landscape just below the
horizon. She hoped Warren and his family would arrive today,
completing the circle of family who had gathered in Candlewood
for her birthday. Later this morning, she would visit with Aunt
Frances and Reverend Glenn to ask them to have Wryn complete
her punishment by doing chores for them. In turn, she hoped they
would each have a positive influence on the young woman. With
Mark and Catherine leaving the day after her birthday, along with
her other sons and their families, she had real doubts Wryn would
be returning to Albany with them and assumed she might have to
remain here in Candlewood.

She let out a sigh and fingered the gold rose she had pinned to
the collar of the dark brown gown she had chosen to wear today.
Covering the pin with her fingers, she closed her eyes. She had
never thought she would be blessed again with the affection and

companionship of a spouse, but marrying Zachary would change her life in ways she'd never had to consider before. When she had married Jonas, he had understood that she would continue family tradition and operate the General Store, just as her mother and grandmother had done, and he would be her helpmate, just as her father and grandfather had been to their wives.

Family tradition, however, had ended when Emma and Jonas had only sons. After her husband died and all her sons married and settled far from Candlewood, she had had no reason to hesitate when she had the opportunity later to sell the General Store and establish Hill House as a boardinghouse.

She had no tradition to consider when marrying Zachary, but she still believed God had led her here to Hill House for a purpose. The life Zachary offered to her now was tempting, but until she discovered how she might serve Him in that life and until she understood which path He wanted her to follow, she was reluctant to leave here.

For his part, Zachary had given her an ultimatum of sorts: Give up Hill House to marry him or remain here at Hill House without him.

She could only pray that the man who had stolen her heart would give her time.

Time for her to pray for God's guidance.

Time for Him to reveal His own purpose for Hill House.

And time for His plans for her to unfold.

Head bowed, she folded her hands together and closed her eyes. "Dearest Father in heaven," she whispered. "I thank you for your constant love and the blessings you have given to me, as well as the challenges. I so want to do your will, but I'm so afraid that I won't know the path you have chosen for me. Please guide me so that I am only your instrument. Help me to be patient, for your timing is always wisest, and help me to make decisions that are pleasing to you. Above all, please show me how to best help those I love and those . . . those who need my love. Amen."

Breathing slowly, she held very still, praising Him and loving Him with every beat of her heart until her anxiety disappeared and she faced this new day with the hope and optimism only her faith could give her.

———————

Full of renewed confidence, Emma made her first visit of the day to Reverend Glenn and Aunt Frances right after breakfast, but she did not have the opportunity to speak to Aunt Frances alone, as she had promised yesterday.

While Reverend Glenn and Aunt Frances held hands and sat together on the settee in the parlor, she interrupted the pleasantries they had been sharing to add a log to the fire to chase away the morning chill from the room. "That should keep you both warm until the sun gets stronger," she said and walked around Butter, who had lain down next to the hearth, before taking a seat across from them.

"You're a blessing, as always, Emma," Reverend Glenn said. "If I got down on my knees to keep that fire going, I'm afraid I'd never get up, even with Butter's help. I don't favor seeing Frances doing the kind of work I should be doing for us, either."

"I don't mind at all," Aunt Frances argued, still obviously troubled by thoughts she had shared with Emma yesterday.

Blessed with the perfect opportunity, Emma wasted no time and introduced the purpose for her visit. She did not mention anything about the change in Mother Garrett's work schedule, out of deference to her mother-in-law so she could tell them herself.

"I wonder if you'd both consider helping me with a problem I have."

Since they both knew Wryn's circumstances through Mother Garrett, Emma started by explaining in detail the mistake she had made when Wryn first arrived, as well as the efforts she had made with Wryn to undo that mistake. "I'm afraid her gifts to you are among those that she's returning, but she also has to work off what she can't return."

Reverend Glenn looked at Butter and shook his head. "Can I assume that includes the beef jerky my loyal friend managed to find?"

"No. Consider that a treat from me for being such a good companion to you," Emma insisted. "I could have her doing chores at Hill House, of course, but I have my own work to do and Liesel and Ditty to supervise, as well."

"So you'd like her to come here to work for us?" Aunt Frances asked.

"I would, if both of you wouldn't mind. You know she can be . . . difficult, but I think she's truly trying to change."

"She's always been quite pleasant while she was visiting us, hasn't she, Frances?" Reverend Glenn asked.

Aunt Frances nodded. "That's true. Maybe it's because we're a bit older. We're more like grandparents than parents to her, which is where the heart of her troubles lies, I would suppose."

"Exactly," Emma replied. "I can't think of two people who might be able to have a better influence on her than both of you. The cottage is very small, and I know it would be an imposition to have someone here all the time, so I was hoping she could come after breakfast, do whatever chores you have for her, and then send her home in time for supper with us. But you have to promise not to offer her anything but your guidance in return. She's doing punishment, not looking for employment."

"How long do you think she'll be on punishment?" Reverend Glenn asked.

"A few weeks, but certainly less if Mark and Catherine decide she's changed enough to return to Albany with them. Otherwise, she'll be staying with me for a while. I suspect that will be the case, but I truthfully have no idea how long she'll be with me," she explained, without complicating the issue by mentioning Zachary or his expectations.

Reverend Glenn turned to his wife. "I think we should try to help that poor girl. What do you think?"

Aunt Frances looked up at him and nodded before she turned to Emma, offering her a smile of gratitude. "I think Zachary Breckenwith is a very fortunate man to have discovered our Emma is as precious as we know she is. Why don't you send Wryn to see us? If we can come to an understanding about what she'd be expected to do, then we can have her start as soon as you like."

———

Walking from the Glenns' cottage to Zachary's house should have taken Emma all of ten minutes, which would have put her there at ten o'clock, exactly as they had planned.

However, she did not reach his house until ten-thirty, through no fault of her own. She had not been walking out and about in town since accepting Zachary's proposal, but judging by the number of people who stopped her along the way, gossipmongers had done quite an excellent task of spreading news of the upcoming marriage between the very eligible bachelor and the proprietress of Hill House.

Quickly banishing a fleeting thought about the kind of gossip that would be ignited if she changed her mind about marrying Zachary at all, she knocked on his door. As anxious to apologize for her tardiness as she was to escape another well-wisher, she knocked again. When he still did not answer, hope that he had not been able to send Widow Ellis on an errand by herself was quickly fading.

She decided to knock once more, and this time, he answered almost immediately.

"I hope I haven't kept you waiting. I was in my office doing some work, and I wasn't sure if that was a knock at the door I heard or not. Please, come in," he said and stepped aside to let her enter.

"I'm sorry I'm late. I had to make a stop at the Glenns' first. They were both agreeable to having Wryn with them during the day, by the way. I thought I'd left early enough to be here on time, but I hadn't counted on so many people stopping me."

Chuckling, he closed the door. "If you're making a list of advantages and disadvantages to living in town, I'm afraid gossip belongs in the latter column. May I take your bonnet and cape?"

"I'd rather not. I really don't have much time. The morning packet is due at eleven today, and I don't want to be late, especially if Warren and his family are arriving. Did Widow Ellis balk overmuch at being sent on an errand for you?"

He cleared his throat. "Not exactly."

Emma chuckled. "Either she did or she didn't. Which was it?" she asked, expecting to hear yet another tale that would dignify her reputation as the most miserable woman in Candlewood.

"She didn't balk. She wasn't here when I got back from walking you home yesterday afternoon. She left this on the table in the kitchen," he said and handed her a note scribbled on a torn piece of brown wrapping paper he had stored in his vest pocket.

Curious, Emma read the brief note:

Mr. Breckenwith:

I refuse to face the humiliation of being let go in favor of Mercy Garrett, despite my superior abilities in the kitchen, when you marry Widow Garrett. I have left Candlewood to secure suitable employment elsewhere. Use the wages I am due to settle my account at the General Store.

A. V. Ellis

Emma gasped. "She quit!"

"That she did," he admitted.

"She didn't even discuss it with you?"

"Not a whisper."

"What are you going to do?" she asked, knowing full well he could not practice law and tend to the kitchen and housework by himself, even if he were so inclined.

He shrugged. "I suppose I'll have to try to find another house-keeper, hopefully one who can cook better than she did, although I'm not sure how long I can promise the position will last. Not until I know when we're going to get married and your mother-in-law takes over the kitchen," he added.

Piqued by his confidence in a decision she had yet to make, she handed him back the note. "If I hadn't just made arrangements for Wryn with the Glenns', I could have had her work here."

He cleared his throat again. "I'm not sure how suitable that would have been. Even if she returned to Hill House at night, her young age and the fact that she would be here alone all day with a man who isn't her relative would be enough to invite gossip."

Emma blushed. "Oh, you're right, of course," she said and began thinking out loud. "Well, then, if you can't use Wryn and you can't hire someone at the moment, you could take your meals at the hotel or carry them home with you like you do in Bounty—but I know Mother Garrett well enough to be able to say she wouldn't stand for that. I'm afraid you have no choice but to come to Hill House for your meals."

He nodded. "I'd rather have your mother-in-law side with me, rather than against me, so I'll accept your offer."

Enjoying the upper hand, however briefly, she smiled. "May I expect you at one for dinner?"

"You may," he replied. "As I recall, supper is at six o'clock each evening. Breakfast is at what time?"

"Eight o'clock. Now, as far as housekeeping chores are concerned," she continued, "I could certainly bring Ditty or Liesel here with me for a few hours each day to keep the house tidy enough."

"I suppose that might work, although I'd rather you didn't do more than supervise the girl."

She ignored his comment and held silent.

"It does seem a shame to waste all that time going back and forth for meals and having your staff do the same to keep this place tidy when there's a simpler solution."

She drew in a deep breath. "Dare I ask what that might be?"

"I was hoping you would. Given my current situation and considering your entire family is here, or soon will be, I should think the solution is very clear. We could save everyone involved a lot of trouble if you agreed to marry me on your birthday so you could move into my home with your mother-in-law," he suggested with a twinkle in his eye.

"But that's . . . that's next week!"

"Which means I'll only have the inconvenience of traveling back and forth between my office and Hill House for my meals for a very short time, and you'll be saved the trouble of bringing your staff into town on my behalf, as well."

She huffed. "You did plan this!"

"Only after I found Widow Ellis' note."

"You should have come to tell me about it last night."

He cocked a brow. "As I recall, you had very specific plans to talk to Wryn last night. Will you at least consider getting married on your birthday?"

"Yes, I'll consider it, but not right now. If being delayed by well-wishers while walking here is any indication of how long it will take, I have to leave to get to the landing. Warren might be arriving, and I don't want to be late," she insisted, slipping past him and out the door.

Mumbling to herself, she rushed down the steps. Widow Ellis' departure was one part of His plan she had not anticipated, but she was reluctant to question God's wisdom or His timing for fear of losing whatever grace she had been given during her prayers. She was, however, growing more and more agitated by Zachary's assumption she would accept his demands. "I'd much prefer a little time between answers to my prayers, or a gentle nudge instead of a shove," she murmured and hurried on her way.

21

WITH SCARCELY MINUTES to spare, Emma was a square away from Canal Street when yet another well-wisher came hurrying toward her.

Widow Franklin, the sixty-something rival for Mr. Kirk's attentions, waved her handkerchief as she approached. "Widow Garrett! I'm so pleased to see you. What wonderful news I've heard about you and Mr. Breckenwith!" she said in her distinctive childlike voice.

Reminded of how she had used the same voice and made a handkerchief into a puppet for little Jonas, Emma managed not to grin. "Thank you," Emma said as she greeted the woman and prayed the packet boat would be a little late, which was not all that unusual.

"Have you set a date yet?" she asked, mopping her brow before she tucked the handkerchief into her reticule.

"No, we haven't. I was just on my way to meet Warren. I'm hoping he's arriving on the morning packet," she said.

"I was just in the confectionary and overheard someone say the packet arrived early today, perhaps twenty minutes ago. Did you say you expect to marry soon?"

"We haven't really decided on a date," Emma reiterated, now doubly anxious to end the conversation. Of all her sons, Warren was the one who would not be forgiving if she was not at the landing to meet him as he arrived with his family. "I really must go. If you'll excuse me—"

"Of course. You must be anxious to see your son and his family. I must be off, too. Mr. Kirk is coming for dinner today, but I wonder if I might stop to see you soon," she said and stepped closer, lowering her voice. "I hope it's not too presumptive of me, but once you and Mr. Breckenwith are married, I was hoping you'd be able to help me with a legal question or two."

"I'm sure Mr. Breckenwith would be delighted to assist you, but I wouldn't be qualified," Emma argued, reminded she had yet to hear from Morning Drummond about her situation.

Widow Franklin shook her head. "There are some things a woman just prefers to discuss with another woman, especially one as bright and capable as you are. I'm certain you'd be able to look something up in the law books as good as any man."

"I probably could, but—"

"Thank you," the elderly woman gushed. "Mildred Perkins was convinced you'd turn me away because of my growing friendship with Mr. Kirk, which is probably very upsetting to your mother-in-law, but please don't say I mentioned her name. Mildred's planning to see you herself. We'll be waiting to hear that you've chosen a date to be married," she said sweetly and continued on her way.

Worried that more than two women in Candlewood viewed Emma's marriage as an opportunity to seek legal advice through her, especially when Zachary was so opposed to the idea, Emma rushed to the corner. After crossing the street to avoid the wagons lined up to load their cargo on the packet boat, she hurried down to the landing, where her worst fears were confirmed.

The packet had arrived early, just as Widow Franklin had suggested, and there was no sign of either Warren or his family. Hoping now that he would not reach Candlewood until tomorrow, Emma retraced her steps and headed toward home. She was halfway down Main Street when she saw Warren struggling with several large travel bags, his family in tow, just ahead on the other side of the street.

As she hurried to catch up with them, memories tugged at her heartstrings. Of all her sons, he looked the most like his father. He was also the most successful of her sons. Warren had parlayed the money Emma had given him into a dry goods business in New York City that was so successful he had built a remarkable new home for his own family just last year.

Warren had always been just as steady and reliable as his father, too, although he had a streak of impatience that was decidedly his own and often accused Emma of favoring his brothers over him. He was also more confident of himself, even as a child, than his father had ever been. He was neither tall nor short, but his body had thickened and his face was rounder than the last time she had seen him, some three years ago. His handsome suit of clothes testified to his accomplishments in business.

His wife, Anna, was walking next to him. Tall and angular as a younger woman, she had filled out a bit, which softened her appearance, but she carried herself with the same gracious demeanor Emma remembered.

Emma's attention, however, was riveted on the two little girls, each holding one of Anna's hands. Deborah, age five, had Emma's blond hair and blue eyes. She had grown so much in the past three years, and Emma could imagine that her own daughter, if she had had one, would have looked just like her. As Emma recalled,

Deborah had one focus in her life—the massive collection of dolls she had managed to acquire in her five short years.

Little Grace, now two years old, was the very image of her older sister at that age. Chubby cheeks. Wispy blond hair. Overwhelming blue eyes.

Nearly there, when Emma crossed the street, Anna was the first to spot her. She nudged her husband to stop and smiled. "Mother Emma!" she cried as she bent down and pointed Emma out to the little ones.

Once she reached them, she tried to catch her breath. "I'm so sorry I wasn't there to meet you," she managed. "The packet was uncommonly early today."

"But you would have been there if you were expecting Mark or Benjamin," Warren snapped as he set down his bags.

Emma swallowed hard. Up close to Warren now, she could see a tension in her son's eyes that had not been there before, but she dismissed it, along with his comment, as simply annoyance that she had not been there when the packet boat arrived. After getting a reluctant hug from her son and a warmer one from his wife, she scrunched down to meet her granddaughters at eye level. "Hello, Deborah. Do you remember me?"

"No, but Mama and Papa said you have a grand, grand house with room for all of us. We're gonna stay at your house. Papa said so."

"That's right," Emma replied and turned her attention to Grace. "I'm your grandmother Emma, little Grace."

Grace held tight to her mother's skirts. "'hickens at your house?"

Emma chuckled. "Yes, we have chickens. We have three nanny goats now, too. I'm hoping that we can pick out some names for them while you're here. Would you like to do that?"

"'hickens! 'hickens."

Anna laughed and patted her little one's head. "All she's talked about during the entire trip is playing with the chickens at her grandmother's house."

"I'm not sure how well they'd play together, but we can collect eggs every morning."

"That should do."

Emma put her hand on Warren's arm. "Your brothers are here already. Since I wasn't certain you'd be on this packet, I didn't order a coach ahead of time. I assume you made arrangements with Mr. Adams for your trunks to be taken up to Hill House later, but you should have had him take those travel bags, too."

"Fortunately, since my brothers didn't see fit to help me home, I spied Andy Sherling. He was about three wagons back, waiting to unload when we arrived. He offered to bring the trunks up to Hill House for us. He wasn't certain how long he'd be, so I thought I'd better bring the bags along with me now."

"Then why didn't you take a coach?"

"Warren and I decided to walk, which didn't seem like a bad idea at the time," Anna offered. "I haven't been to Candlewood for a while, and I wanted to see the changes in town. Besides, the girls have been on the boat for days. I thought a walk might do them some good, although Grace probably won't last much longer."

"We could stop to see Reverend Glenn and his wife so Grace could rest up a bit. I know they'd love to see you and your family, and we could invite them both to join us for dinner. Your trunks will surely be there by then," Emma said.

Deborah tugged on her papa's sleeve. "I want my dollies. Will my dollies be coming, too?"

Warren's face froze for a moment before he relaxed his expression. "No, Deborah. Not . . . . But Mama packed your favorite doll for you in with your clothes so she wouldn't break, remember?" he said. He looked up at Emma and shrugged. "There wasn't room on this packet for everything. Some of our trunks had to be left behind."

"There's a little store here in Candlewood that has lots of pretty dolls you can see. We'll stop there one day soon, but I can show it to you while we walk home," Emma suggested.

Despite her current reservations regarding her betrothal, she was anxious to share her news with her son before anyone else did, knowing it would only give Warren more cause to complain. "Mr. Breckenwith will be coming to dinner today," she began as they started toward Hill House.

"Isn't he your lawyer?" Warren asked.

"He was, and he will be again, but at the moment, he's much more than that. We're hoping to be married soon." She prayed her eldest son would be as pleased with her news as his brothers had been.

Warren froze in midstride, forcing Emma and his family to stop as quickly. His gaze hardened. "Since when? You never wrote a word—"

"I only recently accepted his proposal. There wasn't time to write to let you know."

When Anna took a step closer to him, his gaze softened. "I'm sorry. I'm just . . . shocked."

"I think I shocked myself when I accepted his proposal," Emma admitted, although his recent demands had been more unsettling. "I invited him to dinner so you'll all have the opportunity to meet him. He's a good man," she added, somewhat defensively.

"I'm sure he is, Mother Emma," Anna offered. "Why don't you tell us more about him on our way to see the Glenns."

With seven grandchildren babbling and chattering, Emma's three sons laughing together again, their three wives gabbing, Mother Garrett sharing her news with Aunt Frances, and Reverend Glenn talking to Wryn, there had never been this much commotion at dinner at Hill House. Not ever.

Emma could not have been happier. Warren had not entirely warmed up to the idea that Zachary was going to marry his mother, but he had been civil enough when Emma had introduced them. Setting aside her initial disappointment, she tucked away the experience of having all of her loved ones together again deep in her heart.

When Liesel and Ditty started to clear away the dinner dishes to make room for dessert, Emma glanced at Zachary, who sat to her right at one end of the table.

He smiled and winked at her.

Her cheeks warmed. "I gather you're not intimidated by the size of my family," she murmured.

He leaned toward her. "Quite the opposite. I'm rather anxious to join it officially," he whispered. "Should I presume you've been too preoccupied since we talked this morning to be able to properly consider the solution to my problem?"

Seated next to Emma, Mother Garrett got up to help Liesel and Ditty and picked up Zachary's dinner plate. "What problem would that be?"

Emma rolled her eyes. Although Mother Garrett suffered from a few minor physical ailments, there was nothing wrong with her hearing.

Before Emma or Zachary could reply, Anna got up from her seat, took the dinner plate from Mother Garrett, and urged her to sit down again. "You've done enough for everyone already. Relax and talk."

Mother Garrett sat down again, dashing Emma's hopes they might postpone this specific conversation. When Zachary cocked a brow, Emma shrugged. "You may as well tell her now."

"Widow Ellis has decided to leave my employ to seek a position elsewhere," he announced quietly.

Mother Garrett sniffed. "She probably didn't have the decency to give proper notice, either, did she?"

He smiled. "No, I'm afraid she didn't."

"I can't imagine who would hire that woman. She didn't say?"

"No," he replied. "Actually, she didn't speak to me directly. She just left a note stating she'd left Candlewood to find a position."

Mother Garrett furrowed her brow for a moment and let out a deep breath. "Poor woman. I suppose she knew she had few enough days left before she had no place with you. Naturally, I'll expect you'll be coming here for your meals. I won't hear otherwise," she told him and leaned closer to Emma. "You really ought to think about getting married soon so that man wouldn't have to trudge up and down the hill three times a day just to eat. I don't even want to think about how dirty his house is going to get."

"We're discussing the idea," Emma whispered as she caught the twinkle in Zachary's eyes.

"Cookies! Cookies! Cookies!"

Clapping his hands, Teddy started a chant the other children quickly mimicked when Anna carried in two trays of cookies and set them on the table.

Benjamin grinned. "It looks like Grams has won over another generation."

Mother Garrett beamed, got up, and started doling out the cookies to her great-grandchildren. She traded a kiss for each cookie from them while Liesel and Ditty set out warm apple pie for the adults.

While they all quieted down during dessert, Emma stole another opportunity to study the family gathered around her table. Most everyone, including Wryn, seemed to be relaxed and enjoying themselves, except for Warren and his wife. The slight tension Emma had noted in Warren earlier at the landing and later, when she had told him about marrying Zachary, was still there. Anna was notably more distant with her husband than her other two daughters-in-law were with Mark and Benjamin.

Dismissing what she observed as nothing more than fatigue from the rigors of their travel, if not their different temperaments, Emma hoped a good night's sleep would restore their spirits.

———

Later that day, Emma captured another dream.

Beneath a night sky boasting a grand display of stars that surrounded a glorious moon, Emma was sitting on a quilt with all seven of her grandchildren in front of the fire burning in the outdoor fireplace on the patio.

She had them all to herself.

The youngest ones were within arm's reach. Paul and Jonas snuggled at her thighs on either side of her. Winnie and Grace claimed her lap, albeit a bit reluctantly at first. Sally, Teddy, and Deborah sat at her feet, and they were all listening to stories about their daddies when they had been little boys growing up in Candlewood.

When yawns started passing from one child to another, Emma pressed a kiss to Winnie's head. "Time for bed, little ones. We'll have more stories another night."

"Can I have my dollies to take to bed with me now?" Deborah asked.

"I'm certain your mama unpacked your dolly for you by now," Emma replied for the third time since they had all sat down on the quilt. She shifted Winnie and Grace from her lap to stand up.

Little Deborah pouted. "But I want all my dollies. Papa said I could have my dollies when we lived with you."

"Maybe they'll be on the packet boat tomorrow," Emma said, repeating the same answers she had given Deborah earlier, although she could not fathom why the five-year-old could not have managed a brief vacation from her collection in the first place.

When Winnie dashed toward the fireplace, Emma swept her up to her hip and blocked the others. "I think Big Grams has some milk and pretzels waiting for you in the kitchen."

"Me first!" Teddy cried. When he turned and started running back to the house, the rest of the children followed him.

Emma protected the rear, although she did not have to worry. The promise of more treats from Mother Garrett had all of these little innocents headed straight away from the fire.

Fortunately, Anna, Catherine, and Betsy were waiting in the dining room, as they had promised to do, and they quickly ushered the children to the kitchen after Emma got a kiss from each and every one of her precious grandchildren and said good-night to everyone.

Yawning, Emma arched her back and stretched her legs to get out a few kinks. Exhausted, but joyfully so after such an eventful day, she was anxious to slip upstairs to her bed, figuring she just might manage to do so before her grandchildren were tucked into their own.

She left the dining room and went straight to the center staircase where she found Warren standing with one arm resting on the banister post. She could hear his brothers laughing in one of the front parlors.

"The children are all in the kitchen now, so if you're standing guard to make sure none of them escaped, you can relinquish your duty," she teased.

He did not crack a smile. "I was waiting for you."

"Is anything wrong?" she asked, concerned by his troubled look.

He glanced up and down the hallway. "I wonder if we could speak somewhere more private."

Emma sighed. "We could use my office, but I'm awfully tired. Unless it's something urgent—"

"It's urgent," he said. "Since you apparently invited us all home on the false pretext of celebrating your birthday when you had every intention of announcing you were getting married instead, I believe it's quite urgent. I need to talk to you before you marry that man."

22

WITH HER EMOTIONS SHIFTING from deep concern to heartbreaking disappointment, if not every emotion in between, Emma took a seat behind her office desk, deliberately putting a bit of distance between herself and her eldest son.

In turn, Warren eased into a chair facing her desk, but sat on the edge of his seat. His back was rigid and straight, his gaze dark and troubled.

Out of the corner of her eye, she caught sight of the sampler that hung on the wall. *Honor Thy Father and Thy Mother* were words she prayed Warren would find as meaningful as she had when she had stitched them so long ago.

When Warren did not initiate the conversation, she took the lead. Worried that she did not have the same support for her plans to remarry from Warren that she had received from her other sons, she hoped to clarify the point that the decision to remarry or not was a decision she alone would make. "Do you find the prospect that I'm planning to marry again objectionable, or is it more specifically that I've decided to marry Mr. Breckenwith?" she asked, certain it was the former, since the two men had been strangers until she had introduced them.

Warren hesitated for a moment. "I've only met the man today, but it's clear he's quite different from Father."

Her heart trembled. "Yes, he is, but that doesn't mean I love your father less. I'll always love your father. Always. And I'm never going to forget him, Warren. How could I, when I have three wonderful sons who are just like him in so many ways?" she offered gently. "It's been eight years since your father passed to Glory, and I've discovered that I have room in my heart and in my life for another. Would you deny me the affection and companionship that a spouse can give me?"

"Perhaps not, but since he's a lawyer, I suspect he'll have a good bit more influence with you than my father ever did."

She set aside her son's opinion of Zachary, as well as his father, for the moment in an effort to get at the root of her son's distress. "When Mr. Breckenwith is my husband, we'll make decisions together that affect both our lives, just as your father and I always did."

"That was clearly not the case when you were married to my father," he argued.

"Warren!" She clapped her hand to her heart, shocked that he would dare judge her relationship with Jonas, let alone disparage their relationship to her face.

"Well, it's true enough. As I remember it, you made all the decisions in the family, and he simply agreed with you. Not that I fault him for it. He had nothing but his own hard labor to bargain with. You held the purse strings tight, just as you do now."

Her heart slammed against the wall of her chest, and she had to struggle to keep drawing one good breath at a time. "How your father and I . . . No. I am not going to explain matters that are beyond any concern of yours. It's clear to me now that the only concern you do have is about my fortune, or more precisely, how my marriage to Mr. Breckenwith will affect my fortune and, in turn, your inheritance."

Apparently unfazed by her unusually harsh condemnation, Warren glowered. "I'm the eldest son. I have every right to be concerned, even if Benjamin and Mark don't have the sense to realize what your marriage will mean to us. I can only hope you've taken legal steps to protect your fortune from Mr. Breckenwith the same way you did with my father when he was alive and the same way you continue to withhold any portion of it from your sons."

Raw anger sliced through her efforts to remain calm, if not reasonable. "When each of you reached your majority, you all received an identical and quite substantial sum to start a business of your own choosing. Beyond that—"

"Beyond that, we've received nothing. Mark is barely scratching a living from his bookstore. Benjamin has to toil day after day just to survive in that blasted wilderness he calls home and—"

"Your brothers are happy, contented men who have never, ever come to me to ask for more," she argued, a bit more evenly now that she had refused to let anger control her thoughts or her words. "Our conversation shouldn't be about Mark or Benjamin. We should be talking about you. You have a loving wife and two healthy and beautiful little girls. Of all my sons, you've been the most successful in business. You have a new home you built only last year. What more could you possibly want that I could give you, except more of what you already have? What drives you to want so much more? Is it status? Or greed? Please tell me, Warren."

He looked away for a moment. When he met her gaze again, his expression was hard. "I want what is rightfully mine. I want what you would have given me outright if I had been your daughter instead of a son. I want the respect you never gave to my father. I want—"

"This conversation is over," Emma announced, blinking back

tears as she got to her feet. She held on to the edge of her desk for support. "I'm sorry, but I cannot and I will not sit here and have you say one more cruel and hurtful word. I raised you better. Your father raised you better, and until you remember yourself and your place, I don't think I can continue this conversation," she whispered and turned to leave.

"I'm bankrupt. I've lost my business and I've lost my house."

She swirled about and stared at her son through a haze of disbelief that blurred her vision for a moment.

"Other than the clothes we were wearing when we arrived today, all I can claim to own is packed in the trunks we brought with us. I sold the rest to buy passage here, including my little Deborah's collection of dolls. Unless you help me now, I'm afraid we've nowhere else to go," he snapped.

With his chest rising and falling rapidly and his cheeks mottled red, he threw up his hands. "There. Apparently all I had to do was humble myself and beg sufficiently to get you to listen to me."

Stunned, Emma stared closely at her firstborn child to see that it was shame that colored his cheeks and shadowed his gaze. She also understood that fear was the root of his anger and resentment. Compassion for him soothed away his spiteful words to her earlier. Empathy sent her around her desk to sit beside him.

"I'm so sorry. I . . . I didn't know. Why didn't you write to tell me you were having financial problems?"

He slumped his shoulders and looked down. "I thought . . . I thought I could pull myself out of the mess I'd made of things, but the lawyers . . . those infernal lawyers . . ." He let out a heavy sigh. "I worked so hard and so long to prove myself. For nothing. So here I sit, a man as incompetent in business as his own father, with as little to my name as he ever had. At least he had a roof over his head, which is more than I can possibly expect for myself or my family now that you're about to remarry."

Confused and hurt by her son's perceptions of the life she had shared with Jonas or the place he had in her life now, she shook her head. "I had no idea you were so bitter or that you thought so little of the life your father shared with me, but I am equally distressed that you think I would not make a place for you here because I was planning to marry again."

"Mr. Breckenwith may have his own thoughts about having your grown son and his family living with you," he replied.

Emma set aside that argument, despite the fact that she knew Zachary would have very real objections to the idea. Determined to get to the heart of Warren's expectations, she pressed him to tell her more. "When you came back to Candlewood, what is it you wanted me to do for you exactly, other than give you and your family a place to live temporarily?"

He looked at her, his expression earnest. "I need a stake to start a new business. I know I've made mistakes in business before, but I know better now than to take capital that should have been put back into the business to build a new house. I know how to avoid making those same mistakes. Unfortunately, before and after I declared bankruptcy, that wasn't an argument that was convincing enough for any of the banks to grant me a loan."

She cocked a brow. "The money to build your house came directly from your business account?"

"I didn't want Deborah and Grace growing up over the dry goods store like I did," he explained. "I wanted more for them. At the time, business was good, so I took a chance and lost. We could have had more. Me and Benjamin and Mark," he murmured.

Her heart skipped a beat. "I thought we had what truly mattered. We had each other."

"And patrons arriving, day in and day out, interrupting our meals and putting purchases on accounts they never paid—"

"And yet you chose to start nearly the same kind of business I had here. I don't understand why. If you were so unhappy growing up living over the General Store, why didn't you start a completely different business?"

"It was all I knew," Warren whispered and looked away.

She swallowed hard. "You were the one who insisted you wanted to leave when you could have stayed here in Candlewood. You could have taken over the General Store someday."

"And be a lackey like my father until the day you decided you would turn the business over to me?" he asked and turned to her again. "I'm sorry. It's how I felt then."

"And now," she murmured, her spirit reeling as she juxtaposed her perceptions of her life with those of her son's.

"And now . . . now I knew I had little choice but to return to Candlewood, admit that I failed, and ask for your help. I couldn't see what difference it would make if you gave me money now, since I would only be taking what I'd inherit eventually. But the minute you told me you were going to get married . . ."

"You assumed I would be less inclined to give you the money," she prompted.

"Or a place to live."

"In part because Mr. Breckenwith is a lawyer?" she asked.

"In part. I haven't had a very positive experience with lawyers recently."

She let out a sigh and tried to keep her tattered heart in one piece. "I won't pretend that learning about your financial difficulties won't have an impact on how soon I get married, because it does. I also won't be able to promise that I won't discuss the matter with Mr. Breckenwith, because I will. For two reasons. First, he's going to be my husband, and I know his heart. Second, he's been my lawyer for five years now, and I know his judgment to be as sound as it is fair. For now, I can only hope to reassure you that I'll help you in some way. I don't know how yet, but I will," she promised. "Did Anna know you were going to speak to me tonight?"

He shook his head. "She wanted me to wait a few days, but I was worried. The closer it gets to your birthday, the busier you'll be. I was afraid you wouldn't have the time before then and afterwards, it would be too late."

"It's obvious we have much to talk about and to settle between us while you're here, but let me tell you this right now: Your assumption that I invited you all home on false pretenses is wrong. I only accepted Mr. Breckenwith's proposal very recently, and while we're discussing the possibility of getting married while all my sons are home, that's all it is. A possibility," she murmured and got to her feet. "I . . . I think we've both said enough for one night."

Warren stood up, as well, but he said nothing as she walked to the staircase that led up to her room. She was halfway up the steps when she heard the whisper of his voice.

"I'm sorry, Mother."

She gulped down the lump in her throat. "Me too."

———————

Still fully dressed, Emma slipped under the quilt on her bed and curled into a ball. With one hand, she clutched at the delicate embroidery Aunt Frances had stitched on the hem of her sheet that created the outline of the General Store where she had loved her sweet Jonas and raised their boys, as if trying to hold on to the memories Warren had shattered. With the other hand, she held her keepsakes close to her broken heart.

And she cried.

23

MERE HOURS AFTER HER TALK with Warren, the early morning sky was but a haze of gray that mirrored Emma's spirit.

As the earth quietly strained to escape the darkness of yesterday, Emma sat on the ground in the secluded cemetery behind the church. Leaning her side against her husband's marker, she struggled to escape a numbing sadness that left her weak and confused.

Driven here after a long and difficult night, she had spent her tears and instead offered her prayers. A heavy cape kept her warm from the chill and dampness in the air, but it was her faith and faith alone that kept her broken heart beating steadily.

She stared at her keepsakes, which were now resting on the earth at the base of the heavy tombstone, and caught her lower lip. She had always treasured the memories attached to each tiny piece of cloth. Some, like the piece cut from the work apron Jonas had worn in the General Store, were more threadbare than the rest. Others were new, like the pieces Catherine had cut from the babies' blankets.

All the keepsakes, however, were held together as much by memories as by the threads she had stitched. Warren's bitterness had sliced clear through those memories as cleanly as if he had taken a pair of sewing shears and cut through the cloth itself.

She was still undecided what to do with her keepsakes. The greater part of her wanted to simply bury them here with her past, along with Warren's hurtful accusations and her fears that he might be right: Perhaps she was not the wife her beloved Jonas had so well deserved.

The rest of her wanted to hold on to the keepsakes as reminders that her perceptions of the past her eldest son had questioned were still valid and true.

She traced her late husband's name etched in the granite marker with her fingertips. "Was our marriage as full of disappointment for you as Warren believes? Did I fail you?" she whispered as her mind replayed their lives together.

When no answer whispered back to her heart, she bowed her head. "I did love you. I love you still. If I failed you, please forgive me."

The snap of a twig close by sent her heart galloping, and she flinched. When she looked up, she saw the shadow of an approaching figure that was familiar enough to douse her fears, yet inspired guilt that lifted her to her feet. "Be careful not to trip. Some of the headstones are so low that—"

"I've walked this path too often not to know my way," Mother Garrett replied and stopped at the foot of her son's gravesite. "I was worried about you."

"I'm sorry. I didn't mean to cause you any worry. I left a note on the kitchen table to tell you I'd gone for a walk. Didn't you see it?"

"Yes, I saw it, then I tore it up. I had a good notion I'd find you here."

"How would you know that?" Emma asked. "I wasn't even certain myself I was coming here when I left the house."

"Because I know you, Emma. Better than you know yourself," Mother Garrett countered. "When I heard you crying last night, I went downstairs to fix a cup of tea for you hoping that might help. Warren was just coming up the steps as I was going down."

Emma swallowed hard. "You talked to him?"

"For a good hour or so, over a pot of tea. By the time I got back upstairs with a cup for you, you were asleep. I figured you needed your rest after what he'd put you through. The minute I spied your note this morning, I headed straight out. I knew you'd end up here sooner or later."

Emma rested her hand atop the cold stone. "What did Warren say?"

"He wasn't too forthcoming at first, but I got him to tell me everything, at least his side of the conversation he had with you. I'm disappointed with him, but I can't say I was overly surprised he had behaved so badly with you. I could see he was in a bit of a snit the first moment I laid eyes on him yesterday."

When fresh tears welled, Emma blinked them back, surprised she had any tears left. "He's so very angry with me."

"He's angry at himself, not you."

"He doesn't see it that way," Emma murmured, still reeling with the memory of her son's verbal attack.

Her mother-in-law sniffed. "He does now that I've had a chat with him, but to be fair, he always did listen to me as a boy."

"That's true, but he's not a little boy anymore," Emma said.

"No. He's a thirty-year-old man with family responsibilities, no business, no position, no home, and scarcely a coin to put into his pocket. As far as the world is concerned and as far as Warren can see, he's a failure."

"He's not a failure!" Emma argued instinctively. "I know he made mistakes. Serious mistakes. But it was his business that failed, not—"

"Put yourself in his place," Mother Garrett said. "He's embarrassed. He's ashamed. He comes home for a family reunion, not as the successful man he's become, but a ruined one. He knows he has to face you, but he also has to face his younger brothers and admit he's lost everything. He's praying he can wait until after the celebration of your birthday to tell you his news, only to find that you're about to begin a new life with a new husband. He's gripped with the fear there's no room in your life for him now, and he lets his fear override his common sense. He attacks the one person in his life he could always rely on—his mother—because deep in his heart he knows she's the only one who might ever forgive him."

Emma's heart thudded in her chest.

"He wants to talk to you, Emma. That's why I'm here. He wants to apologize, but I couldn't convince him that you'd want to see him or hear much of anything he had to say."

Emma looked down at her late husband's marker. "I loved Jonas with all my heart. Did he ever come to you for advice because . . . because he was unhappy as my . . . my husband?"

"Never," Mother Garrett replied. "Despite whatever little squabbles the two of you had now and again like most married folks do, he loved you. And I know he loved you because I could see it in his eyes every time he looked at you or those three boys you had together. As short as his life was, I know Jonas was happy with the life he shared with you until the day he died. Don't let Warren's anger fill your head with doubts about that or anything else."

Emma pressed her lips together until she could trust her voice not to break. "I'm afraid it's too late. I keep hearing the echo of

288787877

Warren's accusations that I didn't treat Jonas as my equal, that I treated him as a . . . a lackey."

Mother Garrett walked along the side of her son's gravesite to stand directly across from Emma. "There is a thread of truth in what Warren said, but only a thread. You and Jonas were well matched, Emma, but my Jonas wasn't your equal."

"Mother Garrett!"

"Well, he wasn't. He didn't have your drive or your business sense. In many ways, I believe he relied on you because you had the very strengths he didn't have, but he also gave you his total devotion and support. In return, you gave him the respect and love he deserved as your spouse and the father of your children. That's just how your marriage worked."

Emma's heart swelled, even though she could admit to herself that she did not always succeed in her marriage as well as her mother-in-law implied.

"Not all marriages are like the one you shared with my son. I dare to think most of them aren't, but there isn't a single mold that guarantees success. In some, spouses combine the strengths they have in common to forge a good marriage together, like I suspect you and Mr. Breckenwith will do."

Tempted to share her misgivings about marrying Zachary, Emma held her thoughts to herself. Handling one problem at a time was about all she could muster up the strength to do at the moment.

"No one has the right to say which type of marriage works best because it all depends on the two people who pledge their vows to one another. No one," Mother Garrett continued. "Which is what I told Warren, by the way. Will you talk with him?"

"Yes," Emma murmured, fearful that this conversation with

her son would probably be as difficult as their first. "Of course I will."

Mother Garrett slapped her thigh. "Good. I smell rain coming, so pick up those precious keepsakes of yours and stuff them back into your pocket where they belong and help me get back to the house before we both get soaked. I have a few words to say to that young lady before she leaves to work at the Glenns'."

Emma brushed off her keepsakes and held them in her hand while she walked around to join arms with her mother-in-law. Although she had missed having Reverend Glenn at Hill House, she realized she had grown even closer to Mother Garrett since he had married Aunt Frances and moved into town. "She has a name. You could call her Wryn, you know."

"I could, but I'm holding off," Mother Garrett insisted as they crossed the cemetery and headed for home.

"Why?"

"Because I still don't trust her, and I'm not going to trust her until . . . until Sunday night. By then I'll know if she's being good to Frances and Reverend Glenn, and I'll also see how she leaves my kitchen."

Emma chuckled. "What about breakfast this morning? Will you have time to get that ready for everyone and still have time to talk to her?"

"I left Ditty to help Liesel, which could make a person wonder if I have half a brain left, but Anna was up early, so I put her in charge while I was gone," she replied and patted Emma's arm. "Anna's feeling a bit awkward about what happened between you and Warren, so you might want to talk with her, too."

"You've been awfully busy keeping peace in this family of ours," Emma noted. "I don't suppose you've had the time to give any thought to how I might help Warren, have you?"

Mother Garrett stopped, looked up at the threatening skies, and frowned. "Since you asked, I do have an idea or two, but I'll have to tell you later. We need to get climbing up that hill just ahead before it starts to pour, and I'm going to need every bit of breath in me to get to the top. Just let me ask you to do one thing before we start."

Emma cocked a brow.

"When we get home, get straight up to your room, climb into bed, and stay there. I'll take the little ones out to collect eggs today and send Anna up with a good cold cloth you can lay across those puffy, red eyes of yours. That way, you'll have a moment to talk with her, too."

24

With neither Zachary nor Warren making an appearance at the dining room table, which surprised everyone, breakfast that same morning was the usual mix of hearty food, loud chatter, and good humor, despite the steady rain that spoiled any outdoor plans for the day.

Emotionally drained, Emma did not object when Anna offered to take charge of organizing the day's housework after the table had been cleared and Emma's two younger sons had decided to brave the elements to go into town to order what they needed for the new pen for the goats.

"You play with your grandchildren. Catherine and Betsy and I will take care of everything else today."

When Emma smiled, Betsy laughed. "Don't look so pleased. You have all seven of them to keep happy and there's no patio and no grassy yard for them to run off their energy."

"I have a few rainy-day memories that might help. Just watch the children for me for a few minutes. I need to make a quick change and get a few blankets from the garret," she said.

Fifteen minutes later, she was back in the dining room wearing a pair of men's trousers a previous guest had left behind and carrying eight blankets she had taken out of storage. "What happened to the little ones?" she asked.

Betsy took some of the blankets from Emma. "Jonas and Paul are a bit grumpy. Catherine thinks they're each cutting a tooth, so she took them out to the kitchen with her to keep them from ruining your fun. She took Winnie and Grace with her, too. We thought you might have more fun with the older children that way."

With Teddy and Sally staring wide-eyed at their grandmother's costume, Deborah merely frowned. "Ladies wear dresses. Why are you wearing trousers?"

"I can't very well crawl around in my skirts," Emma replied.

"How come you're gonna crawl?" Deborah asked.

"Watch. You'll see." With Betsy's help, she opened the blankets and draped them across the table so they fell to the floor, transforming the table into a tent.

"If we hear you crying out for help, don't worry. We'll rescue you," Betsy teased as she left.

"Our tent is ready now," Emma announced, and then she got down on all fours and lifted the corner of one of the blankets. "Let's get inside," she suggested, crawling beneath the table and turning around again to hold up the blanket for her three eldest grandchildren.

Sally lifted her skirts and crawled in right before her brother scooted in behind her. Instead of crawling underneath the table, Deborah scrunched down and held herself low by clutching her knees and worked her way inside.

To keep enough light inside the makeshift tent for everyone to be able to see, Emma rolled up the end of the blanket she had been holding and rested it on the top of one of the chairs. "There.

We've just enough light so you won't be afraid," she announced and sat cross-legged with the children.

"Make it darker," Teddy insisted.

Sally yanked the edge of the blanket off the chair. "That's better. Now no one can see us."

"Nobody can hear us, either, if we don't talk too loud. We're inbibbibble," Teddy stated.

Emma caught a chuckle. "I think you mean we're invisible," she corrected gently.

"But I can't see," Deborah whispered.

Emma reached out to take Deborah's hand. "I'm right here, and there are little cracks of light coming between some of the blankets. Your eyes will adjust in a moment, all right?"

Deborah squeezed her hand. "All right."

"Now what do we do?" Teddy asked.

"Tell us more stories, Little Grams," Sally whispered.

Emma smiled to herself as her own eyes adjusted to the dim light. Although she could distinguish between each of her grandchildren, the expressions on their faces were shadowed in the dim light. "I think it's your turn to tell stories to me. You go first, Teddy."

"I don't have any stories."

"I do," Sally whispered. "One day, my mama wanted to make jam, and me and Teddy helped her pick berries, but Teddy . . . he dropped a pail and all the berries fell into the dirt and ruined 'em. Mama made him pick 'em up to feed to the pigs, but he ate 'em instead."

"You ate some, too," Teddy argued. "I got a story now. Sally tried to climbed a tree once and Papa had to get her down 'cause she got scared. That's 'cause she's a girl."

Emma chuckled, in spite of herself. "Do you have a story for us, Deborah?"

"Sh-h-h. I hear someone coming," Teddy whispered, and everyone held silent until the footsteps that entered the dining room faded in the direction of the center hallway.

"I'm too sad to tell a story," Deborah whispered.

"Why are you sad?" Sally asked.

"I don't have my dollies."

"Dollies aren't any fun anyway," Teddy announced.

"Where'd they go?" Sally asked.

"I don't know. I think they got lost. Papa said they'd come back someday when we were living with Little Grams, but . . . but I don't think they know how to get here."

Emma held tight to her little granddaughter's hand and knew Warren must have been desperate if he had been forced to sell his little girl's doll collection. "You still have the dolly you brought with you, don't you?"

"She's lonely. She misses her friends," Deborah replied. "Do you think my dollies are lost, Little Grams?"

Emma struggled hard to find an answer that a five-year-old might accept. She could not give Deborah false hope that she would ever be reunited with her dollies any more than she could admit that they had all been sold. "I think dollies need lots of love," she began. "Sometimes, if dollies do get lost, I think they find their way to little girls who don't have any dollies of their own to love. I'd like to think that's where your dollies are now, wouldn't you?"

"But she loved them a whole bunch, didn't you, Deborah?" Sally asked.

Deborah sniffled. "Lots and lots."

"I know you did, but sometimes, we have to think about other people. We have to share what we love with them, even if that means we must give up something we really, really care about," Emma replied.

Sally let out a long sigh. "I had to share my apple pie once. I think I like apple pie better than molasses cookies, but I had to share mine with Winnie. Then she got sick and heaved it up and made an awful mess. I don't think I have to share it with her again."

"I shared my worms with Billy when we went fishin' once. He caught two fish, but he didn't share none of them with me," Teddy said. "I don't like sharin' much."

Deborah edged closer to Emma. "Do you mean I should share something special, like my dollies?" Deborah asked.

"Yes, like your dollies," Emma whispered, and wondered if she ought to take her own advice where Hill House was concerned. She loved this house. She loved sharing it with her guests and with her family. Now that she had been blessed with the opportunity to marry again and build a new life with Zachary, did she also have the courage to give up something she really cared about by letting someone else discover the love that dwelled here, just as she was asking Deborah to do with her dollies?

Deborah sniffled again. "But I only have one dolly, and she's lonely."

"You can get a new dolly to be her friend. Then she won't be lonely," Sally suggested.

"Yes, you could, and I know you could love a new dolly, too," Emma whispered as her mind wandered from Deborah's needs to her own and back again. "I have an idea. One of these days, we could all go into town together and stop at the store I showed you, Deborah, so you could see if there's a dolly there you could love."

Teddy nudged Emma's knee. "I'd rather stay here and play with the goats."

"Me too," Sally announced.

Emma squeezed Deborah's hand. "Would you like to pick out a new dolly, Deborah?"

"I think so. Can I just look first before I decide?"

"Yes, you can," Emma replied and made up her mind to look more carefully at the home Zachary had offered to her, as well.

"But what if my other dollies come back? Can I still keep my new dolly?"

"Little Grams is nice. She'll let you keep it," Sally offered.

"More footsteps! Sh-h-h!" Teddy urged and scrunched down even lower. Deborah and Sally did the same.

The footsteps sounded as if they were headed for the center hallway, but this time, they stopped halfway through the dining room. Emma caught a glimpse of Mother Garrett's skirts through one of the cracks between the blankets and smiled.

"Big Grams is making pretzels today, and she needs a few children to help her and to taste them when they're done to make sure they're good. I wonder if there are any little children who might want to volunteer."

Three little bodies headed straight toward one of the blankets, which got tugged off the table when they struggled through it.

"I'm a good taster."

"Me too!"

"Me too," Deborah announced before she turned about to peek back at Emma. "Don't worry. I'll share mine with you," she whispered.

"You're a sweet girl. Thank you," Emma murmured.

"I've got another announcement for anyone who might be interested to know there's a very curious gentleman standing right in the doorway, wondering if the woman he wants to marry might be willing to speak with him for a few moments," Mother

Garrett crooned, surrounded by three children anxious to get to the kitchen.

Emma cringed. "Why is he right there? Couldn't you show him to the parlor or . . . or my office?" she whispered, knowing full well she could not escape without having him see her crawl out from beneath the table.

Unfortunately, Mother Garrett chose to usher her little charges into the kitchen without answering, and Emma had no trouble envisioning the look of merriment on her face or Zachary's, either, for that matter.

While she tried to decide how to make as graceful an exit as possible from her place under the table, Zachary peeked through the opening where the blanket had been and grinned. "Are you busy, or do you have a moment to talk?"

She rolled her eyes. "I can talk, but if you would be so kind as to wait for me in the parlor, I'll join you there as soon as I can get more suitably dressed."

Like Mother Garrett, he ignored her request. Instead, he carefully put the blanket back into place before he crawled under the table to sit in front of her. "I haven't been in a tent like this for more than forty years. If I'd known you were having this much fun today, I would have been here sooner."

"You completely missed breakfast," Emma noted, hoping to change the subject.

"Unfortunately, I overslept. Just one of the hazards of living without a housekeeper who used to rise at the crack of dawn and make enough noise to make sure I was up at a decent hour. Those are her words, not mine," he added in a husky voice. "Are those men's trousers you're wearing?"

She rolled her eyes. "I can't crawl about with my grandchildren if I'm wearing skirts, especially in the dark. Now if you wouldn't mind, I think it would be much more appropriate to continue our conversation in the parlor."

"I think I rather like sitting here in the dark with you. We actually have a bit of privacy here, which has been hard to come by lately," he said and cupped her face.

With her heart racing, Emma blinked hard. "If you think for one moment, Zachary Breckenwith, that I'm going to let you kiss me for the first time when we're sitting under a tent of blankets with my grandchildren in the next room and my family running back and forth, I'm . . . I'm . . ."

He kissed her once. Very gently. Very lovingly. Very . . . convincingly.

She sighed, let go of every doubt she had about marrying this man, and kissed him back.

"You were saying?"

"I don't believe I was saying anything," she whispered and made a mental note to cut a bit of cloth from the trousers she was wearing to add to her keepsakes.

Then she kissed him again.

25

WHEN WARREN HAD NOT RETURNED to Hill House by mid-morning, Emma decided not to wait for him any longer.

Her youngest grandchildren were napping, the older ones were busy making pretzels with Mother Garrett, and Anna had nearly everyone else taking care of the day's cleaning. With other important matters pressing to be settled, she also decided not to let the weather hold her back from venturing into town.

Emma slipped out onto the front porch with one of Mother Garrett's canvas shopping bags, which held the legal papers Zachary had drafted for her. The rain had stopped, although the skies held the promise of more rain to come. Raindrops glistened on the budding leaves of the hydrangeas that bordered the porch and the front steps, but the heavy rains earlier had left the front yard littered with puddles. Once she had a route planned out to avoid those puddles, she started down the steps only to hear the front door open behind her.

"I told you she hadn't gotten very far. Wait for us," Benjamin said.

She looked back over her shoulder and saw Mark following

on his older brother's heels. "You just got back from town. Where are you two going now?"

Benjamin grinned and took her left arm. "We're going with you. That hill is pretty slick, and I'd rather not think about what would happen if you slipped. At best, you'd end up sliding straight to the bottom."

She smiled but decided not to mention that she had actually sled down this hill last winter in the middle of the night.

"Main Street is nothing but mud, so we thought we'd better go with you to make sure you don't take a spill before you get to the sidewalk," Mark suggested as he took her other arm.

She smiled again and wondered what either of them would say if they knew how many times she had fallen when she had skated down Main Street, too. Emma was not about to tell them their arguments held any merit at all. Not when the memory of slipping in the mud and pulling Zachary down with her was still so fresh in her mind. "I'm wearing good heavy boots. As long as I take my time, I'll be fine," Emma insisted.

Benjamin looked down at her feet. "Grams said those are the same boots you were wearing when you fell in the mud down by the gazebo."

When Emma's eyes widened, he nodded to his brother. "If we both get a good hold of her arms, we can swoop her right past all those puddles and make sure she doesn't fall."

In the next heartbeat, her two sons lifted her right off her feet and did not set her down again until they reached the front gate.

"There. That wasn't so bad, was it?" Benjamin teased as he opened the gate for her. "After you, Mother."

Laughing, Emma assumed there was little Mother Garrett had not told her sons. She led them through the gate, but Mark held on to her while Benjamin secured it again. "Don't you two have something better to do with your time?"

Mark shook his head. "Not when there's a house full of females cleaning anything that's standing still."

"Or when there's a passel of children in the kitchen with dough up to the elbows. Besides, we'd rather be with you." Benjamin flashed her a smile that soothed her tattered heart as much as their concern for her.

Arm in arm, they started down the hill. To her consternation, she slipped twice, but her sons held her fast and she managed to stay on her feet. After the conversation she'd had last night with Warren, Emma now took full advantage of the opportunity to talk to Benjamin and Mark. "Now that you've been back in Candlewood for a bit, do you find yourself thinking about your father or how it was to grow up here?"

Mark nodded. "When I was in the General Store with you that first time, I almost expected to see him come through the curtain behind the counter wearing that old apron of his. He always kept a few pebbles in his pocket, remember, Ben?"

"He did?" Emma asked. "I don't recall that."

Benjamin cringed and patted the top of his head. "I do. He used one now and then when he caught me outside when I was supposed to be helping him inside the store."

"Or when he caught me in the back storeroom reading a book instead of unloading boxes," Mark admitted.

Emma gasped. "He threw a pebble at you?"

Benjamin chuckled. "Not at us. He'd just toss one close by to get our attention. Now that I think back, I'm sure he missed hitting us on purpose, but once in a while, his aim must have been off and we'd get popped on the head. That stung!"

"I'm not sure who felt worse," Mark added, tightening his hold on Emma's arm as she walked down the steepest part of the hill.

Benjamin shook his head. "He never raised his voice to us. Not that I recall."

"He didn't have to raise his voice. He'd just look at us with those big eyes of his and let us know we'd disappointed him."

"Or he'd toss a pebble or two in our direction," Benjamin added.

Emma let out a sigh. "I do remember how soft-spoken he was, but I never ever knew about the pebbles. Do you . . . do you think your father was happy with the life he led?"

"Why?" Benjamin asked. "Don't you think he was happy?"

"Yes, I do, but sometimes, one person has a different perspective or different memories, like the pebbles I never knew about, but . . ."

"Warren said something to upset you, didn't he? That's why he didn't come to breakfast." Benjamin caught his brother's eye. "I told you he'd said something to Mother," he grumbled. "I know Warren's my brother, but he can be a pompous idiot at times. Don't pay any mind to anything he says."

"Benjamin!"

"He's right, Mother. Warren's my brother and I love him, but that doesn't give him the right to say anything to upset you."

"He has a right to his own memories," Emma said.

Benjamin stopped, forcing Emma and Mark to stop, as well. "You're right. We all have our own memories of Father and of growing up here, but Warren is as blind as he is arrogant if he doesn't remember that Father was a plain God-fearing man of principle who loved his life and loved his sons. There hasn't been a day since I left Candlewood that I don't try to be the man and the husband and the father he was. Not a day."

"He's right, Mother, and I think Warren knows that, too," Mark said.

Emma blinked back tears and hugged her sons' arms closer to her. "Your father would be as proud of you as I am, if he were here."

"I'll talk to Warren," Mark offered.

"No, I . . . I need to do that. Please don't say anything to him. He has . . . he has a lot on his mind right now."

"Must be money. He never did think about much of anything else," Benjamin quipped, looking up at the dark clouds overhead. "But I won't say anything to him. Not unless you ask me," he added and grinned at her. "Now let's talk about something else. Are you going to marry that lawyer of yours while we're all here or not?"

The memory of the kisses she had shared with Zachary made her lips tingle, and she felt her cheeks warm. "Why? Do you think I should?"

"Yes," Mark said firmly.

Benjamin grinned. "I agree, and Warren doesn't have a vote. He's not here, not that it matters much. He'd be outvoted anyway, four to one."

"*Four* to one?" Emma asked.

"Grams gets two votes, and she already voted yes, so why don't you stop at Mr. Breckenwith's and set a date?" Benjamin suggested as they reached the bottom of the hill and turned down Main Street.

Emma gasped. "You two talked to her and took a vote about when I should get married?"

Mark tightened his hold on her arm. "Watch where you walk. The mud's pretty thick along here. Grams thinks you should get married on your birthday. That way we'd have two celebrations instead of one."

"On my birthday? That's less than a week away! There are so many things that need to be settled. I couldn't possibly get everything done by then," Emma argued, feeling pressured to make a decision that was far more complicated than anyone in her family seemed to realize.

"Do you love him?" Mark asked.

"Yes, I . . . I do," she replied, realizing she had never told Zachary she loved him.

Benjamin grinned. "Then what are you waiting for? Go ahead and marry him. There's nothing more important that needs to be settled than that."

Emma swallowed hard, wondering if Benjamin was far wiser than she was.

Emma waited until Benjamin and Mark were a good two houses away before she knocked on Zachary's door. They had promised to wait for her at the Glenns' cottage, which fit well into Emma's plans, since she had wanted to stop and check up on Wryn on her first day doing chores there.

Zachary answered the door when she knocked a second time. "You're a day early. I thought you said you were going to stop to see the house tomorrow."

"If it's an inconvenient time now, I can do that, but since the rain stopped, at least for the moment, I thought I'd come into town."

"I'm expecting a client, but he shouldn't be here for half an hour or so," he said and ushered her into the foyer. "You've been in my office many times, so I doubt you'd need to see that again."

Recalling the office that ran along the side of the house from front to back, littered with piles of legal papers, journals, and correspondence, she shuddered. "I assume it's still as cluttered as ever?"

He grinned. "I work best that way."

"I prefer my clutter out of view," she countered with a grin of her own.

"Should we start with the kitchen, then?"

She wrinkled her nose. "I shouldn't think the state of the kitchen would matter much to anyone other than Mother Garrett, and she would insist on seeing it for herself, anyway. I think I'd rather see the parlor or any of the other rooms on the first floor."

He led her down the hall past the office and a side staircase to a small parlor. "I don't use this room very much, but I should think that would change if we decided to live here—although it's not as grand as either of the two parlors at Hill House."

Emma looked around the room, which held a small settee covered in pale gold fabric. Two chairs upholstered in a bright brocade sat grouped together in front of a small fireplace. Gentle light filtered through lace curtains on two large windows, giving the room a warm, homey glow.

"It's certainly a bit smaller than you're used to at Hill House. I never did replace any of my aunt's furniture, but we could do that, if you like."

"It's charming as it is, although I think a fresh coat might be in order for the walls," Emma suggested as she followed him into the dining room. To her surprise, the room itself was empty, save for a number of boxes lined up against the far wall.

"Aunt Elizabeth took the dining room furniture with her when she moved to Bounty. After she passed away, I didn't bother to bring it back," he explained a bit sheepishly.

"Then I would assume you take your meals in the kitchen," Emma offered with a grin. "Perhaps I should see that after all."

"Right through here," he said and led her through a door into a room that took her breath away. As charming as the parlor had been, the kitchen was even more delightful. A bank of windows ran the entire length of the back wall and provided a view of a large, fenced garden that held every bit as much promise as the terraced gardens at Hill House. Unfortunately, the entire garden was overgrown with weeds, some as high as her waist, but she had no trouble envisioning a colorful garden there.

A large round table that took up a good part of the room could easily seat twelve and had a revolving center section to make serving dishes easily accessible to everyone seated. The cookstove and fireplace, along with other cupboards and counters, looked fairly new, but Mother Garrett would know better about whether or not she would want them replaced.

"It's lovely," Emma offered as her resolve to remain at Hill House began to soften.

He raised a brow.

"I didn't say I was anxious to cook in this room. I said it was lovely, which means I think taking meals here would be most pleasant."

"I see," he murmured. "There are several outbuildings farther back on the property. Since they haven't been used for years, I don't think we need to look at them right now. Shall we go upstairs? There's a narrow staircase here," he said, pointing to the wall next to them. "Or we could go back and use the staircase in the hall."

"We can use this one," she suggested. When they reached the top of the stairs, she found herself in a hallway that ran the length of the house. A lush carpet runner beneath her feet softened her footsteps as they walked, and there was not a speck of dust to be seen.

"There are three bedrooms, but the largest is in the front of the house."

She peeked into the two bedrooms as they passed by. She assumed he had been using one of them, judging by the disarray she noted. She dismissed both rooms as far too small for two people to share, but they were a perfect size for Mother Garrett and for Wryn, if she wound up living with them temporarily. The closer she got to the front bedroom, however, the more she realized the impropriety of being here on the second floor, alone, with a man who was not yet her husband.

"This was the room my aunt and uncle used," he said as he opened the door. "Again, it's probably not what you're accustomed to at Hill House, but we can remedy that easily enough, if that's what you want to do."

Reluctant to enter the bedroom, she remained in the hallway and peeked inside. The walls were painted a soft yellow, just like the water pitcher and bowl that had belonged to her mother, which she kept in her bedroom at Hill House. No rug covered the floorboards, but they had been polished to a sheen. A simple handmade quilt covered the four-poster bed, and she could almost see her trunk set in place at the foot of it. On the far wall, two wooden chests of drawers sat side by side, with a small lady's vanity snuggled in between them. On the opposite wall, a washstand held a large pitcher and bowl, as well as a shaving stand and mirror, leaving room for the well-loved walnut wardrobe that had belonged to Emma's grandmother.

"It's beautiful," she whispered, and stepped back to allow him to close the door again. As much as she had hoped to find this house uninviting, if only to make her decision easier, she found herself standing in the kind of home she had always thought was beyond her reach while she had been living with Jonas and the boys over the General Store. A quaint home. A cozy home. Not a grand showcase like Hill House that she shared with strangers, but a home she would share only with her family.

A real home.

She pressed her lips together and held very still. If she truly believed God had led her to Hill House to provide for the many guests who had sought refuge there, could she not also trust He had led her here now, as well?

The answer beat slowly in the depths of her heart and soul, filling her with great peace.

"Now that you've seen the house, what do you think?" he asked, his gaze simmering with hope, as well as affection.

"I think I like this home very much," she replied. When her heart skipped one beat, then another, she knew that if God had led her here to this man and to this home, He would also guide them both as they built their new life together as husband and wife.

His eyes widened. "You do?"

She moistened her lips. "Yes, I do. As a matter of fact, I think I would like to live here and share this home with you."

"You would?"

"Yes, I would."

"May I . . . may I ask why?" He looked as if he could scarcely believe she had already reached the decision he had asked her to make.

"I could tell you that I think the house is wonderful, which it is. Or I could tell you that I think it would be more convenient for you, which it is. But I should tell you what's more important to me."

She paused, captured his gaze with her own, and held it. "I love you, Zachary. I want to share my life with you. Here."

"You do."

"Yes, I do."

"Are you saying you'll marry me on your birthday as I asked?"

"Yes, I am, although there are a number of issues that still need to be settled, so I'd prefer it if we kept that to ourselves for now," she said. "There's also a problem I need to resolve with Warren, but I'd like to discuss that with you later."

"What about Mr. Larimore?"

She smiled. "I have the papers right here. I was hoping to stop at his office this morning. I don't have an appointment to see him, but I'll try."

He smiled and took her into his arms. "What made you suddenly change your mind about selling Hill House?" he asked.

"I talked it over with a few people this morning, but I haven't really thought it all through yet. I'm not even certain if I want to actually sell Hill House or to keep it as an investment and hire someone to run it."

"Who did you talk to? Your mother-in-law or one of your sons?"

She chuckled. "If you must know, it was a few of my grand-children."

He looked down at her and shook his head. "Your grand-children?"

"Yes, but I talked to Mark and Benjamin, too. They reminded me that if you love someone, you should be willing to give up something that's very dear to you, which got me to thinking about us and . . . and Hill House."

"And here I was thinking that I had been the one to convince you, which made me wonder why I didn't kiss you long before this morning if that's all you needed to help you make up your mind."

"Perhaps you did help," she whispered, "but just to be certain, perhaps you should kiss me again."

So he did.

26

A KNOCK AT THE FRONT DOOR quickly ended their kiss.
Zachary let out a sigh. "Since my client apparently decided to arrive early, it appears we don't have any more privacy here than we had at Hill House. Once we're married, I may have to build another tent here for the two of us."

She smiled. "You may have to do just that. In the meantime, it might be wiser if I took the service stairs to the kitchen and waited for you there while you use the main stairs," she suggested, with no desire to invite any more gossip than their betrothal had already ignited.

He waited until she was safely at the bottom of the stairs before leaving to answer the door. Since she had nothing better to do, she took a peek into the larder. Other than a few staples, there was little else inside, which meant Emma had to get Mother Garrett here to make a list of what she would need to establish herself here in her new kitchen.

Now that Emma had a moment to think what getting married on her birthday would mean in a more practical sense, she realized Mother Garrett would not be able to move in here right away.

Until Benjamin and Mark left for their homes with their families, she would need to remain at Hill House.

Emma had not thought far enough ahead to consider where Warren and Anna would live eventually, but she assumed they would remain at Hill House until Warren decided where and how he was going to support his family. Anna was also more than capable in the kitchen, which would free Mother Garrett to move in here with Emma, and Liesel and Ditty would be at Hill House to help her with the housekeeping.

That arrangement, however, would only be possible until Emma either found a buyer or decided to hold on to the property as an investment. In either case, Emma had to trust God would reveal the answer to her in perfect time—His.

Feeling a bit overwhelmed when she thought about all the lives that would be affected when she married Zachary, she walked over to the bank of windows and stared outside. The garden of weeds encircled a small paved sitting area just beyond the back door. An arbor dressed in a vine of some sort allowed access to a side walkway. Since there were no outdoor chairs in place, only a small bench, she assumed they must still be stored away and made a mental note to ask Zachary about that.

When she heard the kitchen door open behind her, she turned about, saw Zachary entering the kitchen, and smiled. "Are you finished already?"

He cleared his throat. "No. That wasn't my client at the door after all."

"Please don't tell me that Benjamin or Mark came to fetch me. I told them to wait for me at the Glenns'."

"No. The caller is Miss Morning Drummond, but she refuses to speak to me without talking to you first. And she isn't alone.

She brought another woman with her—a woman who insists she wants to speak to you and only you," he said, clearly annoyed.

"I can't imagine why Morning even thought I'd be here instead of Hill House, and I have absolutely no idea why she brought someone else to see me."

He narrowed his gaze.

She narrowed her own. "Are they waiting for me in your office?"

"No, I left them standing in the foyer. I'm expecting a client, remember?"

Emma cringed. "Yes, of course. Why don't you have them come back here to the kitchen where we'll all be out of your way? Would you like me to ask Morning to wait until you've finished with your client to speak to you, or should I simply ask her to stop back another time to make an appointment?"

"Have her stop back another time, along with the woman she brought with her. I have other appointments for the rest of my morning," he said firmly and closed the door again, leaving her wondering where the sweet man she had kissed only moments ago had gone.

Emma hung her cape on the back of one of the chairs and laid her bonnet on a counter. She smoothed her hair and stood by the table to wait for Morning and her companion to appear.

After a soft knock, the door opened, but Morning entered the kitchen alone. Her cheeks were flushed with embarrassment, and she kept her back pressed against the door instead of venturing any farther into the kitchen. "I'm sorry. I seem to have annoyed Mr. Breckenwith by coming here. I know you asked me to come to see you at Hill House, but when I caught a glimpse of you turning down Mr. Breckenwith's street, I thought it might be easier for my friend and me to talk to you here, since it's such a long walk up to Hill House. I don't mind so much for myself, but—"

"Mr. Breckenwith isn't annoyed with you," Emma assured her, all too aware he was annoyed with her. "Where's your friend?"

Morning nodded to the windows behind Emma. "Since Mr. Breckenwith is expecting another client, she decided to wait outside in the garden so I could speak to you privately."

Without bothering to turn around to get a glimpse of the woman Morning had brought with her, Emma pursed her lips. "Although I agreed to make an exception and bring your concerns to Mr. Breckenwith's attention, I thought I made it very clear that I wouldn't be able to give you or anyone else legal advice," Emma cautioned.

Morning paled and her eyes filled with tears. "I know you did. Have you had a chance to tell him about my . . . my problem?"

"Come and sit down. You look as though you're about to faint," Emma insisted and led the young woman to one of the chairs at the kitchen table and took a seat alongside of her. "As a matter of fact, I took a trip to Bounty on your behalf and met with Mr. Breckenwith there to tell him of your concerns."

Clasping her hand to her heart, Morning gasped. "You did that? For me?"

"I did," Emma replied, although she realized now she had also ridden to Bounty to satisfy her own curiosity about whether or not she might be able to help this young woman. Without waiting any further, she quickly explained what Zachary had been able to confirm: Morning Drummond was legally free to marry again.

"You'll still need to speak to Mr. Breckenwith, but you'll have to stop back another time to make an appointment," Emma cautioned. "I'll be there with you when you do meet with him, just as I promised."

Morning reached over, took Emma's hand, and squeezed it hard as tears ran down her cheeks. "Thank you. Thank you."

"You're welcome," Emma murmured, unable to recall when she had felt so good about something she had done for someone else.

When Morning's tears were spent, she wiped her cheeks with the back of her hands, got to her feet, and glanced out the windows to the back garden. "I know you said you couldn't help my friend, too, but would I be able to trouble you to make her a cup of tea before we leave? She tends to take a chill fairly easily. I'm not certain she has much in her larder at home, and I don't have kitchen privileges at Mrs. Sweeney's."

Emma rose. The moment she turned, looked out the window, and saw the elderly woman sitting forlornly on the bench in that garden of weeds, her heart skipped a beat. "She must be eighty years old," Emma murmured. She was unable to take her eyes off the woman wearing a threadbare cape and a bonnet limp with age whose eyes were clouded with disillusionment.

"Miss Burns is eighty-six," Morning explained. "She'd been living with her brother and family, but when he passed a few weeks ago—he was only seventy—his widow told Miss Burns she had to leave by the first of next month, even though her brother promised she could stay and supposedly left provisions for his sister in his will. Can she do that? Can she go against the terms of the will and just turn poor Miss Burns out into the street?"

Emma shrugged. "I suppose that depends on what the will actually says," she replied, trying to remember what Zachary had told her last fall about the will Aunt Frances' first husband had drawn up to provide for her. "Please bring Miss Burns inside while I set some water to boil. There's bound to be some tea somewhere in this kitchen," she said, certain she now knew what He intended for her to do once she was living in town.

Amazed by how quickly God was revealing His plans for her, Emma said a silent prayer that He might touch Zachary's heart and convince him to support her efforts just as quickly.

An hour later, Emma watched Morning slip through the garden holding on to Miss Burns with one hand and a basket of foodstuffs Emma had raided from the little she found in Zachary's larder with the other.

Reminded once again how she had been blessed with a loving family and the financial resources to safeguard herself and her loved ones, she washed up the cups and saucers they had used, rinsed out the teapot she had found in the cupboard, and dried everything. She was just storing the dishes away again when Zachary poked his head into the kitchen.

"Are you alone?"

She smiled. "Not anymore, now that you're here. Have you finished meeting with your client?"

"Yes," he said as he walked into the kitchen. "I trust you've set Miss Drummond and her friend straight and that they'll both stop back to make an appointment with me? In the meantime, I have some time before my next appointment. Shall we go to see Reverend Glenn now to ask him if he's available to marry us on your birthday?"

She smiled again. Convinced she knew how she might be His instrument in the days ahead, her goal now was to convince the man she was going to marry to support her efforts to help the women of Candlewood with their legal problems when they were either too embarrassed or too poor to seek out the services of a lawyer.

"I think we might," she ventured. "Along the way, perhaps you could tell me a bit about the laws providing for the protection of widows, particularly when there's a will in place," she suggested as she donned her bonnet. "I'm not certain I remember exactly what you told me last fall when I came to you to discuss Aunt Frances' problem."

He raised one brow. "Are you interested in the laws in general or in particular?"

"Just in general for now," she replied as he helped her with her cape. "I know you have shelves of law books in your office that I could read—assuming I could make my way to them without tripping over a pile of one thing or another—but it would be much quicker if you simply told me what I'd find there."

He let out a long breath. "Based on what you've asked, I assume Morning Drummond is now as interested in what she might have inherited from her late husband as she apparently was to find out her legal status."

"Then you'd be wrong. In point of fact, I'd like to find out some information for Miss Burns, the elderly woman who came with Morning."

"I thought you said she agreed to stop back and make an appointment with me."

"No, you said that," Emma countered. "Miss Burns hasn't a coin to her name. She can't afford to see a lawyer, but if I could help her—"

He stiffened his back. "I thought I made myself clear in Bounty. You can't dispense legal advice. You're not a lawyer and you can't be a lawyer, as fair or as unfair as you find that reality to be."

"That may be true, but I can read, I can think, and I can reason, and above all, I can listen to women who aren't comfortable discussing certain issues with a man or who can't afford to pay for a lawyer," she stated firmly. "Besides, I don't have to worry about actually being a lawyer. Not when I'm going to be married to one.

You know I wouldn't hesitate to turn a legal matter over to you, if that became necessary."

"What you're asking is . . . is out of the question. Allowing you to give anyone legal advice could get me disbarred!"

Emma's temper flared, and it suddenly became clear that she was the only one willing to make concessions when it came to building a life together. She could not imagine ever having this kind of discussion with Jonas, but she couldn't imagine the future she envisioned for herself with Zachary, either. Not unless he could see her side of things.

"No. It isn't out of the question. It's fair and it's right. I highly doubt anyone who comes to speak to me with a legal problem is likely to make a complaint against you, and I don't think it's too much for you to at least consider the opportunities I would have here in town once we were married," she countered.

As Mother Garrett's words at the cemetery echoed in her mind, she stiffened her spine and forged ahead before she lost her nerve. "When you proposed to me, I thought you wanted a woman as strong in her own way as you are, but it's become abundantly clear that's not what you want at all. If you find the prospect too disturbing that your future wife might be able to use her mind and her wits to help other women, then perhaps you've chosen the wrong one. Perhaps you should marry someone more like your first wife, whose entire world revolved around you, because that's apparently what you expect of me. You want me to focus on you and only you, and you haven't shown one whit of concern about what I might want or need in addition to that."

He froze in place. "That's not true. Not at all true."

She blinked back tears of frustration. As different events during their courtship flashed through her mind, she grew more and more convinced she was right. "Yes, it is, and I should have seen the signs of it before now," she said. "You knew exactly how to sway me to your point of view from the start. I won't bother to mention the mare you gave me again. You've already admitted you had ulterior motives in selecting that gift. Then later, although I didn't realize it at the time, I can see now that showing me the extent of your fortune and drafting a will leaving that fortune to my sons, all the while magnanimously protecting the holdings I have, was meant to convince me how foolish I would be to let a man of your means slip away. You also know how much it would mean to me to wear a pin that belonged to your mother as a symbol of our betrothal, so that I would be only too willing to bend to each of your expectations about what I would have to do in order to marry you. I don't need you to rescue me from the life I have. I need you to love me enough to want to share a life just as meaningful with me here. B-but I wonder now if you truly love me and want to marry me at all, and . . . and unless you can reach a more equitable vision of what we will each bring to this marriage, then . . . then I don't think we should marry at all. And this time," she whispered, "whether or not we should marry is entirely up to you."

Drawing a deep breath, she blinked back tears that blurred her vision. "Think hard before you make your decision, but until you do, I have no desire to see you or to step another foot in this house," she said, then grabbed the canvas bag and let herself out the back door to the kitchen.

Heart pounding, she walked slowly through the garden to go home.

To her great sorrow, Zachary did not stop her and simply let her go.

27

STILL TREMBLING FROM HER ARGUMENT with Zachary, Emma never heard the freight wagon approaching from behind as she trudged back to Hill House.

She never heard the driver cry out a warning until it was almost too late.

Startled out of her reverie when she felt a solid nudge at her back, she looked over her shoulder into the eyes of a pair of draft horses, and literally dove out of the way.

Her cape flew open and she landed facedown on top of her canvas bag and nearly sank in a pit of cold, rank mud.

She sputtered and spewed and coughed and gasped as she struggled to crawl out of the pit and get herself into a sitting position. With her heart pounding, she clawed the mud from her face. When she decided she could safely open her eyes, she looked straight into the frightened face of the driver who had leaped down from his wagon to assist her.

"Mother!"

"W-Warren? Is that really you?" she managed, only to end up with more mud in her mouth once she opened her lips.

He grimaced. "Yes, Mother, I'm afraid it is. I'm sorry. I'm so sorry. Tell me what to do. Please tell me what to do to help you."

Emma stared up from the ground at her eldest son. When mud oozed from the brim of her bonnet into her eyes, she slammed them shut again, yanked off her bonnet, and tossed it away. "I don't know what to tell you to do, Warren. I've never been covered with this much mud before. Not in fifty-one years," she gritted behind closed teeth, convinced her day could not possibly get any worse.

"I tried to warn you that you were too far out into the roadway, but there wasn't anything I could do. The brakes barely held in all this mud, and the horses—"

"Don't worry about blame," Emma said, grateful she had her eyes closed so she would not notice if anyone passed by. "There's enough of that to go around. I'm not even certain I care to know why you're driving a wagon down Main Street when I can't recall a single time you've ever driven a wagon in your life."

"I went to see Andy Sherling this morning to see about getting some kind of work. He sent me to Dan Haley, who hired me just for the day to haul some freight out to—"

"I don't care where you were heading or what freight you're carting about. Not unless you've got a barrel of water on board the wagon that you can dump on me before this mud hardens and I end up looking like a cast for a wax figure that's going to be a permanent fixture on the roadway."

"No. There's no water."

Emma groaned and kept her eyes shut tight. "I've got to get this mud off. What about cider or . . . or anything . . . anything wet?" she asked, pausing between words to keep as much mud out of her mouth as she could.

"Wait. There might be something. Don't move."

She scowled at him and tried not to think about the mud stuck to her teeth for fear she might gag.

"Sorry. Poor bit of advice," he said. "I'll be right back."

Beyond being mortified and shivering with cold, she listened to his footsteps fade and then return a few moments later. "Tuck your head down as far as you can and put your hands on top of your head. I'll try not to let—"

"Stop your hemming and hawing. Just pour whatever it is on top of me," she snapped, but did as he had told her to do.

"But, Mother—"

"Warren Baxter Garrett, if you don't do as you're told this very instant, I'm going to . . . I'm going to write you out of my will!"

"If you insist," he said.

She tensed, expecting to get drenched, which she did. But she also got pelted on her head and shoulders, again and again, with something solid. She did not have to open her eyes to know what those somethings were, because the taste of vinegar and spices that seeped through her lips and stung her eyes was too distinctive.

"Pickles!" she exclaimed, swiping her hands across her face. "You dumped a barrel of pickles on top of me?"

"I tried not to let all of them fall on you. Now hold still so I can wipe your face with my handkerchief, or your eyes are going to sting even worse when you try to open them," he insisted.

She dropped her hands to her lap. When she felt a dozen or so pickles lying there, she pursed her lips while he gently mopped her face.

"There. That should do it. You can try opening your eyes now."

Emma fluttered her lashes and opened her eyes and chanced a quick look at herself. Sure enough, she was rinsed free of mud, at least from the waist up, but her ruined costume reeked of pickles.

She was also surrounded by half a barrel of the nasty things. Poor Warren looked so desperately frightened of what he had done, she reacted instinctively, picked up one of the pickles, and tossed it at his feet.

Warren jumped back. "Why did you throw that pickle at me?"

"To get your attention. I would have used a pebble, but I'm afraid I haven't any in my pocket," she murmured, saw her son's gaze soften with his father's memory, and tossed another pickle at him.

"What's that for?"

"That's for driving a wagon when you have no idea what you're doing."

"In the first place, I already said I was sorry. In the second place, I tried to warn you about the pickles, but you didn't want to hear it. At least I got the mud off of you. Well, most of it."

She threw another one at him. "And before you ask, that's for being rude to me and for being disrespectful and always acting like you're being persecuted . . . and for saying those awful, hurtful things to me last night."

He drooped his shoulders. "I'm sorry. Truly I am."

She threw another pickle at him, which landed on his foot. "That's for being afraid to come to me when you needed help and waiting until you were so desperate you nearly ruined our family reunion and my birthday."

"I wasn't afraid," he replied and held up his hands when she picked up another pickle. "Fine. I admit it. I was . . . I was embarrassed by my failure and I feared that after you married again, you wouldn't want to help me or your new husband wouldn't let you."

She cocked a brow and quickly wiped away a bit of pickle juice that threatened to run into her eyes. "And?"

"And . . . and I let my pride get the best of me. I'd already disappointed Anna and my girls. I . . . I didn't want to disappoint you, too."

She set the pickle back down. "It wouldn't be the first time any one of my sons disappointed me, but nothing you could ever do would make me stop loving you. And that goes for your brothers, too. And I would never, ever marry a man I thought wouldn't come to love you. We'll work things out, Warren," she reassured him, hesitated for a single heartbeat, then tossed one last pickle at him.

Startled, he threw up his hands. "Now what? Am I supposed to confess to everything I ever did wrong in my entire life before you'll forgive me?"

She chuckled. "No, I've already forgiven you. I just want you to think twice before you utter a single word of what just happened here to your grams. Now, unless you want to disappoint me again today, you'll help me up out of this mud before anyone comes along and sees me sitting here taking a pickle and mud bath right in the center of Main Street."

He let out a long sigh of relief, smiled, and bent down close to scoop the pickles off her lap. "You know, Father never had to throw more than two pebbles at me."

She kissed his cheek. "Since I intend to keep a few pebbles in my apron pocket while you're all home, I'll keep that in mind for next time."

"Emma! Wh-what are you doing sitting there with all those pickles!" Mother Garrett exclaimed.

"Don't be a goose, Mercy," Aunt Frances said. "You make it sound like Emma decided to sit in the middle of Main Street in the midst of a barrel of spilled pickles. I wonder where the driver got to," she wondered as the two women hurried toward her as fast as their aged legs and the slippery roadway allowed.

"It's too late to worry about Grams," Warren whispered as he helped Emma to her feet.

Weighted down by mud, as well as pickle juice, Emma held on to Warren for support and attempted a smile.

Until she heard yet another voice behind her.

"Is that you, Widow Garrett?"

Emma slammed her eyes shut, as if she could make Wryn disappear by simply refusing to turn around and look at her.

"I do believe it is you!" Wryn exclaimed. "If you'd told me how much you favored pickles, I would have bought some for you. Oh dear. Isn't that your bonnet lying there in the mud? That's the second bonnet you've ruined since I met you."

When Emma snapped her eyes open again, all three of the new arrivals were standing in front of her. She gave them all a good solid glare.

Warren chuckled. "Better stand back. My mother's well armed with pickles, and she's got a fair aim, too."

Wryn pointed toward the hill. "Look! Here come Uncle Benjamin and Uncle Mark. See? That's Uncle Mark's covered wagon that just drove down from Hill House. I wouldn't be surprised if they've got the rest of the family with them, too. All we'd need now is Reverend Glenn and Mr. Breckenwith. Rather than wait any longer, you could ask Reverend Glenn to perform the marriage ceremony right here and now."

"That's ridiculous," Emma grumbled, too cold and too miserable to even think about telling the little snip that she might not be getting married at all.

"The girl's got a point. You might want to consider it," Mother Garrett offered.

"Maybe you should," Warren concurred, offering a backhanded approval of her plans.

Emma ignored her mother-in-law's comment and turned her attention to Warren. "If I were you, I'd be more concerned about how you're going to explain to everyone why you were driving that wagon over there than I'd be about my plans to do anything other than find my way to a good, hot bath."

Wryn untied her bonnet and handed it to Emma. "Here. You can wear this for the ceremony. You can't get married with your hair so mussed up. I'll go get Reverend Glenn and Mr. Breckenwith."

Emma handed it right back to her. "I can't possibly get married today. And I most certainly wouldn't get married here in the middle of Main Street looking like this!"

Mother Garrett nodded. "Of course you wouldn't, but you've got to get back to Hill House to scrub up real good to get rid of all that mud anyway. There's no sense doing it twice in as many days," she argued. "That makes it nearly unanimous. Get married today."

Emma dismissed her mother-in-law's words as ludicrous and sighed, wondering if there had ever been a woman who had been bullied by her entire family into getting married by taking a vote. Convinced they were all a bit loony, she glanced down at her canvas bag, which was still lying in the mud, tilted up her chin, and used the one argument she could think of that would not force her to admit that she might not be getting married at all. "I can't get married today. I haven't been to see my lawyer, Mr. Larimore. I have some important documents in that canvas bag that he has to review before I can sign them. I can't get married until I do that, and I'm quite certain Mr. Breckenwith would agree with me. In fact, if they have as much mud on them as I do, he may very well have to redraft them," she insisted.

When she saw the look of pure disappointment on the faces

of everyone surrounding her, she tucked it away as one memory she would one day treasure—but not before she washed up and no longer smelled like a mud-covered pickle.

28

THREE DAYS AFTER her muddy disaster on Main Street, Emma slipped through the dining room into the kitchen, anxious to go into town to see if she could gather any information for Miss Burns at the courthouse.

Losing herself in endless work seemed like the easiest way to avoid facing the fact that Zachary had probably changed his mind about marrying her, seeing as he had not shown up for a single meal since she had given him her demands.

She found Warren raiding the larder and chuckled. "Hungry again?"

He slammed the larder shut, then had to chew furiously before he could respond. "Grams makes the best pretzels," he explained, along with an uncustomary blush. "I thought I'd sample a few before I head out to look for another position, preferably one indoors," he added defensively. "Grams gave me a few ideas about where I should look."

"I thought you might be up to something like that."

He shot a curious look her way.

"You're wearing your suit," she said before brushing pretzel crumbs off his jacket. "Let me know if I can be of any help, too. What did Mr. Haley say about the barrel of pickles you weren't able to deliver?"

His blush deepened. "He was pretty decent about it and probably grateful he didn't lose more. Since I wouldn't let him pay me for making the rest of the deliveries, he said that was payment enough for the pickles."

Deborah skipped into the room, interrupting them, and tugged at Emma's skirts just as Anna and Grace followed her into the kitchen. "When are we going to look for my new dolly?"

Emma scrunched down until she was at eye level with the five-year-old. "I have plans for this morning, but what if we go into town right after dinner?" she asked and looked up at her son and his wife. "Would that be all right? I promised Deborah I would show her a few dolls and let her pick out a new one for herself. I offered to take Teddy and Sally with me, too, but they weren't interested."

"It's fine with me," Anna replied. "Warren?"

He swallowed hard. "Deborah would love a new dolly. Thank you."

Deborah's eyes twinkled. "Are you gonna get all muddy and smell like pickles again?"

Emma laughed as she straightened back up again. "I hope not."

Mother Garrett edged her way into the kitchen. "I'm all set to go into town to check on Wryn. If you're ready now, I'll go with you, Emma. I have a mind to stop at Mr. Breckenwith's while I'm in town to find out why he's been so scarce at my table these past few days."

A knock at the kitchen door kept Emma from responding, and Warren waved them off from answering the door. "I'll get that.

You two go ahead, unless you can wait a few moments so I can walk into town with you."

"I wanna go, too," Deborah whined.

"You and your sister need to come with me. There's some explaining to be done about the mess I found in the front parlor," Anna insisted, leading both girls out of the kitchen.

"We'll wait for you in the parlor," Mother Garrett said.

Consumed with finding a way to keep Mother Garrett from visiting Zachary, Emma followed her into the dining room, but before she reached the hallway, Warren called out to her.

"Mother? Would you mind stepping back here for a moment? There's someone here who needs to speak to you."

"I'll wait for you in the front parlor, too," Mother Garrett added.

Her heart leapt with hope until she realized Zachary would not have come to the back door to seek her out. Intrigued by the possibility that yet another woman might have come to seek her, Emma retraced her steps. But when she entered the kitchen, she found Warren standing by the back door, which was closed. "He's outside."

Perplexed that Warren did not allow the man to come inside, she hurried toward the door. Warren opened it for her and followed her outside.

The moment she saw not one man, but two, waiting for her, she realized she had jumped to a hasty conclusion. Zachary was indeed standing there, but there was also a man she had never met standing next to him.

The stranger was about the same age as Emma, and his frame was as straight and thin as his beard, which drooped long enough to touch the middle of his chest.

Finally, she realized the reason Warren had not invited the

two men into the house had nothing to do with his manners at all. The reason—in reality, two very familiar reasons—now made perfect sense.

Her heart sank, but she kept a smile on her lips. She was close enough to Zachary to catch the absolute merriment in his gaze and decided he was enjoying too much pleasure at her expense, especially when she suspected there was one very familiar reason still missing.

Warren held on to her elbow, as if she might need his support.

"This is Mr. Fellows," Zachary explained.

The man tipped his hat. "Ma'am."

Zachary continued. "We were having a discussion at my home about words, which I thought you might find interesting, so I convinced Mr. Fellows to come here to Hill House so you could be part of it."

"Words," she repeated, unable to take her eyes off the two nanny goats Mr. Fellows held tethered together by a bit of rope he held in his hands.

"Would you mind telling Widow Garrett where you found those two nanny goats and why you brought them to my office?"

"They were nibblin' every bit of green out of my wife's garden. We've got a little place at the end of Main Street, just outta the town limits," Mr. Fellows explained. "Before I took 'em both to Sheriff North to investigate, I thought I should stop by a lawyer's to see what I could do about suin' the owner, 'cause there won't be much growin' in that garden now that these two critters had their fill. Some animals best belong on a farm, where they don't bother nobody," he grumbled.

"Exactly my thoughts," Emma whispered. She couldn't decide whether she wanted to strangle Mr. Kirk for bringing those goats to Hill House in the first place, or kick herself for allowing the goats to stay.

Zachary nodded. "I told Mr. Fellows we first had to determine whether the goats were mavericks or renegades before he could entertain filing any sort of lawsuit to recoup his losses."

"A maverick's a critter roamin' round without no owner, which means I got no lawsuit. That much I got before comin' up to your house, which means I'm gonna ask the sheriff if I can just keep the goats. Seems fair enough to me, considerin' what it already cost me," Mr. Fellows offered.

Zachary nodded to Emma. "As your lawyer, as well, I thought you should be here when I told Mr. Fellows that unlike mavericks, renegade goats have a proper owner who bears responsibility for any damage the animals might have done," he said. "Would you please tell us whether or not those are your goats?"

Warren continued to hold on to her as she pointed one at a time to the goats. "That's Ridiculous. That's Outrageous."

Mr. Fellows looked confused. "I beg your pardon, ma'am. Did you say—"

"Those are my goats. The darker one with the odd spots is named Ridiculous. The other one with the overly long coat is called Outrageous," she said, using the names she had given them in jest, since no one had come up with new names for them. "I only got the goats recently and I keep them up at Hill House, which is why my—my lawyer didn't recognize them," she added quickly. "I'm so very sorry, but they must have escaped. My sons were planning to build a stronger pen, but—"

"I got troubles enough bein' bothered with these two critters and what they done without carin' why they got free."

Emma cringed. "Unfortunately, Mr. Fellows, I had three goats, not two, and there's a very good possibility that the other one escaped, as well. I wouldn't be surprised if it turns up in your garden, since it probably isn't far from those two you're holding."

"Will you be payin' up for the damage they done or not? 'Cause if you're not, I gotta see about gettin' myself a different lawyer, 'cause I sure can't use this one. Not if he's your lawyer, too."

When Zachary coughed, Emma could see he was covering up a laugh or two. "You're right, Mr. Fellows. I couldn't represent your interests as well as Widow Garrett's, but I should think we could resolve the entire matter without wasting time on a lawsuit. Would you agree?" he asked, looking directly at Emma.

"Absolutely. I'll be only too happy to cover your losses, Mr. Fellows. Did you have a sum in mind?"

"Can't say I had the time to consider it yet," he admitted, "but if you'll pardon me sayin' so, ma'am, you shouldn't be keepin' goats if you can't take good care of 'em."

Emma grinned. "No, I shouldn't, but I think we might be able to solve that problem, too. If you wouldn't mind bringing the goats around to the other side of the house, there's a walled patio that should keep them from running away again while we discuss the matter. Warren, would you check to see if the third goat is missing or not?"

Warren let go of her arm. "As soon as I help Mr. Fellows here get these two critters on the patio, I'll get changed and take a look, but I have a feeling it's long gone. We'll meet you in the kitchen so you can settle on a sum that he'll find satisfactory."

Mr. Fellows shook his head. "I'm not dressed to come inside no fancy place like yours."

"Hill House isn't all that fancy," Emma argued, anxious to settle the issue as quickly as possible. "I'd really like you to be able to go home knowing all the problems I've caused you today are resolved," she insisted, hopeful this man might also go home as the new owner of three nanny goats.

While Warren led Mr. Fellows and the two adventurous goats away, Emma kept her focus on Zachary. "W-would you like to come in, as well?" she asked.

"I have another client waiting," he offered stiffly.

"Perhaps later."

His gaze softened. "Not today or tomorrow, I'm afraid. I've got too many appointments scheduled, but . . . soon," he said, then walked away.

Her heart ached with hope.

29

THAT SAME DAY AFTER DINNER, Emma kept her promise to let Deborah pick out a new dolly for herself.

Along with Anna, who had asked to accompany them, Emma held her granddaughter's hand. In her other hand, Deborah held tight to her one and only dolly. They approached one of the newest shops in Candlewood, Mrs. Zane's Trinkets and Treasures, which was located almost directly across from the bank.

Teddy and Sally decided to tag along with their father to search for the missing third goat with Mr. Fellows, the proud new owner of all three nanny goats. Fortunately, he and Emma had reached a settlement fair to both of them, which included a bit of cash and all of the materials Benjamin and Mark had bought to construct a pen for the nanny goats.

Anna paused for half a step. "Is that Grams and Aunt Frances going into the bank?"

Emma turned and looked across the street, but only caught a flash of skirts before the door closed. "I couldn't tell, but it could have been. Mother Garrett mentioned she had an errand or two before we left her at the Glenns'," she replied. Unfortunately, she had been too busy with Mr. Fellows to go into town earlier with her mother-in-law, but she remained hopeful Mother Garrett had forgotten all about visiting Zachary to find out why he had not been coming for meals at Hill House. She also had no idea why her mother-in-law would have an errand inside a bank where she had no account, but she assumed one of Aunt Frances' sons might have set up an account for their mother there.

Emma led Deborah into the shop, with Anna following right behind them. Before the sound of the bell over the door had softened to all but an echo, Emma glanced at her daughter-in-law and her granddaughter and smiled. Judging by their awed expressions, they were just as enthralled as she was.

The shop itself was very narrow, no more than ten or twelve feet wide but ran perhaps twice as deep, and a pink-and-blue-striped curtain hung in a doorway at the far end of the shop. A half wall divided the space into two tiny rooms that ran from front to back, giving them all a view of both rooms. There were no display cases or counters; instead, floor-to-ceiling shelves held the most amazing array of toys for children that Emma had ever seen.

In this first room, all the toys on the shelves appeared to be hand-carved from wood or shaped from thin sheets of tin, and the air was heavy with the scent of freshly hewn wood. Puzzles filled one shelf along the wall to her left. Ranging from small to grand, Noah's arks, filled with pairs of animals of every description, sat on another shelf, just below a collection of Jacob's ladders, a series of wooden blocks held together with colorful ribbons. To her right, miniatures of packet boats and horse-drawn wagons and carts on several shelves vied for attention, along with a shelf filled with finger tops and whipping tops. Yet another shelf held marionettes and puppets, all waiting for a child to bring them to life.

Deborah, however, held tight to her dolly and tugged Emma

toward the second room, where the dolls were on display, with Anna following right behind.

Dolls of every size lined the shelves here. On the upper shelves, far beyond the reach of younger children, imported china dolls with glass eyes in various shades of blue were dressed in velvets and chiffon, just like the dolls in Deborah's collection. Below them were shelves filled with dolls just a bit less fragile—dolls with faces made of wax or papier-mâché. Fabric dolls dressed in calico and chintz, their features stitched or drawn by hand, sat on the lower shelves.

Together, they created a colorful display of dolls just waiting to be chosen and taken into a little girl's arms to be loved.

"Be careful not to touch anything," Anna cautioned her daughter.

"I'll be good," Deborah replied and looked up at Emma. "Look at all the dolls, Little Grams! Maybe my dollies found their way here!" she exclaimed before letting go of Emma's hand to wander closer to the dolls.

Emma caught her breath and held it as she turned to Anna. She had not had the opportunity to discuss her conversation with Deborah about where her lost dolls had gone with Anna yet, and she was not sure if Anna would approve or not.

Anna moistened her lips. "Deborah told me what you thought might have happened to her dollies. Thank you. We weren't certain what to tell her . . . until she's old enough to understand," she whispered as Deborah began to wander from shelf to shelf, as oblivious to the presence of adults as the shopkeeper apparently was unaware there were patrons in the shop.

Relieved, Emma let out a long breath. "A new dolly should help for now," she murmured.

Blinking back tears, Anna let out a sigh. "You've done so much for us already by allowing us to stay at Hill House indefinitely. Warren is hoping to find a position here in Candlewood, but we're not certain how long that will take or how long we'll have to depend on your help. If you'd let me, I'm more than willing to take over some of your responsibilities at Hill House so you'd have more time for yourself."

Emma smiled. "Thank you. I have guests scheduled to arrive in a matter of weeks, and I could surely use your help at Hill House then," she replied.

"None of my dollies are here," Deborah announced sadly, interrupting Emma and her daughter-in-law.

"I'm sure you'll find a new dolly to love," Emma assured her.

"Good morning, ladies. I'm Mrs. Zane. I'm sorry to keep you waiting, but I'm so pleased you decided to stop and visit today."

Emma looked over to see the shopkeeper, who had emerged from behind the curtain. To her surprise, the woman was young, about the same age as her sons. Her long dark hair was tied with a ribbon and fell in waves across one of her shoulders as she bent down to speak to Deborah. "I see you brought your dolly with you."

Deborah nodded.

"Does she have a name?"

Another nod. "Her name is Jenny. She's lonely. She needs a friend."

The shopkeeper smiled. "We have lots of dollies here who would like to be her friend. Why don't you look around and when you see one you like, I'll take her off the shelf for you to look at," she suggested before standing up again.

"We haven't met yet, have we?" Mrs. Zane asked.

"No, we haven't. I'm Widow Garrett, this is my daughter-in-law, Mrs. Garrett, and that's Deborah."

"I'm so pleased to meet you."

"You have a stunning display of toys," Anna offered.

"Thank you. My husband carves the wooden toys on display in the other room. Except for a few of the dolls imported from France and Germany that arrive fully dressed, I sew all of the clothes for the other dolls myself. Was there a particular doll you'd like me to steer little Deborah toward?" she whispered.

"No, she's free to choose whatever doll she favors," Emma replied.

"Can I see that one?" Deborah asked.

Much to Emma's surprise, her granddaughter was pointing to a fabric doll on the bottom shelf that had a single blond braid and big blue eyes. The doll was dressed in a dark brown gown topped with a crisp muslin apron and wore a matching bonnet.

Once Mrs. Zane handed the doll to Deborah, the little girl tucked it in her arm. "Isn't she pretty, Mama?"

Anna smiled. "Yes, she is. I think she'll be a fine friend for Jenny."

"Are you sure that's the one you want?" Emma asked.

Deborah grinned. "She's the prettiest dolly here. She looks just like you, Little Grams."

Emma felt that tug on her heartstrings straight to the tips of her toes.

———

En route home, when they reached Coulter Lane, Emma could not resist taking a glimpse down the narrow street toward Zachary's home. When she did, she found Wryn heading straight toward her, although she was still a square away.

"Isn't that Wryn?" Anna asked.

"I believe it is," Emma said, assuming Wryn had just left Zachary's home.

"I'm sure you'd like to speak with her, since she wasn't home this morning when Mother Garrett went into town to see her. If you don't mind, I think I'll take Deborah home while you do."

"That might be best," Emma replied, anxious to find out what Wryn was up to now. She planted a kiss on Deborah's cheek. "Take good care of your dolly until I get home."

"I will," Deborah promised before her mother hurried her back to Hill House.

Wryn held up her hand as she approached Emma. "Don't get all huffy and dithered up. Aunt Frances told me Mother Garrett had come to check up on me today, but she also told me she'd told her she'd sent me out on some errands. I hope your mother-in-law told you that."

"Yes, she did, although she said Aunt Frances was fairly vague about what those errands were."

"If you must know, I returned everything I bought that you asked me to take back, except for the reticule. I still intend to work that off."

"I see," Emma murmured, pleased that Wryn had taken it upon herself to return everything without being reminded. Still, she was exceedingly curious about what errand Wryn might have had at Zachary's. "Is that what you were doing just now at Mr. Breckenwith's? Running an errand?"

"No. When Aunt Frances went out with Mother Garrett a little while ago, she told me I could have some time to myself, which I needed because I had an appointment with my lawyer," Wryn said.

"He's your lawyer now?" Emma blurted, annoyed that he had failed to mention that Wryn was the particular client he was meeting with this afternoon.

"Don't find blame with the man for not telling you. I told him not to tell you, and he has to do whatever I say because I'm his client and you don't have a thing to say about it," she replied boldly.

Emma cast a withering look in Wryn's direction.

Wryn rolled her eyes and sighed. "I mean, please don't be upset with Mr. Breckenwith. He couldn't tell you because I asked him not to say anything, and he was bound to do what I wanted. Does that sound better?"

"I would have preferred to hear you say it that politely the first time," Emma said. "Are you heading back to the Glenns' now?"

Wryn shrugged and shifted her weight from one foot to the other. "Probably. What . . . what would you say if I told you that I wanted to live somewhere else? Would you let me, even if I hadn't worked off what I owe you yet?"

Caught by surprise, Emma could only assume that Wryn meant she wanted to go home to live with her mother if they could reconcile quickly and that Zachary was making efforts on her behalf to do that. "Whether or not you've finished working off what you owe me wouldn't matter. You'd be free to go home, but I don't want you to be disappointed if that takes longer than you'd like."

Wryn shrugged. "I've been disappointed before. Aren't you going to try to get me to tell you why I've hired Mr. Breckenwith to be my lawyer?"

Emma shook her head. "No. Whatever business you have with him is none of my concern. Now if you'll excuse me, I have work waiting for me back at Hill House. I'll see you at supper."

"I won't be coming home for supper. Aunt Frances asked me to stay later today to fix supper for her and Reverend Glenn, but I'll walk Mother Garrett home so no one has to come to town to fetch her," Wryn said and ran off before Emma could argue the matter.

Convinced Wryn was taking only one step back for every two

steps she took forward these days, Emma turned to take one last look down Coulter Lane. Before her common sense failed, if not her convictions, she turned around again to prevent herself from marching straight to Zachary's home and interrupting him in order to get the answer she so desperately wanted from him.

Instead, since she was now alone, she took advantage of this unexpected opportunity to pursue the matter concerning Miss Burns and changed directions completely. She reached the courthouse fairly quickly but left only minutes later. The late Gerald Burns' will had been recorded, by custom, in Bounty, the county seat, and she would need to go there to read it.

By the time she reached the end of Main Street, she was almost as tired as the plump, middle-aged woman with the reddest hair she had ever seen who was struggling her way up the steep hill just ahead of her. The woman, who waddled from side to side, was carrying a basket in each hand.

After mustering up the last of her strength, she hurried to catch up with her. "May I help you?"

"I'd . . . surely . . . appreciate . . . it," the woman managed as she handed her baskets to Emma and tried to catch her breath. "I'm afraid I could never live all the way up there if I had to climb this hill every day."

Emma chuckled. "It's a bit of a challenge for me today, too. My name is Widow Garrett, and I live at Hill House at the top of this very steep hill."

"Then I'm doubly blessed you came along when you did because I was bringing those baskets to you. I'm Mrs. Fellows," she said, pointing to the baskets Emma was holding now. "It's not much, just a couple of loaves of sweet bread to thank you for being so generous to Amos and me."

"I thought I smelled something delicious, but there's no thanks necessary," Emma insisted. "If anything, I'm very grateful that your husband was willing to take all three of those goats. I'm sorry about your garden," she added.

The woman chuckled. "Goats don't eat the roots, so that garden will still grow some. It's just Amos and me now. We'll find a way to make do until it does. I do thank you for saving me some steps, though."

"Are you sure I can't offer you a cup of tea before you go back home?"

She chuckled again. "Not if it means I have to climb the rest of that hill. But I shouldn't dally anyway. I told Amos I was just going to drop this off and come right back home to mend his shirt before he heads out to look for work again. He hasn't found much more than a few days' labor since the match factory burned to the ground, and I'm afraid we'll have to think about leaving Candlewood if he doesn't find something soon."

"I understand," Emma murmured. "If you'd like to wait here, I can take the bread home and bring the baskets right back to you so you can take them home."

Mrs. Fellows waved off Emma's suggestion. "There's no rush for that, but I wouldn't mind if you'd leave them at Mr. Breckenwith's for me. I have to stop back there the day after tomorrow to get the baskets I left there with some goodies for him. I have the opportunity to deliver some pies to the confectionery, but you can't tell anyone. Mrs. Turner doesn't want anyone to know she didn't make them herself, and me and Amos need what little I can make."

Emma smiled. "I won't tell a soul, and I'll make sure the baskets are at Mr. Breckenwith's, too."

"If he's not home when you get there, just leave the baskets on the bench in that garden behind his kitchen. Don't tell him I told you so, but that garden of his looks even worse than mine did after the goats had their fill of it," she noted with a grin.

Emma peeked inside the baskets and saw two lusciously dark loaves of bread. With her mouth watering, she practically ran the rest of the way home. There was only one way to completely salvage this curious day, and she had every intention of doing so by devouring two very thick slices of bread after slathering them with butter.

30

T HE FOLLOWING DAY, Emma was happy that she managed to keep herself busy all morning, especially since everyone else in her family, including Mother Garrett, seemed to have so many plans of their own today without her.

When the front bell rang, she was in the dining room with Liesel polishing the furniture. She waved for Liesel to keep working. "I'll see who it is," she said, hoping Zachary had decided to come to see her today instead of tomorrow. She paused in front of the mirror on the oak coatrack to fix her hair, but she did not need to pinch any color to her cheeks. They were a bit too bright as they were.

When she opened the front door and saw Sheriff North standing there holding Wryn by the arm, Emma was too shocked to be disappointed, but she was alarmed. Wryn's gown was caked with dried mud. She held her soiled bonnet in her hand, but the scrapes and scratches on Wryn's freckled face concerned Emma most of all.

"This young lady tells me she's your niece," the sheriff said without bothering to hide his grin.

"Yes, she is," Emma managed.

"Having you living in town might make my job easier now and again," he remarked as he removed his hat.

"You may be right," Emma muttered, grateful that Wryn had the good sense to have the sheriff bring her here instead of to the Glenns'. She opened the door wide and urged them inside.

"You can't get too mad at me. You had more mud on yourself than I do when you fell the last time," Wryn cautioned.

"That could very well be a matter of debate," Emma countered as she stepped aside to let Wryn pass by. "At the moment, I'm more interested in what happened to you. Why are you all scraped up? And why did the sheriff have to escort you here?"

Wryn tilted up her chin. "I didn't want Reverend Glenn and Aunt Frances to see me like this. You probably think I got myself into real trouble this time."

"I can't say the thought hadn't occurred to me," Emma admitted.

Wryn looked up at the sheriff and grinned. "You'd better tell her. She won't believe me half as quick as she'll believe you."

Sheriff North nodded. "Your niece may have been a bit too foolish for her own good, but she—"

"I caught not one, but two thieves!" Wryn announced, clearly more anxious to spin her tale than she thought. "Two," she repeated and held up two very dirty, scraped fingers.

Emma gasped. "You what?"

"Your niece caught two young men sneaking out of the back window down at MacPherson's Apothecary with a week's worth of receipts."

"I wrestled the two of them to the ground, too."

"No!" Emma exclaimed, shocked more by the danger her niece

had encountered than the impropriety of wrestling with not one, but two members of the opposite sex.

"They made such a fuss, there was a crowd in no time," Wryn continued. "Some men stepped in to help me, and then Sheriff North came and hauled those two riffraff off to jail. I thought the crowd would never stop applauding, either. Mr. MacPherson was so upset, he decided to keep his funds in the bank from now on, and he was so grateful for my help that he gave me a reward. I put that right on your account at Mrs. Kelly's to pay for the reticule I bought, and I still have a few coins for myself. Mrs. Kelly didn't even complain about all the dirt I tracked into her shop, either," Wryn blurted.

When she finally stopped to draw a breath, she looked down at her skirts and frowned. "I think I might have ruined this gown, though. Do you think the mud stains will come out if I set it to soak? It's my best gown, and I'll need it if I have to testify in court if those two stupid men don't decide to plead guilty."

The sheriff coughed. "There's not much chance that will happen. From what I got out of those two, being bested by a female once is embarrassment enough. Now if you'll both excuse me, I'd best be getting back to the jail," he said and shut the door behind him.

Rendered speechless, Emma struggled to gather her thoughts. Seeing Wryn as a heroine took some doing, although the young woman's feisty nature had served her well this time. There was no question the entire episode had given her the acceptance she so desperately desired, although Emma would have much preferred a more subtle solution. She looked at Wryn and smiled. "I'm proud of you. I'm also frightened just thinking about what could have happened to you, and we should probably discuss what is and what isn't appropriate for a young woman to do when she's up against a couple of thieves. But I am truly, truly proud of you."

Wryn grinned. "Me too."

Emma cocked a brow.

Wryn tilted up her chin. "Well, I am. I wasn't sure if I could get the best of those two men, but I sure couldn't let them steal from Mr. MacPherson. He's been awfully good to Reverend Glenn. But the minute I spied that bag of money they were stealing, I thought of you and I just knew I could stop them if I tried hard enough."

"You thought of me?" Emma managed. "Why?"

"Because you're the strongest, smartest woman I've ever known," Wryn said. "You really are."

———

After supper that night, once Emma's grandchildren had been put to bed and Wryn's heroics had been told and retold, the adults who had gathered together in the east parlor were ending the day with quiet conversation. Emma sat next to her mother-in-law on the settee, while her sons and their wives sat in chairs across from them, side by side as couples.

Benjamin lifted his hand to still the chatter about the latest topic of conversation, which had Emma sitting on the edge of the settee. To her, Zachary's absence these past few days had been palpable, but she had not realized how much it had been a topic of concern. Until now.

When everyone quieted, Benjamin grinned. "None of you should be surprised at all that Mr. Breckenwith has made himself scarce these past few days. Once he's married my mother, he'll have little time to himself, especially with all of us around," he teased.

"The man's a lawyer. He has clients to contend with," Mark added, supporting his brother's argument.

Warren cleared his throat to get everyone's attention. "It's getting late, so rather than spend any more time discussing a man who isn't here to defend himself, I have some news I'd like to share with all of you."

Ever grateful that he had steered the conversation in another direction, Emma was able to relax and sit back in her seat again, fully aware that Mother Garrett was watching her closely. She glanced at Anna and knew from the smile on her face that Warren had already shared his news with his wife. Judging by the satisfied expression on Mother Garrett's face, she had been told already, too.

"As of Monday, I'll be gainfully employed at the First Bank of Candlewood," Warren announced and blushed when the room erupted in cheers and applause. He waved them to quiet. "I might have been the first one to hightail it out of Candlewood, but I'm also the first one to decide to live here again permanently, too. Since you all know why Anna and I had no choice but to come home, I can see now that living in Candlewood is going to be a blessing for me and my family," he said.

Emma's heart swelled.

Warren looked at Mother Garrett and smiled. "Thanks for speaking up for me with Mr. Wyatt, Grams."

Mother Garrett beamed. "He didn't take much convincing once Frances and I reminded him of a few things."

Emma had been unaware that her mother-in-law even knew the owner of the bank, but she realized now that it was Mother Garrett Anna had seen going into the bank the other day. "What 'few things'?"

"Frances and I simply reminded him that folks like Mr. MacPherson still don't trust banks, and if he had a mind to convince them otherwise, he'd best hire someone like Warren. Besides, Frances and I have gotten friendly with his mother. She moved here with her son and his family, and we see her a lot at the General Store. I believe she spoke to her son about Warren, too."

Satisfied, Emma turned back to Warren. "Exactly what kind of work will you be doing?"

He grinned. "Eventually, I'll be reviewing loan applications. Unlike those big city bankers, Mr. Wyatt figured I had enough firsthand experience to know exactly when a request for a loan should be denied."

Emma chuckled, along with everyone else, including Warren.

When the laughter died down, Warren turned to Benjamin. "I know you like a whole lot more space around you, but there's plenty of good farmland here."

Benjamin grinned. "Maybe so, but I'm still heading back to Ohio. If I can get my brothers-in-law to help me out again, we'll be back to visit more often," he said, and Betsy nodded her agreement.

Warren turned to Mark next. "When you left to open that bookstore of yours in Albany, Candlewood wasn't much more than a simple farm town. The canal's changed that, and I'm hoping you'll think about coming back, too."

With his face flushed, Mark looked at Catherine and smiled. "As a matter of fact, Catherine and I have spent the past few days talking about doing just that."

"You have?" Emma blurted, unaware that her youngest son was entertaining any thoughts about moving back to Candlewood.

"We have, Mother Emma," Catherine assured her. "Now that my parents are both gone, you're the only grandparent our children have left, and we'd like them to be closer to you."

Emma clasped her heart, overwhelmed to think that not one, but two of her sons might call Candlewood home again, which meant she would also have most of her grandchildren here, too.

"There's more than enough business here now to support a store like mine, but I need to work out a few details first before I make my final decision," Mark cautioned.

Warren grinned. "I'll be glad to consider your loan application, if you need to borrow any funds."

Mark laughed. "You might have to do just that, but I should get enough from the sale of my store to avoid borrowing anything. I've had a few offers in the past, so I don't think I'll have much trouble selling out. As a matter of fact, the young man who's tending the store while I'm gone might be interested. I'll talk to him first, of course, as soon as we get back. In any case, I should expect we'd be able to come back to Candlewood by midsummer at the latest."

"Well before the baby is born," Catherine added as she placed her hand atop her tummy.

"Catherine and I will need a place to stay, just temporarily, until we can get settled in a place of our own. We were hoping we could stay here at Hill House," he said, turning toward his mother.

Emma swallowed hard and wondered if God's plan for her had been to stay right here, with her family, all along. "You're all welcome to stay here," she assured him. "What are you going to do about Wryn?"

Mark swallowed hard and took his wife's hand. "I'm not certain her mother would quite believe the girl's reformed herself as much as she has. Not this quickly."

Catherine nodded. "Mark and I will speak to my sister, of course, but if she's still not willing to have Wryn return home, then she can stay with us once we get settled."

"Would she be able to stay here with you when we first go

back to Albany? I'd rather not have Wryn travel all that way, only to be disappointed again," Mark said.

"Of course she can stay with me, but you'll have to talk to Wryn yourself so there aren't any misunderstandings like there were last time," she replied. "You'll be staying here at Hill House for a while, won't you?" she said, turning to Warren.

"We probably need to stay for a few months, at least," he replied.

"Naturally, I'll continue to help out, for as long as we're here at Hill House. I should probably say good night, though," Anna said as she got to her feet. "Dawn comes earlier and earlier these days, and I'd like to finish a few chores before we go visiting tomorrow."

"We're leaving right after breakfast, too," Catherine added.

Betsy nodded and stood up. "Us too."

Warren joined them, along with Mark. "We should probably all call it a day. What about you, Mother? Grams?"

Mother Garrett shook her head. "I still have a bit of energy left. You all go on to bed. Your mother will sit with me, won't you, Emma?"

Disappointed to have yet another day alone tomorrow, Emma managed a smile. "We won't be much longer, but you could save me some steps if someone could lock up for me."

"I'll do that," Anna volunteered and led the younger adults out of the parlor.

"We're very blessed, aren't we?" Emma murmured as she listened to the echo of their footsteps as they mounted the stairs

"Having those boys home with their families. Knowing both Warren and Mark are back home again for good. You and Mr. Breckenwith getting married. Blessings all. Life always manages to fall into place, one blessing at a time," Mother Garrett replied and patted Emma's thigh.

Shaking her head, Emma drew in a long breath and turned to face her mother-in-law. "Life doesn't always fall into the place we've expected," she said, unable to keep the burden she had been carrying secret any longer.

Mother Garrett cocked her head. "Having second thoughts about marrying that man, are you?"

Emma nodded. "A few more than that," she admitted and slowly explained her situation, starting with her decision to live in town with Zachary and either sell Hill House or keep it as an investment and ending with the ultimatum she had given to Zachary.

"You never mentioned moving from Hill House to me before. Not seriously," Mother Garrett murmured.

"I wasn't certain myself that I could leave. Not until just a few days ago. But since you'd said you knew you had a place with me wherever I lived, I didn't worry about it because—"

"Because you weren't sure that man wanted a woman with a real backbone or not, and he hasn't let you know that he's figured out that he does," Mother Garrett offered.

"You don't know he's come to that conclusion."

Softening her gaze, she took Emma's hands in her own. "He's a smart man. He'll come around to it, and when he does, I don't want you worrying yourself about me. I'm perfectly content right here with you, but if you do patch things up with him and want to sell out, you won't be able to do that right away. Not with Warren and Mark needing a place to stay for a while, which means . . . I'd like to stay."

Emma's heart skipped a beat. "Here? You'd want to stay here at Hill House, rather than with me?"

"Anna can't run this boardinghouse, even with Liesel and Ditty's help, and take care of her husband and her little ones and have a new cook in the kitchen, too. My place is here, helping Anna, just like I've always helped you."

Stunned, Emma struggled to keep herself sitting upright. "You . . . you wouldn't want to come live with me?"

Mother Garrett cupped the side of her face. "I love you dearly, Emma, but I couldn't move into town with you. Not now. Warren and Anna both need me much more than you do," she whispered, then wrapped Emma in her arms and held her close.

They cried together, and Emma knew this very precious, precious woman was more than the rock that had held her life steady for over thirty years. She was the one true cornerstone of Hill House, too.

And one day soon, when Zachary finally gave Emma his decision, Emma prayed her mother-in-law would be there to support her—either way her life unfolded in the days and months and years ahead.

31

A T FIRST LIGHT, Emma stood with her back to the kitchen door and glared at her mother-in-law. "Everyone else seems to have plans today that don't include me. Why shouldn't I ride to Bounty? Give me one good reason why I shouldn't. Just one."

"What if Mr. Breckenwith is planning to come see you today?" Mother Garrett argued.

"I said a good reason. Moping about hoping the man might come isn't good enough," Emma countered. "Besides, if I leave now, I can be at the courthouse practically when it opens and ride back well before late afternoon."

"If I were hoping for a visit from my future husband, I'd want to be here and be gussied up a bit when he got here, too."

Emma lowered her voice. "But I don't know if he's coming today or not, and I don't know if he's going to be my future husband or just . . . just a man who used to be my betrothed. And neither do you."

"Suit yourself. You usually do anyway," her mother-in-law quipped. "I hope you've got a few extra coins in that reticule of yours. He's not in Bounty this time to come to your rescue."

Emma tilted up her chin and jiggled her reticule until the coins rattled. "I don't need him to rescue me. Not today. Not ever."

"At least take this with you," Mother Garrett insisted, pressing a small canvas bag into her hands. "Since you won't stay to eat some breakfast before you leave, take this snack to eat along the way."

When Emma's stomach growled, she frowned.

Mother Garrett chuckled. "It's the last of that bread you brought home from Mrs. Fellows. I slathered it good with butter for you," she said and pressed a kiss to Emma's cheek. "You take care of yourself today."

"I will, but if I'm not back by supper, please don't worry about me. If need be, I'll spend the night in Bounty and be back sometime tomorrow," she replied and headed for the livery to get Mercy.

Armed with a copy of Mr. Burns' will, which provided very nicely for his aged sister, Emma arrived back in Candlewood the next day fully confident she would be able to convince Miss Burns' sister-in-law to abide by the terms of her husband's will without involving a lawyer.

She arrived at the livery and dismounted just as the town clock struck four o'clock, a good hour later than she had planned. Hopeful she would have enough time to at least get rid of the road dust she was wearing before supper was ready, she handed Mr. Adams the reins. "Mercy gave me quite a comfortable ride again today. I think she deserves some extra oats, if you wouldn't mind."

Frowning, he took the reins for a moment and handed them back to her. "Didn't Mr. Breckenwith tell you?"

"Tell me what?"

"He came by just about noon today. He told my son he's not boarding this horse of yours here anymore."

Emma felt the blood drain from her face and tightened her hold on the reins. "No, he didn't. Did he . . . did he say why?"

"I couldn't say. My son's right out back in the corral. You want me to ask him?"

"No, I-I'll stop on my way home and ask Mr. Breckenwith myself," she replied, wondering why Zachary did not have the decency to wait until he spoke with her before changing the arrangements he had made for Mercy—unless he no longer felt responsible for the gift he had given her.

"I could keep her here for you, rub her down, and feed her while you're gone."

She handed him the reins again. "That's a good idea. After I talk to Mr. Breckenwith, would I be able to board her with you if I need to?"

"Sure thing," he said and led the horse around the livery to the corral.

Too piqued to care about her vow not to return to Zachary's home until he had told her of his decision, she avoided Main Street and took a shortcut through several side streets to get to Coulter Lane. Every step she took only increased her determination to get an explanation for what he had done.

She paused for a moment on his front stoop and removed her riding gloves and her bonnet to freshen her hair a bit, pleased that only a few hairs had escaped the braid she had fashioned that morning. After moistening her lips, she knocked firmly on the door, waited no more than a heartbeat, and knocked again.

"The least you can do is be home so I can get an explanation," she grumbled.

The door swung open, unleashing luscious smells of supper cooking in the kitchen, before the echo of her words had faded.

Zachary had not answered the door, but she recognized the woman who did. "M-Mrs. Fellows?"

"Indeed it is. Come in, Widow Garrett. We've been expecting you."

"You have?" Emma asked, dumbfounded.

"Let me take your things and hang them up," she insisted, waiting for Emma to slip out of her cape, as well. "I'll let Mr. Breckenwith know you're here."

"That won't be necessary," Zachary said as he stepped out of his office. "I heard a knock, but Mrs. Fellows answered before I could."

Mrs. Fellows disappeared down the hallway without saying another word, leaving Emma alone with him.

She took a deep breath, surprised at how her heart started to beat a little faster the moment he looked at her. "I see you have a new housekeeper."

"And a groundskeeper, as well," he said. "The Fellows are good people."

"Unlike a certain gentleman I know who gives a lady a gift, then doesn't bother to tell her he's decided to change the arrangements he made for her to keep that gift."

His eyes started to twinkle. "I thought that might get your feathers ruffled enough to make you stop here on your way home. Apparently I succeeded."

She dismissed wondering how he knew she had been riding in favor of why he was so intent on annoying her. "Indeed you did, although you might at least have the courtesy to tell me why it was so important to you to annoy me."

"Truthfully? If I had asked you to come here instead of meeting with me at Hill House, I didn't think you'd come for the simple reason you told me you wouldn't."

She tilted up her chin, reluctant to admit he was right. "Is there a reason why you felt it was so necessary for me to come here instead of your coming to see me at Hill House?"

"No," he whispered. "Not a single reason. There are several, actually, but the most important reason is that I knew I didn't have a prayer of convincing you to forgive me for being such a lout during this entire courtship of ours unless I showed you proof that I want you to be my wife. Because I love you, Emma. I love the woman of faith and character and substance you've been since we met, and I love you for the woman you'll be as my helpmate and companion in whatever time we are given together as husband and wife. I want you, Emma. Only you."

She blinked back tears, unable to think past the notion that he loved her for the woman she was.

"Here, let me show you. I've made a number of changes to the house that I think will convince you," he said and gently guided her into his office.

She looked around, but had to blink hard several times until her blurred vision cleared. The last time she had taken a peek into this room, only days ago, stacks of magazines and journals had littered the entire room, leaving only a narrow aisle that led to his cluttered desk.

Now, only half the room remained cluttered; the other half, which held a lady's desk positioned close to his, was as neat as her office at Hill House. No magazines. No journals. No law books were scattered about; rather, even the library of law books on the shelves alongside the lady's desk stood neat and tall.

"You may not be able to practice law, per se, but there's nothing in the law that prevents you from studying the law. You proved your ability to be discreet when you were operating the General Store, and you've always protected the privacy of your guests at

Hill House. I'd be a very foolish man indeed if I didn't trust you to be equally discreet about my clients or to take advantage of the help and the insight my very bright, very intelligent wife could give me," he said.

"Truly?" Emma managed, afraid she might wake up to find this was all a dream. "You'd want me to study the law and work right here alongside you?" she asked, overwhelmed he would help her to fulfill a dream to choose law as her domain and use what she learned to help other women.

"I'd be honored to teach you and work with you and live with you here, if that's what you really want to do," he said, turning her toward him and gazing into her eyes. "If not, if you think you'd rather stay at Hill House, then that's where we'll live and my clients will simply have to get used to the idea. Or you can sell the place or keep it as an investment, and we can live here. It's entirely up to you. All I know is that I can't imagine living anywhere . . . not without you."

Her heart swelled with joy that she sent directly to God as a prayer of gratitude. Cupping Zachary's face with her hand, she let her tears run free. "Nor can I, but I would very much like to share this home with you as your wife," she whispered as he caught her in his arms and held her close.

With her cheek pressed against his chest, she felt his heart beating as fast as her own but found it impossible to believe that he had been able to convert his office to accommodate her so quickly. Curious about the other changes he mentioned, she looked up at him and smiled. "Did you say there were other changes you wanted me to see?"

He kissed her. Hard. And then again. "Yes, madam. There are, although I'm a bit too distracted at the moment to be able to think of one."

Grinning, she kissed him back. "Try."

"As you wish," he grumbled, although she sensed his grumbling was a bit feigned. He took her hand, led her out of his office, and closed the door behind them. "You've met Mrs. Fellows, of course. She and her husband are working here now, although I wasn't able to promise them much beyond this week since I didn't know how you'd react to my apology."

She chuckled. "Actually, you might want to ask them to stay on permanently."

"What about your mother-in-law?"

"She's going to stay at Hill House with Warren and Anna," she replied, quickly sharing all her family news with him. "I'm not so sure now that I should actually sell Hill House, but if I do, I know it will take time to find a buyer I could trust to keep Hill House as the very special place it's been for everyone who has called it home. By then, hopefully both Warren and Mark will have found homes of their own."

He nodded and led her through the parlor, which did not appear to have changed except for a fresh coat of paint on the walls. "One of the outbuildings at the rear of the property is a cottage. The Fellows might want to move in there instead of going back and forth to the place they've been renting," he suggested.

"Don't forget about the goats," she cautioned as they left the parlor and walked into the dining room, which remained as empty as it had been the first day she had seen it. As they neared the kitchen, the smell of roasted chicken grew even stronger.

He laughed. "I don't imagine they'll leave those critters behind, but there's a strong fence around the garden behind the kitchen. Mr. Fellows already has that area weeded out and planted for his wife. And just in case you're wondering, I'm not keeping our horses at the livery because Mr. Fellows will be tending to them in the stable behind the cottage."

He paused in front of the kitchen door. "I have one surprise left for you. Care to guess what it is?"

She took a good whiff of air and grinned. "Supper."

"Not exactly," he teased and opened the door. "Supper with your family would be more correct. It's the least I could do, since they've spent the better part of the past two days helping me get the house ready for you."

Before his words could fully register, she saw her sons and their families, Wryn, Mother Garrett, and Reverend and Mrs. Glenn standing together in the kitchen. Each and every one of them, down to her youngest grandchild, was beaming with anticipation.

"Well?" Warren prompted.

Grinning, Zachary took Emma's hand. "She said yes."

"Y-you knew what he was doing? All of you? You knew?" Emma managed as she held on to his hand for dear life and scanned every face in the crowd.

"Not until yesterday when you rode off to Bounty," Mother Garrett offered. "That's when we decided to lend a hand and help get this house fixed up for you."

"What we didn't know was whether or not he could convince you that he would be making the worst mistake of his life by letting you go," Benjamin told her, winking at his brothers.

Wryn clapped her hands. "Marry him. Right here and right now, Aunt Emma. We're all here, and Mother Garrett and I helped Mrs. Fellows fix a supper that's as fine a wedding supper as I could imagine."

Mother Garrett nodded her approval. "She's right, Emma. There's no sense waiting any longer, is there?"

"All in favor say 'aye,' " Wryn cried.

"Aye!" was the unified response of her sons and their wives and her grandchildren.

"Aye!" cried Mother Garrett and Reverend Glenn and Aunt Frances.

"Aye!" whispered Zachary as he pressed a kiss to the back of her hand.

And marry him she did.

Right then and there, in front of all of her loved ones. Right then and there, in the presence of God, who had guided her to this moment. Right then and there, holding hands with the man who cherished her.

Widow Emma Hires Garrett, the proprietress of Hill House, quickly became Mrs. Zachary Breckenwith, wife, helpmate, and companion, but foremost always, His faithful, beloved servant.

The Beginning

Epilogue

EMMA'S BIRTHDAY CELEBRATION exceeded every one of her expectations.

As planned, she arrived at Hill House with her husband on her birthday at noon, only to find the wrought-iron gate and fencing in the front of the boardinghouse decorated with white and yellow ribbons. Although the hydrangeas planted in the front garden had yet to blossom, the tulips planted only last fall had bloomed for the occasion. More ribbons had been tied to the railing on the wraparound porch where her entire family, including Reverend Glenn and Aunt Frances, was waiting to welcome her.

After Liesel and Ditty cleared away the remnants of a scrumptious picnic dinner they had all shared on the grassy plateau and Emma opened her gifts, the games began and the air was filled with the sounds of laughter and joy that would echo in her heart forever. Three-legged races for Zachary and her three sons and the eldest grandchildren. Ring toss and hide-and-seek for Emma, her daughters-in-law, Wryn, and the younger ones, while Mother Garrett, Aunt Frances, and Reverend Glenn sat together in the gaily decorated gazebo and cheered them all on.

Finally, before the adults were too exhausted to help and the babies had to be put to bed for their afternoon naps, Emma gave each of her grandchildren a gift of her own. Before long, seven wondrous kites were flying high in the flawless blue sky over Hill House.

Blinking back tears of joy and gratitude for the blessings of this day, Emma stood just beyond the gazebo and watched in awe as the wind played with each of the kites floating above her loving family. As one kite would dip, another would be swept up in a swell of air or still another would strain to go still higher. Yet all were kept aloft by the existence of the wind, made visible only because of the movement of the kites above the earth.

Convinced such was the nature of God, with His existence made even more visible in this world through the people He had created to love Him and serve Him, Emma bowed her head. She prayed that He would continue to bless her children and grandchildren with a faith that would be strong enough to hold them steady through the joys and sorrows life held for each of them in the years ahead.

Mother Garrett stepped out of the gazebo, walked over to Emma, and put her arm around her waist. "That's some special family we have here, isn't it?"

Emma glanced at them all and smiled. "Yes, it is."

"Did Wryn talk to you yet?"

"She did," Emma said. "I have to admit I'm not surprised that she's decided to accept Aunt Frances and Reverend Glenn's offer to live with them. They seemed to have had an affinity for one another from the day Wryn met them," she said, slipping her hand into her pocket to retrieve the slim packet she had stored there. Anxious to make her birthday even more memorable, she handed it to her mother-in-law. "This is for you."

Staring at the packet, which Emma had hastily tied with one of the ribbons she'd snatched earlier from the gazebo, Mother Garrett tilted her head. "It's your birthday, not mine."

"It's not a birthday present. It's just a gift . . . a very long overdue gift. Open it."

Mother Garrett shook her head as she untied the ribbon and stuffed it into her apron pocket. "I can't see why you need to give me a gift for anything."

"It's not for just anything. It's for everything you've done for me and for so many others," Emma whispered, watching Mother Garrett as she unfolded and began to read the papers Zachary had drawn up for her.

"But this says . . . this says Hill House . . ."

"Hill House is yours now, or it will be as soon as you sign those papers and Zachary files them with the court," Emma offered. "I've set up an account for you at the bank, too, so you don't have to worry about replacing something if it breaks or if the roof starts to leak or if—"

"I can't accept this," Mother Garrett argued and handed the papers back to Emma.

Emma wrapped her hands around her mother-in-law's and smiled. "Yes you can, because . . . because I can't let just anyone take over Hill House. Besides, it's high time you had a chance to set the rules around here, isn't it?"

Mother Garrett's eyes began to twinkle. "I would get to set the rules if I owned it instead of you, wouldn't I?"

"Yes, you would."

"And I'd get to decide who needs to work here, not that I have a mind to let Liesel or Ditty go. They're good girls, and I wouldn't trust anyone else to keep an eye out for Ditty, but I've been thinking we might need another pair of hands to help when guests are here since Anna has the girls to take care of, too."

"You'd be the owner. You could hire anyone who suits you."

Mother Garrett began to smile. "If I did own Hill House, Warren and Anna just might want to live here with me permanently now that I'm getting up in years and couldn't possibly manage running the entire boardinghouse on my own."

"I have a feeling they might," she replied, confident Mother Garrett would make sure the property would remain within the family when she left this world to reap her final reward.

"And Mark and Catherine wouldn't have to worry about finding a place too quick, either, if they decide to move back here, too," Mother Garrett suggested as her smile widened.

Emma chuckled. "For a woman who didn't want to accept my gift, you certainly have come up with more than enough reasons to make you change your mind."

Mother Garrett huffed. "There's lots to consider. Not that I have to worry about Wryn anymore. She's doing fine with Frances and Reverend Glenn, and I have a feeling she won't be too disappointed if she ends up living there permanently. But I haven't even thought about what you'd be doing with yourself if you didn't have to worry about Hill House."

"I'll be busy enough," Emma replied. Plans were already underway for her to start studying law with her husband. "There's only one slight problem."

Mother Garrett cocked her head.

Emma groaned. "Those three goats have already escaped from their pen twice. I don't suppose I could talk you into taking them back here, could I?"

Mother laughed out loud. "Not if I live to be a hundred, but I'll have a chat with Anson Kirk. I expect he'll be by to see me pretty quick once he finds out I own Hill House now," she said and stuffed the papers into her apron pocket. "I think I'll wait until that husband of yours is finished helping little Grace with her kite before I sign the papers and give them back to him," she said, wrapping her arms around Emma to hug her tight. "Thank you, Emma. You're a love. Just a love."

"And so are you," Emma whispered, her heart full, her spirit humbled but content now that Hill House finally had the owner He had planned for this very special home all along.